Lifelines

Shireen Magedin

AUSXIP PUBLISHING

Lifelines, 1st Edition

Edited by Rosa Alonso
Cover Design by Mary Draganis
Interior design by AUSXIP Publishing

Paperback: 978-0-6451084-3-9

AUSXIP Publishing
www.ausxippublishing.com

DEDICATION

I would like to dedicate this book to my mother, who has always been my inspiration and who never stopped encouraging me. No matter what.

You will be missed, Mama.

ACKNOWLEDGMENTS

Writing has been an amazing experience for me. From the beginning, when I first came up with an idea for a plot, through the development of the story and all the way to the last page of the novel. It's almost like living through a turbulent pregnancy and finally giving birth. What a relief!

First of all, I would like to thank Mary D. Brooks, who encouraged me at all times. My writing experience was limited to just writing for medical journals or the odd newspaper article, and I don't think I would have been able to put these words down if it weren't for her support and belief in me. She pointed me in the right direction of Rosa Alonso, who, as my editor, helped format the canvas on which I painted the words to bring the story to life. Sometimes I think my writing was a bit too gory because, to my amusement, Rosa's strikethroughs would be predominantly focused on the macabre details. Rosa, thank you for bearing with me.

I would like to also thank Allison Slowski and Linda Psillakis, who read my chapters right in the beginning, before they even had much substance, for always being constructive with their critique.

Taylor Rickard sensed that I was anxious about writing romance, so she talked to me about my characters in such a way that they became real and not two-dimensional people being haphazardly described. I was able to get into their heads as they were in mine. Thank you!

Last but not least, I appreciate the time that Dr. Sohaila Alam and I spent together reminiscing and discussing the cases mentioned in this book.

Though my characters are fictional, the cases mentioned here are real and have been handled or experienced by myself.

PAKISTAN

(ISLAMIC REPUBLIC OF PAKISTAN)

SARAH AND TANYA'S JOURNEY

CHAPTER 1

SOMEWHERE IN SINDH WITH SARAH

"For a woman to succeed in a man's world, she has to be twice as good as a man. Luckily, this is not too hard." — Anonymous

The bus seemed to have lost its shock absorbers somewhere on the pot-holed road. I felt as if every bone in my body including my *malleus, incus*, and *stapes* in the middle ear was shaken to bits. Just so you know, these are the small bones in the middle ear that help in the conduction of sound.

I was sure I would feel the effects of being roughly jostled and flung about later on, but I ignored my discomfort because, as I looked out the window, I was fascinated by the changing and very varied landscape—scorching deserts in a dusty, shimmering haze, and then tantalizing mirages in the horizon followed by oases with fruit-laden date and coconut palms. Alternatively, we would burst upon green banana plantations or lush mango orchards. Then again, we would come upon the seemingly endless mustard fields whose yellow foliage was nearly as breathtaking as Wordsworth's daffodils. I was pleasantly surprised at the varied and bountiful areas we were passing through. Indubitably, this area was heaven's fruit basket, but with the weather from hell.

My name is Sarah Shahzad Shah. I may sound randomly exuberant, romanticizing what would seem to others a mundane journey, but I would like to make a point that I was absolutely thrilled that day because I had passed the requisite grueling exams and had been admitted to the medical college I was travelling to. If I sounded as if I was rambling or overawed, it was because my life's ambition was about to be realized. I was leaving home, my pet iguana, my older twin brothers, Adam and Azan, and all that I held dear to embark on this interesting journey to become a doctor. I was scared, and yet, there was a feeling of anticipation that gnawed on my innards that day. I was travelling to an unknown town in an area I had never visited before. My father told me about the rich heritage of the places and the people we saw, and that only made them more real to me. More authentic. It even instilled a love for them, as I was also of their ilk, even though I had hardly lived there.

My college was situated in the province of Sindh, which is supposed to be well known for its Sufi saints and poets. Many bards have sung their praises and kept their mystique alive through the ages. We did pass a few well-kept Sufi shrines, their white marble domes shining like pearls in the sun. They were nestled in dense foliage, surrounded by parks where there were always some devotees who prayed and sang the devotional songs of the resident saint of that particular area. They reveled in the music, the recitation of poetry, and folk dancing and singing along with the artistes who came from all over Pakistan to participate in festivals commemorating the saints.

"What are you looking at so intently?" said my father as he leaned over me to peer out of the window. I turned and smiled at him while I gestured to the ornate shrine we had just passed.

"Sarah, you seem quite enthralled with the land and the scenery. Are you finally happy to go to college here? No more doubts?"

"Baba, it will always be difficult for me to leave home, but you have always told me of the rich heritage of the area, so I am trying to absorb as much as I can. And yes, I am excited to start college." I made a funny grimace that told him that I was trying to be brave.

"Did I ever tell you that it was here where Sindhi folk songs emerged, and they are liked to this day, even though they're centuries old?" He asked with a smile. My father was pleased that I was at least showing interest in the province of his birth, and even though the diesel engine was very loud, and conversation was difficult, he tried to point out landmarks and added a few anecdotes to make them entertaining.

When the bus finally stopped for refreshments in one of the towns famous for one of these Sufi saints, we heard strains of the distinctive music played by the acolytes at the nearby shrine. My father, a staunch aficionado of Sindhi and Farsi poetry, cocked his head towards the dulcet sounds and said, "Sarah, listen! That is the real authentic sound of Sindh. The music and poetry of the famous mystic and poet Shah Abdul Latif Bhitai."

The wind was moving towards us, and the music was quite poignant and had a sort of spiritual essence that seeped into one's consciousness and created a feeling of calm, just like the ripples on a pond in a gentle breeze.

I noticed that many of my fellow passengers were just as enthralled as I was, but soon the driver started to urge everyone to hurry up and board the bus again, and we had to resume our jarring, potholed journey.

While passing through the small towns and villages, I was struck by the different crafts we saw that were inherent parts of the identities of the towns.

While we passed through them my father informed me that one town was renowned for its blue ceramics, especially the tiles and urns which reflected the influence of Turkish and Persian invaders from nearly 1,500 years ago, while others were known for their block printing, which was supposed to be over 3,000 years old, and the artisans were still using the same vegetable dyes and designs to make the intricate shawls of pure cotton or silk known as the *Ajraks*, which are a sign of the Sindhi identity and nationalism.

Passing through yet another change in the landscape, I noticed, to my delight, that the workers in the fields were predominantly women. The traditional clothes they wore would give the peacocks languishing in the shade competition.

"Baba, aren't these women beautiful?" I raved. "I can just imagine what a colorful calendar could be created if one just took their time to capture the colors and the culture."

My father smiled at my interest and said, "Did you know that in many Sindhi tribes married women had to wear ivory-colored bangles that covered their arms? Your great grandmother used to wear them. She told me that an ideal set would have included seventeen bangles worn on the upper arm and nine on the lower arm; a total of fifty-two bangles on each arm." *My great grandmother?* I listened with interest.

"They were never removed, not even during sleep, and were worn during a woman's entire married life," my father continued. "It is said that they have magical properties that protects the wearer against the evil eye and supposedly ease birth pains. Obviously, due to the preservation of elephants, and after outlawing the sale of ivory, the expensive bangles of yore have been replaced with cheap plastic ones."

We watched the women work, cheerfully singing folk songs and filling the baskets on their backs with raw cotton bolls.

I tried to look for the menfolk and correlate their involvement in family and rural cultivation affairs, but, when I did spy anyone of the male gender, they were either squatting on the roadside watching the traffic go by or gathered at the thatched roadside tea cabins that popped up like mushrooms on the highway. I am sure if women didn't exist here, these men would be extremely helpless and definitely would have still lived in caves.

Our destination was a small town called Nawabshah. It

was famous for its sugar cane and mangoes, and also a national hub for cotton and banana production. In essence, a regular rural/urban fusion town. As the years passed, it established itself as a university town with many reputable educational institutions, including our destination, the College of Medical Sciences, which was established by the government exclusively for women.

While sitting on the uncomfortable seat in the bus and trying not to slip off with every heave and lurch, I continued to quietly look out of the window. Conversation was difficult over the noise of the heavy diesel engine, and anyway, I was so excited that I hadn't slept well the night before, so conversation wasn't a priority for me. There was a pleasant and yet nervous feeling within me that quietened only when I took a deep, calming breath and assured myself that I was finally on my life's path, on my way to medical college and hoping against hope to come away as a competent healer in the future.

The reason that my excitement was tinged with a touch of apprehension was because this was the first time that I was going to live in the desert and plains of Sindh. I had spent most of my life in the mountains, be it Europe or the North of Pakistan, so I was not sure whether I really wanted to be here in the oasis/desert province. I loved greenery and cool climates, and due to my father's work postings, I had attended my premed college in Peshawar, up north in another mountainous province, so the additional dilemma was that I didn't even know anyone here and was worried, just like any other teenager, whether I would fit in.

All of a sudden, the bus gave a jolt, and a horrendous screech jolted me out of my reverie. Then, with a final heave of its broken shock absorbers, it shuddered to a stop and let a few passengers off. The driver became more energized once the town's outskirts came into view, and he started to yell at the top of his voice that the next bus stop was for the "ladies' medical college."

We had finally arrived in Nawabshah! This little burg was supposed to have a hot desert climate, and I had heard from my father's friend that the town was considered one of the hottest places in Pakistan, with temperatures soaring as high as 530C in the summer. Due to my excitement, I did not realize how hot it was the day we travelled there, but someone mentioned later that the temperature on that auspicious day was over 500C!

As predicted by the loud driver, the bus conveniently stopped right in front of the college gate. Gathering my bags and my trunk, which contained most of my life and what was necessary for the next five years, I nearly fell out of the bus in my haste. I was coated in dust and felt quite ripe. I saw that many of the other passengers disembarking from the bus turned out to be fellow students. It was amusing to see that they looked just as overawed and grubby as I did.

Well, here we all were, standing in front of a high wall with equally high ornate gates barring the outside world from the perceived rites of academia inside. It was nearly overwhelming to think that behind those ostentatious gates was my future. Once I stepped in, there was no going back. I had to make a choice, and quick. Would I act like a child and hang on to my father as he turned away to take the bus home? Or would I go forth and earn a name for myself?

No, there was absolutely no option to act like a child. I wanted this too much, and I could almost taste it!

I cast my eyes above the gates and saw a semi-circular dark blue sign that proclaimed that we were entering the College of Medical Sciences for Women. There was a kind of logo that looked quite elegant with the requisite caduceus, the river Indus, and an open book. There even was a Sindhi couplet from Shah Latif Bhitai which loosely translated meant: *"You are the Greatest, You are the Healer & You are the Panacea of all ills."* The poet was obviously referring to God when he wrote that.

I stood there in wonder, staring open mouthed at that symbol of hope and learning, just savoring the moment. That first impression meant a lot to me, and to this day, I still see in my mind's eye the young and impressionable me standing there, absolutely fascinated. I was so enthralled that I didn't realize I was blocking the way for others who wanted to pass by me to enter the college.

Suddenly, I heard a car slam on its brakes. The tires screeched like a banshee forcing everyone to look at what the commotion was all about. A police jeep nearly had a fender bender with the bus, which had come to an abrupt halt and then tried to pull away from the curb without signaling. I was instantly drawn to the policewoman driving the Jeep. She had the most beautiful brown eyes peeping out from under the smart peaked cap. Who was she? How had she chosen such an unusual job for a woman in a remote town? Rather than being irritated, she had an amused look in her eyes. I kept staring and wished I could meet her one day. As if she had read my thoughts, she caught my stare and didn't look away, seemingly as captivated by me as I was by her. I felt a pleasant lurch in my stomach. I was inexplicably drawn to her. Which didn't make any sense at all. I didn't even know who she was. She suddenly started as if coming out of a daze when the pressure horn of a bus blasted behind her to give way.

I was also brought out of my trance when I felt my father quickly nudge me forward, wanting to hurry things along. I think the unbearable heat and the swirling dust made him feel tired and a tad irritated. Since the gates were closed, we looked around to see how we could attract the attention of anyone to let us in. I finally noticed that there was a huge bell embedded in one of the columns on the right side of the gates. I promptly darted forward and reached out to ring the bell before anyone else could. (Competitive? Or just superstitious? Was ringing the bell before anyone else supposed to be lucky for me?)

As if he was waiting for us, a doorman immediately opened the gates and ushered us in with a welcoming smile. I felt as if I was in one of those slow-motion movies where the scene is gradually revealed by the smoothly opening gates. I was in awe! Here in the desert, there was an oasis! They had told us in the brochures that the college was built on 200 acres, give or take, but once the gates opened, our first impression was the sight of the beautiful buildings surrounded by high walls that were lined with rows of massive *Neem* trees. These trees are unique to the area. Their bark, leaves, and seeds have ancient medicinal qualities, and its extracts have been recommended for a wide range of ailments.

Most of the gardens were still dug up and under development, but I could see that they had been well designed and were in the process of being laid as planned. They would eventually turn out to be cool havens for us on hot summer days. The quaintest part was the lush sunken lawn just near the entrance, which was surrounded by many colorful rose bushes already in full bloom.

My earliest impression of the college was that the buildings were older than expected, though they were extremely well maintained. The architecture was similar to the Art Deco style of the turn of the 20th century. The bass reliefs and plaster decorations were typical of the era. I was told by a teacher later that the place had belonged to an old boarding school for boys before they had moved out to a new campus across town, leaving these stately buildings for our use. They had been very beautifully restored and seemed to glow in the sunshine; it was probably the heat shimmering off them, but the overall effect was aesthetically pleasing.

I hardly noticed my father in my admiration of my surroundings, but I did vaguely sense that he beat a hasty retreat after giving me a perfunctory kiss on my forehead and wishing me luck. He may have been in a hurry to catch the next available bus and make the five-hour journey home before sunset. We had opted to travel by bus that day instead of driving in ourselves because we were initially unsure where to go, and my father also wanted me to get familiar with the route and the modes of transportation because that was the way that I would be commuting on the weekends, while living in the dormitory in college.

Regrettably, at that time, the airlines hadn't started flights to this (as yet) insignificant university town. It was still too small and not commercially viable. However, as the area developed, we were grateful to be able to reach home within a short 30-minute flight, but till that happened we had to slum it in the buses or the trains for five grueling hours each way.

As the fleeting sense of loss caused by my father's sudden departure receded, I became even more acutely aware of my surroundings and the teeming masses of happy students around me. I think that could have been one of the reasons of my father's hasty retreat—probably too much excitable estrogen in one place.

Looking around to see where everyone was congregating, I followed the obvious queue to a special booth set up to register the students as they arrived. I was trembling with excitement while I tried to find my name in the admissions list. After getting the requisite welcome pack and a name tag, I found a nice shady corner and amused myself with people watching. Friends were greeting each other only as young girls of that age could. There was a lot of screaming, shouting, hugs and jumping up and down. That didn't bother me at all, but I still continued to stay in my corner because I really had no clue what to do, and there was no list for room allocations to guide me.

Apparently, they thought we would all pair up with friends as and when we met them.

Well, it was nearly sunset when I realized that I couldn't continue to stay in my comfortable nook, so I dragged my psychedelic trunk over to a room where someone in passing had mentioned there might be a vacancy. Shyly peeking in, I saw three pleasant looking girls deep in conversation while unpacking and getting themselves settled. Clearing my throat to get their attention, I asked the girls whether there was place for me to be their roommate, and I was welcomed with open arms.

"Come on in! We were wondering who our fourth roommate would be," said the tallest of the three girls, who I later got to know was called Sana. "Nice to meet you."

We all introduced ourselves and shyly spoke about where we were from, and how much we were looking forward to our new "careers."

The room allocation for that wing was four students to a room because the rooms were quite large. Again, the Art Deco influence was predominant here. The floor was quite remarkable and was made of interlocking red stones that were common to the area. They were skillfully cut, probably by hand since the building was about a century old. They were fashioned into large flagstones and polished to a sheen that was in all probability due to a combination of age and a power polisher. There were eight large rooms on that floor, and all were already occupied. Sounds of laughter and merry conversations were heard from every room as the occupants were happily settling in. The uncanny thing about these rooms was that they were quite cool as compared to the scorching weather outside. Later on, I found out that our wing was on top of the dissection hall and the morgue. The flagstones were retaining the cold from the refrigeration unit below, so that's why we were "fortunate" to have the advantage of air-conditioned decadence while the others broiled.

Getting to know my new roommates was as awkward as going to a cocktail party where the hostess throws you together with her other guests but forgets to introduce you to one another. Apparently, the other three students knew each other from pre-med college, so I was the only fish out of the water. I had the mistaken impression that it was going to be an uphill task to get myself accepted here. Looking on the bright side, I was fortunate that my roommates spoke fluent English and I was able to converse comfortably with them, since my Urdu skills at the time were sadly lacking proficiency.

My new roommates were from Karachi, the same town where my parents were living, so we gradually started to connect. Soon we were chatting away as if we had known each other for years.

Sana was tall and willowy with straight long hair tied in a messy ponytail. She was the brooder and scholar of the group, while Ghazal had a dusky complexion, and was short and stocky with her hair cut into a shiny bob. Soni thought that her long curly hair was her crowning glory and therefore her best feature. Looking into every mirror she passed was compulsory for her, and soon became a reason to pull her leg. But she was always noticed because of her clear skin and shining eyes. In fact, she was quite gregarious and was always looking for comic relief when study times were stressful. That made her popular with the rest of the students in our class. Quite the balance if I may say so.

"Let's unpack quickly and then look for some food," said the ever-hungry Ghazal. That was one thing that we all definitely agreed with as it was nearly dinner time.

While I was unpacking and making my bed, I suddenly felt a cold wave of a strange sensation come over me and I started to shiver in spite of the heat of the day. My hair stood on end at the nape of my neck and I had goosebumps on my arms. I felt as if there was a presence there. It was not malevolent, but I sensed that it was not of our world. I tried to see whether the others were aware of this entity or if they had similar sensations, but they seemed oblivious to my discomfort. I tried to shake off my feeling of… no, I can't call it foreboding… I didn't at that point know what to call it. I still hadn't put a name to these weird feelings that I had regularly had since I was a child. I decided to ignore them for as long as they let me, like mentally sweeping them under a proverbial carpet. Just as suddenly as it appeared, the sensation went away. Maybe making me aware of them was their way to greet me and send out feelers whether I was the right person to help them. It was a relief to feel halfway normal again.

Okay! Step one taken; I had found my niche, my haven for the days to come. The next step was to locate the cafeteria to see where the hungry hordes would be fed. After dinner, since the college was new, the powers that be had arranged an elaborate inauguration followed by a variety stage show to welcome us, the first batch of the new medical college. Evidently, the politicians and VIPs of the area, including the current Prime Minister, were invited. There was going to be a lot of security. A thought suddenly came to my mind. *Will "my" policewoman be there as well?*

After a few false turns in the convoluted maze of corridors, we finally located the cafeteria. The first impression we had was that it was a massive hall, probably the size of two tennis courts. It was literally teeming with students of all shapes and sizes. The noise was a veritable cacophony with everyone excitedly trying to get a word in sideways. The explosion of color was nearly blinding since the dress code of the evening was formal because of the auspicious occasion. It was fun to see that the sheer joie de vivre floating around was infectious.

The impression I initially had when entering the massive hall was one of sterility. The walls of the cafeteria were completely covered from top to bottom with white ceramic tiles and the floors were polished marble. All the better to keep clean, I presumed. For our comfort while having our meals, there were long wooden tables with white marble tops flanked on either side by chairs. Most of them were already occupied by the happy, incessantly chattering students. It was on the whole quite aesthetically pleasing, and there was the overall impression of cleanliness and hygiene as per the standards that one would undoubtedly always expect in a *medical* college.

Just inside the entrance of the cafeteria, we noticed that there was a marble-topped counter on the laden with trays, plates, and cutlery arranged in colorful plastic crates and tubs for easy access. A kitchen staff member was doling out something that looked like a spicy chicken curry from an immense cauldron. Behind the counter, fresh *naan* was being baked in the sunken clay ovens as fast as possible. Each and every one was supposed to get a piece of piping hot leavened flatbread, called *naan,* fresh from the tandoor oven.

"Oh, yum! I love the aroma of naan!" Ghazal's mouth was literally watering as we watched the nearly automatic speed at which the naans were being prepared.

"He does look hot, doesn't he? I do hope he is drinking

enough water, otherwise he will get dehydrated," said the ever-pragmatic Sana.

We enjoyed the food and decided to take the fruit that served as dessert with us to the auditorium where the inauguration was to take place. The idea was to snag some good seats. We thought that if we were early enough for that, we could ensure that we enjoyed the festivities in a fitting style and not cramped behind the columns where the stage would have been obscured from our sight.

The auditorium was situated in a beautiful baroque building that had a plaque indicating that it had been built over 250 years ago. It was a bit mismatched compared with the other art deco buildings, but it had a dignity of its own. The vibes emanating from it were friendly, as if it held memories of many happy occasions. The main hall inside had been fitted out as an auditorium, with an ornate first-floor wooden gallery surrounding it. The balustrade around it was highly polished and elaborately carved teak wood. The front of the hall had a massive stage replete with electronically controlled velvet curtains and a built-in sound system.

After we looked around the ground floor and found nothing to our satisfaction, it was unanimously decided to sit upstairs in the gallery so that we were able to have a bird's eye view of the stage. In that way, were able to comment and be as lively or loud as we wanted because we were out of the way and (hopefully) the noise we intended to make wouldn't carry so well to the front.

"This is fun," said Soni. "We have such a good view of the stage. It is as if we are sitting in the royal box in a theater." Even though it wasn't that funny, we were caught in the ambience and the feeling of festivity of the evening and couldn't stop giggling.

Leaning down to see what was happening in the lower seats, I saw a feminine figure in a formal police uniform. Maybe this was the woman I had seen in the morning? She was bending down, speaking to her team, but once she stood up straight, I saw that she was tall and looked quite sophisticated in her uniform. Her hair was neatly braided in an intricate French braid that went well with her hat and fell gracefully down her back. I have always loved people in uniforms, whether they were men or women. It made them look smart and in charge, if you know what I mean.

She was glancing around as if she was expecting to see someone. When she looked up, she found me staring at her and our gazes locked once more. Her eyes were mesmerizing. I really wanted to get to know her. I had never wanted to meet a person as desperately as I wanted to meet this mysterious policewoman. It was as if she held part of my soul. I had never thought of such things before in my life. My focus was school and then college. I didn't even know whether I was attracted to men or women, but I felt this inner restlessness that compelled me to keep looking at her. I just couldn't tear my gaze away. My intuition was telling me that we would be at the very least good friends. Maybe she would teach me to braid my hair like hers one day, I thought.

My roommates saw who I was looking at so intently and started once again with their funny remarks and comments. Soni said in a loud voice, "Leave the cops alone, Sarah. My dad says that neither their friendship nor their enmity is a good idea. Best to just stay away!" We settled back in our seats giggling as only giddy teenagers could.

Waiting for the tardy politicians and VIPs was a pain, but finally the program lurched to a start. We had to initially suffer through a typical formal inauguration ceremony that is usually the norm in educational institutions, especially when they want to pander to the alleged movers and shakers. There were a lot of speeches from pompous men that were all puffed up in their own importance. The peculiar thing was (and it did irritate quite a few of us) that all of the speakers were men at an inauguration for a women's medical college! Not even one eminent woman in sight. Except of course "my" smart policewoman on duty.

After all the posing and pretentious speeches were over, we were regaled with a show by local artistes and were introduced to Sindhi folk music and culture till quite late into the evening, or should I say till the early hours of the morning. My gaze kept looking for the policewoman, "my" policewoman. I saw her in the distance with the VIP guests, but she was kept busy and didn't come near us again.

I did enjoy myself, more so because I had started to bond with my roommates, but I wanted the night to end soon because my focus and anticipation was directed towards the next day, when we would formally start our official career as medical students.

Towards the end of the program, when the belly dancers came on stage and started their gyrations and the male members of the political entourage were enjoying themselves a bit too much for our comfort, we realized that we were quite fed up with their shenanigans and tired after the long, dusty journey that we had undertaken that day. Therefore, by unanimous consent, many of us decided to sneak away and stumble sleepily to our rooms.

Sleeping in the same room with strangers for the first time was a bit disconcerting, especially as I was used to having my own room at home. Funny and weird thoughts started to pop up in my mind, which I am sure would have made everyone laugh if said out loud. Would I snore? Would I be able to sleep well? Would my roommates make weird noises while asleep? In fact, it turned out that the only irritating thing was changing our clothes in the showers if we wanted a modicum of privacy.

After a much-needed shower, I lay down on the halfway comfortable *charpoy* bed and mulled over the day. To my consternation, while drifting in and out of the twilight between wakefulness and sleep, I felt the same presence I had felt before. I still didn't know what it was and why I was trying to convince myself that the entity was harmless, even a friend. My confusion kept growing and my uneasiness lingered on. At the ripe old age of 17, I was not even aware that there were levels of spirituality, extra perception, and empathy in the world. I wish I had had a guide or a teacher at the time. How I would have enjoyed this facet of healing and helping people. Instead, I had to flounder through my varied sensations and emotions, learning as I went on.

Later in life, I found out that I was clairsentient. I feel and sense things that cause me to stop and think about what I have to do next. The point is that whenever I ignored these feelings or warnings, I used to land in deep trouble, and when I followed my gut, I would be a winner. I also found out that I am now on a lesser level clairvoyant as well. Weird. I probably would have been burnt at the stake in medieval times. I do thank my maternal grandmother and my paternal great grandmother for these gifts that were passed on to me. I did wonder then how I could apply them in my medical world and where they would ultimately take me.

I would like to say that such gifts should not be considered as creepy or unusual. Many people have some sort of psychic ability, whether they know it or not. These skills are more obvious in childhood, but as they grow up, many adults start to block out their abilities to the point that they become non-existent. When I eventually realized what was going on in my head, I was able to develop this ability, especially when I intuitively use it to diagnose and treat my patients. But I digress…

Police Headquarters: Arriving In Nawabshah With Inspector Tanya Kareem

Finally, I had arrived at my destination. It was so hot that day that I was sure even the devil would have fainted if he had ventured out. They just had to post me here in this hellhole! The thrill and the pleasure of finally being promoted to inspector had faded away when I received my posting orders. The chief inspector was quite condescending, as if he was doing me a great favor by sending me here to Nawabshah. What in God's name did he think I would do here? No doubt I had been given my own precinct, which I was told for a female was quite good.

(Female? Now I am a species, not a person?). Well, at least they made my precinct responsible for the new Women's Medical College down the road. There was only the first batch there, so I doubted that a bunch of studious teenagers would be in any serious trouble. Or would they? One never knew where the twists of fate would take us.

The heat was so oppressing that I was extremely uncomfortable and I wanted to just get out of the uniform. The shirt was a crisp elegant gray with my shiny new silver pips on the shoulders, but that was when I first wore it in the morning. Since then, I had started to wilt, as I had come directly from the train station to the precinct to report for duty. Looking around, I saw the constable that had met me at the station and I called him over. I gestured to my luggage and told him that I was ready to get settled in my new quarters.

Hefting my suitcase, he gestured that I should follow him. He was still shy, which I felt was not unusual since I was the first senior policewoman to be stationed in these backwoods. I am sure the place will soon have a spate of culture shocks when the medical students, and later when they morph into doctors, start invading the town. Now, that would be something to tell his clan when he went home. The constable walked briskly towards a fairly new looking Jeep Wrangler that was fitted with the requisite antennas and broad band radios necessary for a police vehicle. It sported the police livery and the relevant badges. Putting the suitcase not too gently in the back, and still not talking, which I found to be quite amusing, he gestured that I should sit in the passenger seat.

"Who does this jeep belong to?" I asked. Looking

startled, he answered that it was meant for the use of the inspector.

"And that would be me?" I said in an amused voice.

"Yes," he said. Finally! I got him to speak! He speaks! I could not help smiling.

"Well, then, give me the keys." He looked at me with a shocked expression on his face. It was such an expressive look that I nearly burst out laughing. In his mind he could not fit the blocks of contention together to make his brain realize that this person standing in front of him was not only a female, but she was also going to drive the jeep! How could she do that? What would people say?

"You seem to forget, Constable, that not only am I your superior in rank, but that jeep has been requisitioned for me, so kindly hand over the keys immediately. You may sit on the passenger side and show me the way to my accommodations." Much as I didn't want to throw my rank and my weight around, I concluded that if I didn't, I would not be treated like my peers with the same rank. I had to show them that I was even more capable of carrying out my duties than my male counterparts.

I think it finally dawned on him that I was not just a helpless woman and meant business. My orders and directions were to be obeyed. Therefore, he nimbly hopped onto the passenger side of the jeep and waited for me to start it. Thankfully, even though it was an unknown vehicle, it was fairly new and started quite smoothly. The constable, whose name was Abdul Shakir, indicated that I should turn left when we exited the gates of the precinct. I found that we were driving down a tree-lined boulevard. Even though the day was scorching hot, it was quite cool under the shade of the trees. Given the height of the Jeep, I was able to look over the wall that made up most of the right side of the road. I could see that the compound within was teeming with a lot of girls, some chatting with each other and some lugging heavy baggage. So, this was the medical college my precinct was attached to. Interesting.

Since I was momentarily distracted, I nearly didn't see the gaudily decorated bus that screeched to a halt in front of the college gates. Slamming on the brakes, I came to a complete stop. The bus was disgorging its passengers, most of them making a beeline for the college. Then I saw her. She looked dazed and in awe and kept looking up at the college coat of arms as if she wanted to imprint that symbol on her brain and never forget it. She stood out from the crowd and I wondered if I would get to know her one day. Her auburn hair had just caught the rays of the afternoon sun and was shining as if it was on fire. She looked innocent, maybe even naive, but then, what could one expect from a sheltered 17-year-old student who would no doubt be even more sheltered the next few years while studying in an all-girls medical college? All of a sudden, she looked towards me and it seemed as if a connection was forged between us. It was disconcerting and yet felt as if it was meant to be. As I looked at her, I realized it was the first time in a while that I felt any attraction to anyone. How cruel the fates were to let my dormant feelings emerge for an unknown person in the middle of the road. Would I ever see her again? Would I feel this sharp tug to my being once more? For some odd reason, thinking that I might not see her again hurt. I didn't know what was happening to me.

"Pull yourself together, Tanya," I sharply admonished myself.

I was jolted nastily out of my reverie when the pressure horn of a bus blasted just behind me. I nearly jumped three meters high. The constable could not help smirking. I gave him that much and chuckled along with him.

Navigating through the crowd and the buses that kept disgorging their passengers, many of them for the college, we turned into another tree-lined road. This was a quiet area where the families of the Army and police officers lived. The cookie cutter houses were all constructed by the military, but even though they were similar to each other, the families living there had individualized them by cultivating their front gardens. Some even had vegetable patches in the back yards. They looked rather pretty, especially as the lush bougainvillea and the jasmine flowers were in bloom.

Constable Shakir directed me to a fairly new looking house that had a forlorn looking front and back yard. Well, someone had painted it a pleasant cream color, which was acceptable. It just seemed that I had to personalize this place and make it my home, just like the others had.

Opening the front door, I was glad to see that the place was at least spotless clean and smelt of the pine disinfectant that was probably used to wipe the floor.

Hello, what was this? Wasn't I supposed to get furnished accommodations?

"Where is my furniture, Constable Shakir?" I asked. My irritation was growing, and the heat was not making it any better.

"Inspector... Sir... the house is furnished... look," he stammered.

Hm, let's see. If you can call one chair in the living room, a gas cooker in the kitchen (no fridge or air conditioner), and a rickety charpoy in the bedroom furnished, then yes, it definitely was.

"Where are the curtains?" I bellowed at the hapless constable. "Do you expect me to expose all of my glory to the neighbors?" Now I was on the verge of losing my temper. Believe me when I say that I am known for being even tempered.

"Who is responsible for requisitioning this house and furniture?" It was nearly the end of the day. I wanted a shower and then a short nap. On top of that, I was on duty that night. The inauguration of the medical college had attracted a hatful of politicians. Obviously, it was up to us to take care of their security. I was thankful that my predecessor had already arranged the duty rosters of the policemen and women who would be attending the function.

Constable Shakir was by now quite nervous and lurched towards the telephone that was conveniently placed on the floor. He dialed a number and started to talk in the local Sindhi dialect. He probably thought that I would not be able to understand what he was saying. Well, he was in for a rude shock. I was well versed in a few colloquial languages. No one could hide anything from me by trying to speak another language that they thought I didn't know.

"Inspector, Sir, there has been a budget allocated for your furniture," he stammered nervously.

"Then where is it? Or better still, where are the so-called furnishings?" I tried to hold on to my temper. It was obvious that it wasn't his fault, but someone was trying to test my patience.

"Sir, the sub-inspector told us not to requisition any furniture for you because you are a woman and would not like the things that we men would get for you." He was so nervous I am sure if he didn't have better control of his bladder, he would have wet pants there and then.

"And when were you going to tell me that? How do you think that I am going to spend the night? Connect me to the sub-inspector; I will talk to him myself. It's no use if you are an intermediary. I need to let him know that this is unacceptable."

I held out my hand for the telephone receiver once he dialed the number. "Sub-Inspector Malik, this is Inspector Tanya speaking…"

"Oh, welcome, welcome to Nawabshah," he greeted me in an oily voice before I could say anything. "I hope you are settled in and are keen to start your work?"

"No, I am not settled in, and I think you know why. How dare you let a senior officer who is travelling from one city to another be accommodated in an empty house? You were told categorically to get the place furnished before I moved in!" I wasn't shouting, but there was a grim tone in my voice that was immediately understood by the sub-inspector, who had also broken protocol by not meeting me when I reported to the precinct. "I will be spending the night in a hotel and it will be expensed to the precinct. You can make the expense report and the explanations to the head office. I will expect a meeting with you tomorrow, and

I will also want the funds that were allocated to furnishing my house to be handed over to me immediately."

Without waiting for his reply, I put down the phone. As I was his superior, he couldn't refuse me. But I was suspicious now. He had been the top banana of the precinct for a few months till they appointed a new inspector. Maybe he thought he would be given the slot permanently. Now he had either misappropriated the funds or he was trying to make my life miserable till I requested for a transfer elsewhere.

Well, he hadn't yet met Inspector Tanya Kareem. I had already been told by the chief inspector that I was allowed to create my own team. I was going to give the present staff time to prove themselves, but it seemed that I needed to exert myself from the first day onward.

CHAPTER 2

THE DISSECTION ENCOUNTER

"Any fool can know. The point is to understand."
— Albert Einstein

Sarah's First Medical College Encounter

There was controlled pandemonium the next day. Everyone wanted to use the showers at the same time to get ready for class. Bathroom doors were thumped and there was a lot of good-natured yelling and laughter. The welcome pack had indicated that we were required to wear our white coats for our classes. Maybe it was to give an impression of uniformity, like at a private school, but in reality, everyone was quite proud to wear their coats like a badge, confirming our medical student status. At least it felt that way on the first day and that feeling has happily lingered on for years.

Fortunately, I was able to get my coat custom-made by my father's military tailor and was pleased that it fitted me quite elegantly. Especially on the shoulders. It did look different to the mass-produced coats that were available in the college tuck shop. Knowing that, I am embarrassed to say that I pulled back my shoulders and strutted around with a bit of pride.

To give you all a slight perspective of who I am, I would like to say that when I started medical college, I was young, just seventeen years old. I had happened to skip a couple of classes in school. People told me that I was halfway attractive, and some had even called me pretty, but at the time I was so self-involved with my surroundings and my studies that I did not consider myself vain. Actually, I was not aware that I was good looking. My mother used to discourage looking in the mirror for long and told us that the devil would peep out if we were too focused on ourselves. That scared me for years.

My thick auburn hair was shoulder length with a slight wave, and because of the heat, was most of the time tied up in a neat ponytail. It had natural red streaks that lightened when I went swimming in the summer. I definitely had my own panache that made me stand out and I was quite amused when my style was copied many times over. But that's another story.

Actually, to tell you the truth, I didn't have time to focus on such mundane thoughts. I was impatient to dip my toe in the perpetually moving stream of materia medica. There was so little time and so much to do! One thing I would like to point out is that I never had the time or the inclination for a relationship. I just wasn't attracted to the type of people who my parents thought were suitable. I didn't think there was anything wrong with me; it was just that my goals and my impending career meant so much to me. And yet there were those brown sparkling eyes haunting me... Why had this thought popped up?

It was nearly overwhelming to watch the students, all in their new shiny white coats, streaming out from every possible nook and cranny. Everyone had one single goal—to have breakfast!

"Isn't everyone looking smart?" said Ghazal.

"Yes, everyone looks like reverse penguins in the summer," laughed Soni. Reverse penguins? Weird. Whatever did that even mean? But then, that was Soni.

Surprisingly, the discipline in the cafeteria that morning was remarkable. Everyone waited in line to be served the simple but nutritious breakfast. This time the cook was becoming red-faced once again by frying omelets over a massive skillet that was at least a meter in diameter. The speed at which he flipped the eggs from the skillet onto the plates was impressive.

Teapots of prepared milky tea were set on the tables and they were seamlessly replenished in remarkably short periods. The tea was aromatic and was quite strong, probably from being constantly boiled on the massive stoves, but the saving grace was that they had added a lot of milk, like I usually liked to drink my tea, and it went down bearably well with the rest of the breakfast.

"Do you think they would give me another egg?" asked our ever-hungry Ghazal.

"Go over and stand in line once again," said Sana laughing. "I am sure they can't differentiate or recognize us. After all, it's just the first day."

Finally we went to look for our classes-allocation on the notice boards... crunch time! Yes!!!! I was to report to the dissection hall! The myth of dissecting a human body was going to be revealed, and the trepidations of touching a dead human body, zombies, and things that go bump in the night would be debunked. I would like to say that I had never seen a dead person in my life. The pinnacle of death that I had ever encountered was when my goldfish went belly up and were flushed down the toilet. May they float in peace.

After all the pre-conceived ideas, creepy stories by senior students and young doctors, most probably to scare us, it was surreal entering the dissection hall. It was massive, and there were ten tables, each at a distance of about three meters from each other, placed in two rows along the opposite walls of the hall. Six of the tables had cadavers that were ready for dissection on them. Three of them were empty, and one in the farthest corner had a shrouded figure on it. The smell of formaldehyde was overpowering, and though I am sure it affected everyone, we all tried to look and act cool as if it were no big deal. We all behaved as if we saw dead bodies laid out on stainless steel tables all the time. I for one couldn't look at the remains as the specimens or the tools of learning they were supposed to be. It was sad to see the poor shells of humanity lying there, waiting to help us with our education, whether willingly or by default.

The surroundings, the smell, the whole place actually

was disconcerting and overpowering, but with all of my colleagues around me, I started to feel a modicum of ease. Heaven forbid that I would be there alone! It would have been terrifying, whether it was day or night. However, in all its splendor and reverence there was still an underlying disquiet that kept popping up in my mind. Just as I was getting to be a bit more comfortable with my surroundings, I heard an eerie quavering voice call out, "*Look at me... Look at me... I need... Respect! Respect!*"

These words kept weaving in and out of my mind like in a ghostly loom. They seemed so real, but as before, I noticed that I was the only one who could hear the voice. Was my anxiety morphing into some form of neurosis? Or was someone playing a practical joke on this clueless first year (first day) medical student?

I shook my head to clear it and started to focus intently on the cadavers lying there. They closely resembled the Egyptian mummies that had fascinated me when I first saw them in the British Museum. I was actually a bit disappointed. I thought they would look more... how do I say it? Human? Their skins were dark, leathery, and their jaws were open, frozen in a permanent macabre scream. The eyes were either non-existent or sunken. It was difficult to imagine that these empty vessels used to be people who once lived... and loved. They had favorite foods, worked for their living, and basked in the warm sun. Just like us. It was sad as well as horrifying. Is this the first lesson a medical student learns? To look dispassionately at the "specimens" with the intention of learning? I thought there had to be more to this. How could we be compassionate to the living if we weren't to the dead?

As we were not going to start the actual dissections that day, our visit to the dissection hall was just to make us feel comfortable around the bodies. Our professor wanted us to learn where they were stored and where and how they were mummified. I listened intently to the morgue technician as he explained the preserving process to us. He showed us how most of the blood was drained from the large blood vessels and replaced with the embalming fluid that was pushed in so that it was disseminated to all parts of the body, making the tissues hard and thus easier to dissect.

Our concentration was broken by the sounds of nervous laughter. Obviously, there were the class clowns like Soni who made fun and had smart remarks to bandy about to lighten the portentous atmosphere, but on the whole, everyone tried to convey a studious persona.

All of a sudden, the nape of my neck started to prickle once more and my hair stood on end as I became aware of the presence that I had felt in my room the night before. Now it was getting to be a bit annoying, especially as I was initially clueless as to why I was getting these messages from the unknown. These feelings somehow made me very aware of the body that was lying on the farthest table in the hall, and my eyes were repeatedly drawn to the shrouded figure that seemed quite out of place there. I started to walk toward the covered figure with a feeling of trepidation. It was as if I didn't have a mind of my own and was slowly pulled in that direction. I had no choice but to be there. I was in a daze. The feeling was compelling, even hypnotic. I stood there for a while, then I took a deep breath, reached out, and gently drew the shroud away from the face of the person lying there. I let out a gasp of surprise. He looked normal, and if I didn't know better, I would have thought he was just fast asleep. He hadn't been preserved or mummified yet, so I was able to see that his features were very noble. He was scruffy, and his clothes, though dirty and torn, were apparently of a good quality. I was mesmerized and kept staring at the man lying there as if I was trying to memorize and imprint his features on my mind. He had a flowing white beard and a brown birth mark shaped like a small leaf on his forehead. Clearer and louder, but still as if through a fog, I heard the quavering voice once more, and it seemed to be coming from the old man himself. It was such a sad voice. Full of longing, full of despair.

"Help me! Help me! I need... Respect! Respect..."

I was so deep in thought that I suddenly jumped when I felt a hand land heavily on my shoulder. With a pounding heart, I turned around to see the laboratory technician, who must have followed me.

"Are you alright?" asked the technician. "You seemed lost in your own world."

I bombarded him with questions and he patiently explained that the body had just come in that morning and was considered "fresh." It still needed to be preserved and prepared for dissection. Some municipality workers had found the old man lying on the roadside under a makeshift shelter. Apparently, he had died in his sleep a couple of weeks before. He was in the police morgue awaiting identification, but, since no one came forward to claim him, he had landed in our dissection hall.

The technician said that most of the bodies in the morgue were either homeless or persons that had donated their bodies to science. The police usually brought the homeless bodies to the morgue after ensuring that there was no one to claim them.

As we talked, I felt the strange fog surrounding me once more. I had a vision of a young man with an anguished look on his face. It seemed that he was looking for something or someone frantically. Then I knew exactly what I had to do. I was supposed to seek this young man out and bring him to the old man's body. My dilemma was how could I do that if I didn't know anyone there. I had been in this college for less than a day! Nevertheless, something nudged me on. I felt that time was of the essence. Well, I guess it was because the lab technician was about to embalm the old man's body. I didn't have any authority to stop the process, but once a body was dissected, no one could have identified or claimed it at all. It was gone for good. What a sad predicament.

I left the dissection hall as if in a dream or a trance. I started to walk resolutely towards the administration office, where I felt compelled to look for the young man I saw in my vision.

After I randomly looked around and having basically explored most of the offices in the building, I started to get anxious. It was getting late and I was worried about missing my other classes. It wouldn't look good if I were late on my first day. Just as I was about to give up, a young man rushed into the office and nearly bowled me over. In trying to avoid me, he dropped the stack of files he was carrying. Apologizing, I bent down to help him sort out and pick up his papers and was shocked when I looked up and immediately recognized him as the same man from my vision. This was a delicate situation that would need subtlety and sensitivity. How could I go about that? Should I take the direct approach or should I try to talk to him in a roundabout way? There is no easy way to say "I might have found the body of someone you know!"

Tentatively, I introduced myself to him and asked whether he could help me with an issue in the dissection hall. He was a bit reluctant and tried to fob me off to someone else. It seems that the myths and dread of dead bodies were still alive and kicking, but I persevered and when he persisted in his reluctance to help me, I finally had to let him know the reason why I needed him in the dissection hall. Not wanting him to think I was foolish, I just told him about my concerns.

"There is the body of an alleged homeless, unidentified old man in the dissection hall, and I was wondering that, since you are working in the administration department, maybe you could have a look before the body is dissected." I went on to assure him that I wasn't accusing anyone of negligence. I was sure everything had already been done to confirm the "homeless" status of the body.

"The thing is that I did have an uneasy feeling about him because he looks like someone from a well to do family. Could you just humor a nervous rookie medical student and come and have a look, please? I want to be sure that all has been done to find the family of that man and that everything is well above board."

I was ready to keep on trying to shake him out of his reluctance to come with me when he suddenly stood stock still in the middle of the corridor and became very pale. For a moment, I thought he was going to pass out. He lifted his hand to stop me from speaking, took a deep shuddering breath and said in a sad, unsteady voice, "My father has been suffering from dementia and is missing from our home for the past six months." He took a deep breath and went on, "He just left the house one day and never found his way back. We have been looking all over for him."

He went on to tell me that the family was frantic with worry. They had notified the police and posted advertisements in the local newspapers. They even drove around town and the outskirts to look for him, but no one had seen or heard of him. They were getting desperate for news of their sick father.

After he told me his story, he was suddenly galvanized and immediately hastened towards the dissection hall with me trailing cautiously behind. As he reached the covered body, he slowly lifted the shroud with trembling hands and looked at the revealed face for a few moments. It was then that he started to sob piteously. It was his missing father! I thanked God for the mysterious voice that led me to the son, otherwise the old man's body would have been "disrespected" by being dissected, and his family wouldn't have been able to either trace him or hear of him anymore. While it was a tragic situation, it was nice that the family was able to have closure and give their missing father a proper funeral.

After a short argument and the hustle and bustle of trying to prove the identity of the man, the lab technician handed over the body of the father to the son, but as was to be expected, there was a myriad of red tape and paperwork. The police were informed by telephone and we were told that someone would come over to verify the information and take our statements.

My next class was about to start so I tried to inconspicuously slip out of the door, but I was noticed by the technician and was told that I had to stay to give my statement to the police when they came. The college wanted everything to be legal and above board. More so as they wanted to put down specific guidelines to avoid similar situations in the future.

By now the anatomy professor had also been informed of the situation and he also hurried into the dissection hall. There was a small curious crowd listening to what everyone was saying and trying to find out what the hullaballoo was all about. He told me he would let my other teachers know that I would be skipping my classes that day. According to him, since it was just an introductory class, I probably would not have missed anything of significance.

"Why don't you sit in my office and wait for the police?" the professor told me. I was apprehensive because I had never dealt with the police before and my knowledge about them was only from the television or movies.

There was the echo of footsteps outside the office, and with a smart rap on the door, two policemen entered followed by the policewoman I had seen the day before. She looked impressive and very much in charge. And of course, she was taller than I was. Seems like everyone was taller than me! Did I mention that I liked her uniform? I must have, because she was the epitome of elegance and it seemed custom made just for her. She looked so comfortable. As she entered and laid her eyes on me, she did a double take, as if she recognized me and was surprised to see me there. Then she walked directly up to me and said, "Sarah, your professor gave me your name, it's nice to finally meet you. My name is Inspector Tanya Kareem. I have been seeing you around."

I was startled at her forthrightness, but then started to laugh. "I have noticed you too," I said, trying to stop laughing since it was supposed to be such a solemn situation.

"Well, now that I am here, let me first talk to the college administration and the son of the deceased. I will need to take your statement and then you are free to go," said Inspector Tanya.

After she finished interrogating the others, Inspector Tanya came and once more sat down in the chair next to me.

I told her what had occurred that morning. Obviously, I left out the weird feelings that drew me to the body, but I don't think anyone noticed that. To everyone it seemed a fortunate coincidence that I had seen the body and had questioned why it was in the morgue.

"By the way, I saw you the first day that I arrived in Nawabshah," I told her. "Your jeep nearly collided with the bus. I was glad that you were all right."

"The driver was lucky that I was in a good mood" she said good naturedly. "Coming back to our weird encounter today, I am very happy that we were able to get closure for the family. It would have been devastating for them if they never heard from their father anymore."

That was a sobering thought. She was right. I could not even imagine going through life wondering where any of my parents were.

"This has been a terrifying incident," I told Inspector Tanya. I was trembling. Most probably from a delayed reaction. I could not even fathom what the family was going through.

Inspector Tanya nodded her agreement, and unexpectedly took my hand when she noticed that I was trembling.

"You have had quite a day, haven't you?" she said sympathetically. "I would suggest that you have a cup of hot tea with lots of sugar in it. It always helps me when I feel a bit wobbly," she went on.

I would have loved a cup of tea, but the guilt of skipping my classes weighed heavier on me.

Bidding the Inspector a reluctant goodbye, I was finally able to make my way to my classes. What a relief!

Because of the events of that day, we were one workstation short and the technician was grumbling about it, but he was also happy that the family was reunited. I didn't tell my friends, teachers, or even Inspector Tanya about my encounter with the "twilight zone" because I was puzzled and quite disturbed at the way things had worked out. The positive outcome was amazing, but the encounter itself was quite startling.

That night, before I went to sleep, I felt the benevolent presence once again, and the words "*Thank You, Thank You*" kept echoing in my head.

Well, what do you know! That was an auspicious start to my medical college journey, wasn't it? I seriously wondered what other wonderful and strange things I would encounter in my chosen career. I also hoped that whatever the cases might be, I would be able to contribute positively to whosoever's path I might cross. Oh, and I might have made a new friend here. Inspector Tanya was quite interesting when I talked to her. Let's see how that turns out…

Inspector Tanya: Strange first day at work

I woke up with a dry mouth and a headache. These rickety air conditioners usually do that to me. My alarm went off well after I had a much-needed trip to the bathroom. I picked up the phone to call room service, but I guess that was too much to ask from a small rest house.

"Reception, can you connect me to room service, please?"

"I am sorry, madam, we don't have room service," answered the man on the other line. "What do you want?" Not the politest person around, but I guess one had to make do.

"I would like to order some breakfast, and before that, I would appreciate a cup of strong tea." I literally growled into the phone. I felt that if I didn't have my daily caffeine dose, my headache would get worse.

Finally, I was able to make the rough and ready person that the rest house owners in their wisdom had put at the reception to answer the phones, understand what I wanted. After a quarter of an hour, I was able to get surprisingly quite a good cup of tea. My breakfast of fried eggs and toast soon followed. I was now ready to go and try to unravel the Gregorian knot that the precinct seemed to be tied with.

Locking my room behind me, I was pleasantly surprised to see Constable Shakir polishing the windshield of my jeep. Seeing me approach, he saluted smartly. Hm… someone has been talking about my disciplinary preferences, I thought to myself with a smile.

"Salam, Inspector, sir!" said the Constable.

"Salam. Let's go; there is a lot to do today."

Since it was fairly early in the morning, the drive was peaceful. The air was fresh and free from the fumes of the massive diesel buses. It was quite pleasant.

On reaching the precinct, I was effusively greeted by the sub-inspector and shown into my office. This place was also in shambles, and the air conditioner made wheezing sounds as if it was a cow in labor. It was very distracting and not at all effective. I switched it off and started the ceiling fan. That felt much, much better.

The sub-inspector was lounging in front of the desk in a very insolent and languid pose, which was unfitting for a subordinate when meeting a senior officer.

"Stand up straight and show me the daily crime report!" I literally barked at him. I was getting quite irritated with his attitude.

Once he had handed the files, he pulled a chair towards him, wanting to sit down. I looked up and gave him a stern stare.

"Do you always sit without permission in the presence of a senior officer?" I asked. "Is this the discipline they teach you in the Police Academy?" Believe me, I didn't want to be like this, but I needed to draw lines from the beginning or things would become quite difficult. I wanted… no, I needed to have a well-run precinct. So far the challenge was an uphill task.

"No… Sir… uh… Madam…" the sub-inspector stammered. He stood to attention immediately. I didn't invite him to sit down. I wanted to have the advantage of seniority over him when I was going to ask the difficult questions. If I had shown any weakness, he would have definitely taken advantage of it.

Now for the difficult questions…

"Sub-Inspector Memon, first of all, why was I shown to an empty house when you had been categorically instructed to provide me with a furnished house?" Though I spoke in a modulated voice, my facial expression did convey my irritation.

Before he could open his mouth to speak, I went on, "I believe you have a check for the allocated funds for my furniture. Please, kindly hand it over to me." He became red in the face and then unexpectedly, absolutely pale. If I didn't know any better, I would have thought that he was afraid of something… or someone.

He turned around and left the room as fast as his chubby legs would allow him. After about ten minutes, he came back and handed me a personal check from his own account. The amount written on it was much less than what I had been informed by the chief inspector. It confirmed my suspicion that some underhand embezzling had definitely taken place.

"What is this?" I barked. "Where is the check that was sent to you from the Police Headquarters? Bring that to me immediately!" By now he had started to sweat and was fumbling in his pocket for something to wipe his damp brow. *Aha! I caught you now*, I thought.

"I... I... don't have it, sir. I deposited it the bank as soon as I received it..." He stammered.

"And of course, you deposited the money into your personal account... Tell me, doesn't the precinct have a dedicated account in the bank?"

He obviously had no answer to that. I ordered him to bring me the complete sum by the afternoon. I had already made up my mind that he would be reported. There seemed to be many infractions against him. I needed people around me that I could trust. This was one staff member that I would gladly replace.

I met everyone individually and spent some time with the precinct accountant. There seemed to be many misappropriated funds. Somehow, being in the backwater gave them the impression that no one would care at all if funds were skimmed off in a few places.

Just as I was about to sit back and take a deep breath, the phone rang. Constable Shakir picked it up and spoke briefly to the person on the other side. Then he looked at me anxiously.

"That was the medical college, sir. They would like us to come over to validate an alleged homeless dead body that we had sent over yesterday. It seems the relatives of the deceased have finally identified him. We need to go over there to verify the identification and to sign off the relevant paperwork."

The medical college had called. Interesting. Maybe I would see Sarah again. I doubted that. It was their first day and everyone would be in their classes. Anyway, even though I wasn't obliged to personally go on this errand since I was the senior officer, I still decided to tag along. I wanted to see how my staff handled this unusual situation. Were they at the time absolutely sure that the deceased was homeless? Did they investigate properly? Was this another indication of the sub-inspector's incompetence?

Setting my peaked cap on my head, I drove the jeep with two of my policemen to the college. We were almost immediately ushered to the office of the Anatomy professor, which was situated near the dissection hall. As I walked in, I did a double take. Sarah was sitting in the chair opposite the professor's desk looking pale and mildly distressed. Tilting her head, she looked at me with a quizzical expression. She had seen my double take. *Smooth, really smooth, Tanya.* Anyway, I walked up to her to shake her hand and introduce myself. I was startled to feel a zing when I held her hand. "Static electricity," I thought. Sarah tried to suppress her laughter, but she looked adorable trying to look serious.

We started to question the college officials about the relevant paperwork that was needed to accept a donated or unclaimed body for dissection. It all seemed to be above board. The papers were all in order and meticulously filed and referenced. They were aware of the legal implications if a body was accepted by the college without proper paperwork, or if there was any doubt that the body in question was embroiled in covert illegalities.

I needed to talk to Sarah and the son of the deceased. I talked to the son first because I saw how distressed he was and how he just wanted to take his father and go. He reassured me that there wouldn't be any legal charges levied by his family because it was a bizarre but understandable situation since his father was mentally ill. They only wanted to lay him to rest and have closure. Once I had spoken to him, I finally turned my attention to Sarah, who had started to fidget in her seat.

"I am sorry to have made you wait," I said.

"That's all-right, Inspector Tanya, but please be so kind as to hurry up. I am missing some classes because of this inquiry." Clearly, Sarah was uncomfortable with the situation. There seemed to be something that was not quite right, but I just couldn't put my finger on it. What wasn't she telling me? Why did I feel there was more to the story?

"What made you realize that this was not a usual homeless or unidentified, unclaimed person?" I finally asked her.

"Well, as I looked at him, I thought that even though he was scruffy and evidently had been living on the road, he had very noble features. I also realized that he was wearing designer clothes. They were of an expensive brand that my father also wears, and they aren't the type that one would just give away to a homeless person," she explained.

Sarah also told me how she went to the administration to try to find out whether there were any investigation guidelines regarding the bodies that were received in the dissection morgue. It was fortunate that while she was talking to the young man in the administration department, he had a sort of epiphany and ran off to see whether the deceased was his father. Apparently, he had been suffering from Alzheimer's and would often forget where he lived. Poor man must have been frantic in his last days.

Well, that was a macabre start of my work in

Nawabshah, but as we continued to talk with each other, going from the present predicament to other subjects, we realized that we were both on the path to be friends. We had so much in common. It seemed that my posting in Nawabshah was going to be very interesting indeed.

CHAPTER 3

DR. MARINA'S NARROW ESCAPE

"She nourishes the poison in her veins and is consumed by a secret fire." — Virgil

Sarah

Anatomy is not the only subject taught in the first two years of medical college. We were also immersed in the intricacies of Physiology and Biochemistry of the human body as well. In fact, I loved the Physiology Practicals. They were lots of fun because here, in the laboratory, we learnt baseline clinical skills, like measuring our blood sugar or blood pressure.

To gauge the difference between resting and post exercise blood pressure, we had to run laps around the college, and it was entertaining when the weather was good, not so when it was 45 ^{o}C in the shade.

Another somewhat entertaining practical that would appeal to creepy little boys was to dissect live frogs. We did it not to identify the anatomical structures like when we dissected them in school, but to understand physiological processes. Our frogs were "grown" in an immense amphibian tank outside the laboratory, near the college courtyard, under a large shady banyan tree. Therefore, we had quite an adequate supply of the live amphibians for our experiments, but since we didn't want to unnecessarily hurt or decimate them, we tried to keep the numbers down as much as possible. Some people, like my unamusing lab partner, used to get their juvenile thrills by putting frogs into their neighbors' pockets. Not funny! "Grow up, Simran!" would be heard from nearly every corner of the laboratory. What an idiot!

Our Physiology demonstrator was a larger-than-life woman. She had a cheerful personality and got on well with most of the students. Whenever we were stuck with mounting our specimens or needed any other help, she would be quick to help us. Dr. Marina must have weighed approximately 150 kgs and was blissfully unapologetic about it. She loved her food, and it was quite common for her to order various delicacies from the nearby restaurants and kiosks. Her laboratory partner and co-demonstrator, Dr. Shehla, was, on the other hand, nondescript and seemed like a wilted young woman. She was one of those people who would act older than their actual age. She wore dull pastels and always seemed to want to fade into the background, even when she lectured us. Her lectures worked well for sleep deprived students. I always thought that I should have worn tinted glasses in her class so that I could have comfortably snoozed while she droned endlessly on.

I never really liked her because I could feel the strong negative vibes emanating from her whenever she looked towards Dr. Marina, especially when she thought no one was observing her. On the other hand, she acted all cheerful and chummy towards her when she assumed that she was being noticed. I genuinely thought that what bothered her must have been that Dr. Marina was more popular than her, both in the classroom and outside it.

"Dr. Shehla doesn't seem like a nice person," I told Sana one day during one of her boring lectures. "I just get an evil vibe off her." I shuddered.

"There is nothing wrong with her." Sana tried not to laugh out loud. "The only crime she would commit is to kill us with her droning voice and her dull lectures."

Soni and Ghazal nodded while pretending to be engrossed in a lecture on amino acids. Soni tried to hide a yawn while holding up her notebook. It was quite comical because it was very noticeable. Dr. Shehla did hear our not so sibilant whispers and sent one of her poison stares in our direction but continued with the lecture.

As the year went on and we switched study groups and subjects, there were long periods when we didn't meet our previous demonstrators. In addition to that, with the carelessness of youth, we did not even think about trying to find out where they were and how they were doing, even though we were living on the same campus. We were just too busy with our own issues and studies.

Trying to find respite from our frantic days, I loved to study in the garden during the summer evenings. The balmy air was lovely and a relief from the scorching days. Even though the weather used to be ridiculously hot during the day, the nights were quite pleasant, especially when there was a gentle breeze. We were fortunate that the lawns were well lit by immense halogen street-lamps, so visibility was surprisingly good, even at night. It was nice to see that a few more students had copied me and were taking advantage of the good weather as well. Occasionally, someone would call out a question and an impromptu discussion would occur. Some other students would even bring over some tea or coffee for their friends who were studying late and needed their extra caffeine boost.

One fine summer evening, while I was absorbed in my books and the background noises had faded into a pleasant hum, I felt that oh-so-familiar prickling at the nape of my neck. Startled and disturbed, I looked up to see Dr. Marina standing in front of me. She had a strange expression on her face and she seemed to be trying to tell me something, but I couldn't hear her. Even more strange was that she looked transparent and quite emaciated, not at all like her usual self. That good natured woman who was usually so comfortable with her weight looked alarmingly gaunt!

All of a sudden, with a visible undulation in the light, she became a bit unfocused, but her eyes bored intently into mine and I saw her lips move. Although I strained to listen, I still couldn't hear anything. She closed her eyes as if she were concentrating, and then I heard her words in my head. She looked at me with a desperate expression on her face and simply said, "Help me!"

I looked around to see whether anyone had seen Dr. Marina or heard her desperate plea, but everyone else was engrossed in their books or their animated discussions. The second I looked away, she disappeared just as suddenly as she had appeared before me. Curioser and curioser.

Without further ado, I gathered my books and started to walk towards my dorm, but the deep uneasy feeling remained with me. On an impulse, I turned and walked to the other side of the campus, where the teachers' apartments were. I thought I would talk to a friend of mine who was also a teacher at the college. Maybe she would know what was going on.

Thankfully, Dr. Naheed was in her apartment, and she welcomed me into her cozy pied-a-terre even though it was quite late. She had made the cookie cutter accommodation that the college allocated for the staff into a comfortable living area, with a few knick-knacks and colorful cushions brought over from her home.

"Come in, come in, Sarah!" she said happily. "I haven't seen you in a while. It seems that the clinics have been keeping you quite busy. Or is there some handsome doctor that I don't know about?" She laughed at my nonplussed face.

"It is nice to see you. And the fault is absolutely mine." I agreed with her. "But you know how focused medical students get. Nothing exists outside our sphere of concentration." We both laughed knowingly.

"Naheed, I have come for some information. Can you tell me where Dr. Marina is? I haven't seen her for a while."

"She is admitted in the hospital! Didn't you know?" exclaimed Naheed. "She has been ill for at least three weeks, and she doesn't seem to be getting any better. The doctors are confounded. They don't know what is wrong with her in spite of the numerous tests that they have done."

Apparently, many people on campus already knew about her condition, but I hadn't heard anything at all about it.

I felt as if I was hit by a thunderbolt as I heard my friend tell me the details of what she knew of Dr. Marina's illness. Feeling a wave of nausea come over me, I started to get into the "zone," as I used to call it. This was where I would experience situations intuitively, but I pulled myself together and left as soon as I politely could. I didn't want to space out and have a mistaken diagnosis of petit mal epilepsy slapped on me. I can assure you I don't have that condition... yet… if ever.

We weren't allowed out of the college premises after 10 pm, so it was frustrating for me to have to wait until the morning, but there was nothing I could do about it unless I jumped over the gate or the wall. And that wasn't worth the risk of my being suspended, or so I thought at the time. I lay down on my bed and started to "look around" and focus on the sick doctor. The strange thing was that I couldn't "see" Dr. Marina at all. All I could see was the angry face of her laboratory teaching partner, Dr. Shehla, furtively mixing a dry, gray powder in her tea. We had just finished studying toxicology that semester, and the only powder, to my knowledge, that caused such rapid weight loss was arsenic.

I opened my vademecum of poisons and did a quick check to confirm my suspicions. There it was in black and white! Dr. Marina showed all the symptoms of arsenic poisoning, including abdominal pain and significant weight loss.

My "vision" and my cautious theory that she was being poisoned did sound dreadful, but the poor lady was not getting any better. I had to put on my Sherlock Holmes hat to investigate, so I planned to speak either with her or her doctor the next day. There was one voice of caution repeatedly flitting through my mind. I shouldn't do this alone; I needed to speak to somebody who could help. Moreover, Tanya needed to be informed as soon as possible. Fortunately, I did have her office phone number. However, I didn't want to call her on an unfounded suspicion or a whim, but I made a note in my diary to call her immediately after I had seen Dr. Marina and formed a solid opinion.

The next morning, I skipped breakfast and ran over the connecting bridge from the college's main building to the hospital. Thankfully, the nurse at the Intensive Care Unit's counter knew me from our clinical rotations and was helpful with the information I needed. She was kind enough to allow me to see the Dr. Marina for a few minutes.

I knocked on the door of Dr. Marina's room and heard a weak voice inviting me in. I was shocked when I saw her. I had to control my tears and put on a brave face so that I didn't startle her. She looked emaciated in that large hospital bed. She was happy to see me, but I could see that she could hardly talk, and when she did try, her words came out with such great effort that she nearly passed out. The IV fluids and medication that she was getting were the only the reasons that she was still holding on.

The nurse told me who her attending physician was and

I immediately went to look for her. I had had a few clinical rotations with Dr. Farah and she knew me well. We had a good rapport because we had done a small clinical trial together and I had helped her compile the study data and write an article on the findings so that they were published in a well-known local medical journal.

Dr. Farah was finishing her paperwork in her office when I knocked hesitantly on her door, not wanting to disturb her in case she was busy. She looked up, quite surprised to see me.

"Come in, Sarah, sit down. Let me finish these files and then I will give you my full attention." She smiled and was once again engrossed in her work.

When she finally finished, she looked at me with a questioning look. "Why are you in the hospital at this time?" she asked. "Aren't you supposed to be in class? I thought your year had clinics only in the afternoons and evenings."

While we were drinking the inevitable cup of tea her assistant brewed for us, I told her why I was there and what my concerns and suspicions were. We discussed Dr. Marina's case at length.

"I am sure you have done all that is required to diagnose Dr. Marina's illness, but have you thought of doing a toxic screen? Maybe focus on a poison like arsenic?" I asked tentatively since I didn't want to second guess or offend her.

"Funny that you mention that," she mused. "I sent her blood as well as her hair for toxic screening just an hour ago. Good catch!" I was pleased that she wasn't offended like some senior professors would be if a student enforced their opinion on them. "I just took over the case from Dr. Iqbal, who is on emergency leave, and I was wondering why these investigations hadn't yet been done. Dr. Marina's symptoms of poisoning were masked by the similar symptoms of gastroenteritis. Therefore, I am sure that any suspicion of poisoning wasn't deliberately overlooked." She was quite worried, but till she had her suspicions confirmed from the laboratory, she couldn't do much to help Dr. Marina. Just as we were chatting, her phone rang. It was the laboratory. To our dismay, they had found significant amounts of arsenic, not only in Marina's blood stream, but also in her hair follicles and nails, which indicated chronic arsenic poisoning. Apparently, this had been going on for a long time!

The odd thing with Dr. Marina's case was that her symptoms still persisted after three weeks in the hospital. In all fairness, her symptoms should have declined if she was away from the alleged source. Now it was time to talk to Tanya.

"Her symptoms should have abated by now," I said. "Yet, she's deteriorating rather than getting better. My friend is police Inspector Tanya of the local precinct; may I bring her in to investigate Dr. Marina's case?"

Dr. Farah thought it was a good idea, especially since we knew Tanya and were sure to be kept in the loop as the investigation went on. She informed the head of her department and I called Tanya.

"Hey, Sarah! How are you? I haven't heard from you in a while." Tanya sounded pleased to hear my voice.

"I am so sorry to bother you, Tanya, but one of my teachers is being poisoned with arsenic. We weren't sure before, but the laboratory has just confirmed the presence of arsenic in her blood. Please, could you come over and do the needful?"

She was able to come to the hospital immediately. In her usual persuasive way, she talked to the staff and could put together some pieces of information through their statements to construct a sequence of events.

The head nurse knew who was visiting Dr. Marina regularly, and her statement was the most useful and focused the case in the proper direction.

"Dr. Shehla has been bringing soup and tea from her home. I find it quite nice of her to make sure that Dr. Marina drinks whatever she brings in front of her. She insists on feeding the sick doctor herself. Everyone thinks it is sweet of her to care for her colleague." She went on with a worried expression on her face. "We all did notice whenever Dr. Shehla left, she would feel extremely ill once again."

As luck would have it, there was an empty flask on the bedside table in Dr. Marina's room. Inspector Tanya picked it up after she put on the latex gloves that she conveniently carried in her pockets. The dregs of the flask were sent for toxic screening to the police laboratory and the flask was examined for fingerprints.

As you might have guessed, the fingerprints matched Dr. Shehla's. But then, why wouldn't they? The flask was hers and she was bringing some form of nutrition for Dr. Marina, wasn't she? However, the police laboratory's toxic screen revealed that the dregs in the flask did have small doses of arsenic. It was impossible for her to explain that away.

We were lucky that we were able to diagnose Dr. Marina's ailment in time and treat her immediately. The culprit, Dr. Shehla, was promptly arrested, and Tanya told us later that, after a quick trial, she had been jailed for attempted murder. She was sentenced to fifteen years incarceration with hard manual labor.

The question in everyone's mind was why Dr. Shehla was so jealous of Dr. Marina. It was puzzling because they seemed like such good friends. They used to be seen together all the time. Obviously, they had to work together in the laboratories and set the lesson plans together, and that took most of the day, but they were also seen in the cafeteria or in the recreation room playing table tennis on many occasions. I wondered what would come up in Tanya's investigations.

Dr. Marina was shocked at the hate and malevolence emanating from her so-called friend. She was upset at the blatant duplicity that made her suffer and nearly kill her. For a while, she was understandably depressed, but her usual exuberance and resilience didn't let her down. She bounced back healthy, joyful and slimmer! She would joke with her students about being bankrupt because she had to get a new wardrobe. The happier outcome was that the tragedy brought her and Professor Imran closer, and their friendship blossomed into an endearing love. After a few months of courting, they did tie the knot and, to my knowledge, are still happy together.

When I last saw her, Dr. Marina hugged me and thanked me for saving her life. Of course, I modestly said I didn't do anything… much. She insisted that I had, because while she was ill and in a semi coma, she had "seen" me studying in the gardens and somehow knew that I would be able to "hear" her. It was that "visit" that triggered further investigation into her case and her life was saved. Though I was still wary about these psychic incidences, I was happy to help in any way. No one should take a human life, no matter what the circumstances or the reasons. Everyone has a right to a life filled with health and happiness.

I was proud of Tanya and the way she handled the case. This was the first time I could see how a murder investigation was conducted. Though I didn't do much, I did bask a bit in Tanya's glory.

Tanya

Work at the precinct had become mundane. Minor crimes were committed every day, and the daily crime reports were handed over to me by the sub-inspector. I still didn't like him. But as long as he behaved.

I hadn't heard from Sarah for a while. I suspected that she didn't want to disturb me while I was busy. I couldn't dispute that because my work did have erratic hours, and a call could be the deciding factor between life and death if it came at an inopportune time. Therefore, I used to call her whenever I was able to. For her to call me during work hours indicated that there might be something seriously wrong.

"Tanya, I am so sorry to have bothered you." She was very apologetic, but firm. "One of our teachers is being poisoned and she is not doing very well. Thank God we were able to diagnose the condition and identify what poison was being given to her. But now it's touch and go. I do hope the doctors can help her." She was quite upset. Understandably so.

On the bright side, well, at least we were being pulled out of the doldrums and there was a proper case to sink our teeth into. Well… just saying.

My trusted constable and I reached the hospital and started our investigation by talking to the treating physician of the victim. Sarah met us at the gate and introduced us to the doctor.

"It's so nice of you to be so prompt," she exclaimed. "Let me introduce to you to Dr. Farah. She has been very diligent in getting samples of blood, vomitus, and hair ready for you to take to the police laboratory."

Laughing at the mock disgusted look I had on my face, Dr. Farah asked me to sit in her office. Over a cup of tea, Sarah and she brought me up to date regarding the condition of the patient and their suspicions. Dr. Farah was quite indignant. "Why would a colleague do that to another?" she kept asking till I became irritated. I would have said something acerbic, but just at that moment, I caught Sarah's eye and she almost imperceptibly shook her head as if she knew what I was going to say.

"We will investigate the case to the best of our ability," I finally reassured Dr. Farah. "We need solid facts for them to be accepted in court. If Dr. Shehla is found guilty, she will be punished."

After two days, our police laboratory confirmed the findings of the hospital laboratory. Dr. Marina was definitely poisoned, and from the long-term administration of arsenic, it was confirmed that someone near her must have administered it on a regular basis. The fingerprints and the witness statements were enough to arrest Dr. Shehla. As she was awaiting trial in one of our lockups, it was easy to question her further.

"Do you know why you are locked up and in our custody?" I asked for the tenth time. I was slowly getting frustrated, but I knew she was on the verge of telling us her grim story.

Finally, after about a week in the lockup, Dr. Shehla said she would sign a confession. Her only stipulation was that I interrogate her.

"Well, I am glad that you have finally decided to tell the truth," I said. I am sure she heard the fatigue tinged with relief in my voice. This wasn't a case that I wanted to pull along unnecessarily. Dr. Marina deserved justice.

"Yes, I have decided to talk." She sighed. "I don't like the lockup here and I am sure the conditions at the central jail will be worse, but I need to tell my story. I am feeling guilty and that just gets worse day by day. There doesn't seem to be any relief whatsoever." She tried to look forlorn, but I felt it was just an act to gain sympathy.

"My story starts with the oldest negative emotion of all time—jealousy. I was jealous of Marina's popularity, how she was able to make friends so easily, and how she spoke without guile and self-consciousness with the man that I'm in love with."

I was astonished. Had this mouse of a woman performed a crime of passion? Maybe, but the way the poison was administered means the crime was well thought out. A crime of passion is usually spontaneous, isn't it? Or at least it is most of the times.

"I fell in love with a colleague, Professor Imran of the Pharmacology & Toxicology department in our college." Her eyes became dreamy as she thought of him. "I became obsessed with him, but what could I do? He is so handsome, and his fair features mirror his ancestors from the north of Pakistan, who were said to have settled in the area with the soldiers from Alexander the Great's army. His green eyes are always twinkling as if he's thinking cheerful and positive thoughts all the time." She sighed. "Yes, he is a happy person. That draws people to him, many of them seeking his friendship and wise counsel."

Listening to Dr. Shehla was like hearing the script of a cheesy soap opera. I knew that the story would be convoluted, but I needed to know how it played out. For the sake of my curiosity, and of course, for the closure of the case.

Dr. Shehla started to flag with fatigue, but we needed her complete statement for the preliminary hearing in the morning. There was to be no rest for her, and obviously none for me and my stenographer either.

"His kindness and friendly demeanor caused me to mistakenly have stars in my eyes and I was already planning my wedding in my mind. He has never given me an indication that he is interested, but I mistook friendship and kindness for romantic interest," she went on.

Dr. Marina wasn't aware of Shehla's obsessive infatuation and was quite pleased with her own platonic friendship with Professor Imran. They would occasionally spend time discussing and debating on a myriad of subjects ranging from physiology to mythology over a cup of coffee. Since Dr. Shehla didn't share their diverse interests, she felt at times ignored when she was left out of the discussions.

"I thought, maybe imagined, that I was being deliberately snubbed," Shehla continued. "I know now that there was nothing more than a casual friendship between Marina and Imran."

In her fevered mind, she was sure that Dr. Marina was her rival, so she devised a plan to get rid of her without any suspicion pointing towards her. She wanted to plan the perfect murder. Being a lecturer in human physiology, it was relatively easy.

Dr. Shehla researched different poisons in the library under the guise of getting her lesson plans ready for the week. She learned that arsenic given in small doses created symptoms similar to severe gastroenteritis and thought that was perfect. That ailment was quite common in the area, and Dr. Marina was known to love street food without being too picky about hygiene and cleanliness, so no one would suspect anything. Everyone knew that Dr. Marina would actually laugh when she ate at the street kiosks saying that the flavor of the food was enhanced with the bacteria and dust. So, simulating lethal gastroenteritis was the best option with minimal odds of anyone ever suspecting Dr. Shehla.

"Answer the million-dollar question. How did you get the poison?" I asked. I was astonished at her audacity and her single-minded planning of the alleged murder. "It's not as if you could just walk into any shop in the market and ask for it."

"I did think for a long time. I wanted to get the poison without leaving a trail that would point to me," she said slowly, weighing her words. "Then it struck me! It was my eureka moment. Professor Imran had access to a lot of chemicals and toxins. My source was right under my nose!" Her voice was tinged with triumph, as if she was internally congratulating herself for a good job done.

After careful planning, Dr. Shehla "coincidentally" met Professor Imran in his laboratory and accepted the inevitable cup of green tea that he was always willing to offer his visitors. While they sat there savoring the hot brew, Shehla started to ask him about the chemicals on display. Slowly, the subject moved towards poisons and their effects.

"I mentioned that I had a lot of cockroaches in my apartment and no matter what I did, they didn't seem to go away. I asked Imran whether there was any toxin that would get rid of the cockroaches for good." One could see that she enjoyed the ingenuity of the story, that the pseudo-remorse just seemed to melt away. Her narcissistic trait was slowly peeping out of her persona.

"Imran said that arsenic would do the job and explained to me in detail how it should be used. I asked if I could have a small amount to try and see whether the pests in my apartment could be exterminated that way. He readily agreed and went to the back of the room and opened a cabinet with a key that he had hidden on top of a nearby cupboard." By now, Shehla was so engrossed in her story that the previous signs of fatigue had melted away.

"Imran took a round glass jar from the cabinet with a dark gray powder in it and shook out a small amount into a little envelope. Without any thought of having to hide what he was doing, he replaced the key on top of the cupboard with a wink and a grin. He explained that he had lost the key many times, so this was a safe place, since the main door of the laboratory and the office was anyway locked in the evenings."

Dr. Shehla went on to say that she quickly finished her tea and left, supposedly to kill the pests in her apartment. She was trembling with excitement and in a hurry to start her nefarious plan. Little did Imran know that she was planning on exterminating another kind of "pest" from her life.

That evening, Shehla stealthily put a small pinch of the poison into Dr. Marina's tea. She made sure that the amount was minute, and the taste was masked by the two spoons of sugar Dr. Marina usually stirred into her brew. Shehla didn't know then that arsenic is tasteless. The next morning, as expected, Dr. Marina woke up with severe symptoms of gastroenteritis. She could not keep anything down and felt extremely ill.

"Seeing her suffer, I did feel sorry for a few minutes," Shehla said. "But then I imagined her and Imran together, and my jealous rage built up inside once more."

The fleeting feelings of compassion that Dr. Shehla might have felt for Dr. Marina were wiped out with the triumph of her success.

"I realized that I didn't have enough arsenic to achieve my final goal, but now I knew where Imran stashed the poison." She was almost triumphant while disclosing her plans, as if she was begging for acceptance, and even admiration for her genius. "My next step was to get enough of the poison to make Dr. Marina first chronically and then ultimately fatally ill," she said without a shred of remorse.

As Professor Imran had said, the laboratories were locked when the persons responsible were not available or there were no study groups and/or projects going on. Therefore, the best time to carry out her plan was in the evening, when no one was around, and the night watchmen were making their routine rounds in the college corridors.

"How did you do this?" I asked. "Were your plans spontaneous or did you work out a strategy of some sorts?"

She looked slyly at me and explained that it took her a few days to study the duty rotations of the security personnel. She wanted to identify someone who would be most responsive to her plan, especially making it a point to know whatever she could about that person's life. Finally, she thought that one of the nighttime security guards, Babar, was the best person to help her, albeit without letting him know exactly what was planned. It took a few weeks, but whenever she met him, she would ask how he was and about his family. She wanted to find out if he had any particular weakness or requirements. The poor man thought that she was genuinely interested in his life and circumstances.

Babar finally opened up and told her that his daughter was suffering from acute leukaemia, and the monthly chemotherapy sessions were awfully expensive. He didn't want to stop the treatments because he didn't want his child to suffer even more. By a fortunate twist of fate, he had asked Shelah if he could do some odd jobs for her to earn some extra money. Seeing her opportunity, she readily agreed, and he was grateful for her continued help and interest in his daughter's health. Little did he know that in her mind he was the perfect person to act as a scapegoat to carry out her nefarious plan.

On the fateful night when she finally procured the poison, she lurked in the shadows till she saw Babar walking down the dimly lit corridors, checking the doors and rattling the locks to make sure they were properly locked. When he was near enough, she suddenly ran towards Professor Imran's laboratory, acting as if she was flustered and upset. Babar stopped her and asked where she was going and whether he could help her.

"I tried to sound worried and told Babar that I had lost an important file and believed I might have left it in Imran's laboratory earlier that day, Shehla said. "I explained I urgently needed that file for an important early morning meeting. I insisted that my career depended on it."

I could almost picture Shehla turning her watery eyes towards him and asking to be allowed into the office.

Babar must have known this was against the regulations, but I imagine he thought Dr. Shehla was a kind person who had helped him with the treatment of his daughter, so he couldn't refuse her this small favor, so he unlocked the door and let her slip inside.

Shelah found the key on top of the cupboard, just where Professor Imran had left it. She took the arsenic and poured an adequate amount of it into a plastic bag that she had hidden in the deep pocket of her shirt.

"When I stepped outside, I lied to Babar about not having found the missing file after all and asked him not mention to anyone that I had lost it. I then thanked him and went home, satisfied that he wouldn't betray me and ready to carry out my plans."

During her trial, the testimonies of Babar and Professor Imran corroborated the sequence of events. The fingerprints found on the key and on the container in the laboratory, and the poison found in the flask were the deciding factors to Shehla's guilt. Fifteen years' incarceration is, to my mind, too little when one willfully wants to harm another human being…

I am grateful that Sarah was able to help with the investigation. If not for her timely suspicion of the diagnosis, we would undoubtedly have had a tragedy on our hands.

CHAPTER 4

MAI BHAGI

"I am a mystic gypsy called Qalandar.
I have neither fire, nor home, nor monastery.
By day I wander about the world, and at night,
I sleep with a brick under my head."
— Shabaz Qalandar, mystic Sufi of Sindh

Sarah

Most of the girls in the college were residential students. Before they started living in the dorms, many of them were spoiled with the luxury their parents had provided for them their whole lives. Sometimes the rustic living conditions in the dorms got on their nerves. They were as comfortable as possible, but on the stark side. Therefore, the highlight of our weekends was to take the five-hour journey to go home and recharge our batteries. After all, as hostel students, it was mandatory for us to restock our snacks, replenish our pocket money, and, of course, to have our enormous piles of laundry done.

There used to be this whole drama where we had to get our leave applications signed by the hostel warden, and permissions were doled out according to her whims and fancies. The funny outcome of this strictness was that some students went to their grandparents' "funerals" many times before they were caught fibbing. After we received the coveted signature, we would hop along, happy to have the clearance to stuff our bags with our dirty laundry and decide with our friends what mode of transport we would use to get home that day.

Sometimes, if there were enough passengers going in the same direction, we would charter a minibus. That was fun. We could be as loud as we wanted as there weren't any other passengers to bother, except for the poor bus driver. But more often than not, the drivers were happy to ferry a busload of young, ebullient girls and would every so often contribute their own cassettes when we wanted to listen to popular cheesy film music. The other option was the public bus service that definitely guaranteed sore muscles by the time we reached home, and last, but not least, we had the luxury to travel by train.

Choices, choices… I, for one, liked to travel by train because it gave us more freedom to move about, instead of suffering a sore derriere by sitting in one seat for five hours. Additionally, all of us liked people watching and enjoyed the unique entertainment provided by the colorful characters that used to hang out around the station. Since they considered us regulars most weekends, we formed a wary but friendly… I wouldn't call it friendship… let's just say a connection with them.

One such character stood out in her utter uniqueness. She was a regular fixture at the railway station. Her age was actually indeterminate—she could have been anywhere between 25 and 55. We all presumed that she was homeless because she had set up her shelter under an overpass bridge near one of the abandoned railway tracks, although some gypsies said that she occasionally lived at their camp if there were extremes in the weather. Even though everyone knew her, no one actually knew anything about her. Most of the time she would be seen dangerously hopping up and down the tracks, begging for food and alms, even doing odd jobs for money. She terrified me with the chances she took. She was quite confident about her ability to skip over the rails, but was narrowly missed a few times by speeding trains passing through. We all began to think that she was an adrenaline junky because she used to grin and fling her arms up in triumph after her near misses.

This intrepid but reckless woman was also somewhat vain and very finicky with her appearance. In contrast with other vagrants and gypsies at the station, she was always dressed in clean clothes, even though they were old and mended in a few places. Her colorful tie-dye outfits with the requisite Sindhi ajrak as her scarf, were eye catching, and she always had a happy smile for us. It was no surprise that we nicknamed her Mai Bhagi, which meant Happy Lady in Sindhi. When she first heard it, she was delighted and reveled in her new name. Soon everyone started to call her by her new moniker. It's quite sad that we really never got to know her real name.

While we were waiting for the trains to take us home for the weekend, our whole group used to chat with her. We often sent her on errands and generally made excuses to tip her so that she wasn't overwhelmed or took it for granted that we would give her some charity or alms every time we met her.

"Mai Bhagi, why do you hang around the railway station and risk your life by hopping over the tracts?" asked Soni one day.

"Yes, you could be run over by a fast-moving train that doesn't stop here if you are not careful," chipped in Ghazal. We were all worried because she had been dodging a few trains in front of us that day. And it was terrifying. I don't know about her, but at least my adrenaline was switched on high.

To make her stop darting around, we bought her some food and made her sit with us while we waited for our train. It was difficult, since she was such a restless soul, but hunger won the battle and we watched her devour the food as we spoke with her.

"I have lived most of my life here at the station. Don't worry; nothing will happen to me," she said with bravado. "You city people are not as brave as I am." She started to laugh mockingly at us. "Wasting such a lot of time dragging your heavy bags over the overhead bridge. It looks quite painful!"

Mai Bhagi's life as a gypsy was interesting, and she was savvy in the ways of the world. She made her living predominantly as a beggar, though she did accept small jobs and assignments, but only if and when she felt like it.

Sana was interested to know how Mai Bhagi kept herself so clean in spite of living out in the open.

"That's no mystery," Mai Bhagi smirked. "I use the shower in the transit rest rooms. The bathrooms also have running water. I like being clean. I wash my clothes in the sink and dry them in the field behind the station, but I have to keep a look out for them. There are many sticky fingers around." She laughed heartily at her own joke.

We also got to know that one of the benches in the station was "hers." She slept on it quite comfortably when she wasn't hiding under her bridge. Because she was so friendly with everyone and so well liked, very few railway officials had the heart to shoo her away once she went to sleep.

All of us were scared of the risks she took at the station and continued to admonish her time and again to stop hopping onto the tracks because we never knew when the trains, due to their sporadic timings, would come barreling into the station. I was one of the most vocal of people when we cautioned her, probably because my intuition and clairsentience used to be on high alert whenever I saw her and my anxiety would be almost suffocating. I would have a feeling of disquiet whenever I saw her. I felt that I wouldn't see her on this earthly plane for long. My relief whenever I saw her at the station used to be palpable, and sure enough my roommates had fun at my expense as well. I started to feel irritated with myself. This was not on. I just couldn't sit there and predict the demise of everyone around me. It was too upsetting in every way.

One day, while I was going on and on about her risks and safety like a broken record with her, she put her hand on my arm to stop me. She looked at me in the eye and said quite seriously, "Doctor, I am well aware that you know what's going to happen to me. I am a gypsy from an ancient tribe, so I recognize that you have the 'eye' like I do. You feel things that others don't. What has to happen will happen. Just promise me that when I need you, you will come and hold my hand."

Her words stunned me! I just stared at her, my mouth opening and closing like a grounded fish gasping for air. Before I could answer or say anything coherent, our train chugged into the station and I had to board it before it left without me. She ran after the moving train calling out, "Promise me!" She nearly tripped over a brick while she ran, but she was persistent. It was only after I tersely nodded in agreement that she was satisfied and stopped running.

The usual revelry we had while going home couldn't pull me out of my melancholy. My friends tried to lighten my mood with jokes and funny songs, but nothing felt right at the time. I knew deep in my soul that I would be meeting Mai Bhagi again in circumstances that would give me goose bumps. I was not looking forward to that.

As the days went by, I immersed myself in my studies and the various college activities. I had nearly forgotten about the last time I had seen Mai Bhagi when a few weeks later, I was posted as a student observer in the Emergency Room and was called to help a senior doctor with a severe trauma patient. We were told by the EMT present that the female patient they had just brought in had been run over by a speeding train. To my horror, but regrettably not to my surprise, it was Mai Bhagi, who had tripped on the tracks as she was trying to cross them, and a fast-moving train that wasn't scheduled to stop at the station had run over her legs when she fell in her haste to sprint over the tracks. Both of her legs were completely severed except for the one delicate sliver of skin that they were both hanging from.

I was just a third-year student with limited skills and the only thing I could do was try to comfort her with soft words and hold her hand as I had promised her. The others in the trauma team were trying to treat her shock, stop her bleeding, and make her as comfortable as possible. The doctors tried to reattach and repair her legs, but they were unsalvageable. The only thing we could do was clean the wounds and try to stop the bleeding to the best of our ability. The trauma team had to give Mai Bhagi as many intravenous fluids and blood transfusions as possible to try to save her life. Sadly, our efforts were unsuccessful and she died while we were still working on her. The cause of death was registered as severe accidental trauma and shock due to acute blood loss. That she was also anemic and malnourished clearly did not work in her favor. Maybe, if she had been in better health, she would have had a better chance. The if's and why's would keep on haunting me, and to this day I still see her face smiling in delight at me when we bought her lunch at the station.

As was the usual standard operating procedure, the Emergency Room at the hospital had to inform the police and the coroner about the poor woman. We were therefore visited by Tanya and her team. While it was nice to see her again, I wished it would have been under more pleasant circumstances.

Since she was in the hospital in an official capacity, she

just waved at me and smiled before she started to take statements from the ER doctors and the EMTs. As per the requisite protocol, Tanya took our statements as well, first together, then individually, which indicated that she was comprehensive and methodical. I told her later that I was very impressed with her.

"Inspector Tanya!" I said addressing her formally because of the situation. "Could it have been foul play? Do you think that someone might have pushed her onto the path of the ongoing train?"

She looked at me with understanding and compassion because I had previously told her about Mai Bhagi. She knew that I had liked the eclectic gypsy and that her passing had upset me.

"I can't say at this point, but I will definitely let you know once I have finished my investigation." She squeezed my shoulder to indicate that she empathized with me before she followed her men to the waiting Jeep.

The police interviewed some witnesses at the station, including the stationmaster himself. It took some time to collect all the relevant information because, as it often happens all over the world, maybe more so in this neck of the woods, people were wary of the police. They did make some headway because of Inspector Tanya's smooth yet persuasive way. When she finished analyzing the data they had collected, she promised that she would let us know her findings so that we could put Mai Bhagi's body to rest, wherever that might be.

After just a few hours, we had another visit from Tanya. She had completed her inquiry and wanted to let the medical team know about her findings. Her investigative team had combed the area where the accident had occurred. The meticulous investigation was undertaken because initially, like I did, the police had suspected that she could have been pushed by someone onto the path of the oncoming train.

"Sarah, Mai Bhagi's death was a tragic accident. We looked around and found a ripped piece of cloth similar to what she was wearing tightly wedged between the rails. Her clothes probably got caught in the groove between the metal joints. Witnesses said that she tried to free herself, but she couldn't pull her clothes out in time when she saw the train coming. It all happened so fast..." Tanya was nearly as upset as we were. She told us that she had also talked to Mai Bhagi a few times at the station and had developed a soft spot for the vagrant as well.

While waiting to hand over her body to her relatives, the police kept Mai Bhagi's body in the morgue, which stretched to over two months, but unfortunately, no one came forward to claim her. A few of us tried to help with Tanya's investigation by cutting classes to ask the people in the surrounding gypsy camps about her. We also questioned the other drifters at the station on whether they knew if she had family or ties to anyone. We thought they might be more open talking to us instead of the police, but no one knew anything significant about her. It was heartbreaking that even in death she remained a mystery.

Fortunately, Tanya was able to gather her meager belongings from her makeshift shelter before anyone else claimed or stole them, but they offered no clue of any specific identity or information about any next of kin. Mai Bhagi didn't even have the mandatory identity card that everyone was supposed to have. The police were just as clueless as we were.

Finally, to the satisfaction of the other junior students, there was a rare female body to dissect. I was just grateful that I had moved on to the next professional year and wasn't one of those students. My friends and I wanted to remember her as the laughing woman we used to see at the station, risking her short life hopping from one platform to another over the perilous tracts. I said a little prayer for her while standing outside the dissection hall. I didn't go inside. Seeing her lying there would have been too much for me.

The whole situation was surreal. It was as if she knew that her life was going to be short and she made sure that she lived it to her fullest capability. She was also aware that I had "seen" her and she had tried to comfort me in advance, instead of the other way round. Holding her hand as her breath gently left her body was not only a comfort for her, but, oddly enough, also for me. I was grateful that I was able to provide solace, ever so small, to a dying woman. However, the burden of guilt was heavy. Could I have been firmer when admonishing her? Could I have made her understand the risks she took in a better way? The only answer that comes to me, and reassures me, is that it was her time to move on.

For a class welfare project, we contacted the railway authorities to review the safety parameters of the railway station. After much lobbying and with the help of Inspector Tanya, we finally did get the stationmaster to put up strong iron fences in between the tracks to encourage passengers to use the overhead pedestrian bridge and not take short cuts and hop over the tracks. He also affixed prominent signage with warnings about the risks of crossing the tracks. The police and the railway authorities collaborated to levy heavy fines in case of violations, though I wonder if any were enforced or paid. Hope prevails that these small safety measures would have to some extent prevented similar tragedies in the future.

Mai Bhagi, you were a short-lived light in this world and brought smiles to many faces because of your sunny disposition and humor. Your unfortunate accident ensured that many travelers are safer. This is your legacy. I hope you are happy wherever you are now, may God bless you.

Tanya

The heat had been oppressive for days. It was the hot, humid type that wanted you to stay in and not venture out at all. I was by now quite comfortable in my house. With whatever I could manage with the police budget, I was able to get it stylishly furnished. The best thing was that a new air conditioner hummed quietly in the bedroom. I really didn't want to go to work that day. Since I was the boss, there was no way out of it. I just had to get ready and go.

When I opened my front door, I was hit by a blast of heat. My aviator glasses immediately fogged up with the humidity, and I could just make out Constable Shakir's form. He had made it a morning ritual to polish the windshield of my Jeep. Stepping quickly to the vehicle, I reciprocated his brisk salute and we both drove to the precinct.

The usual crime reports and conflict management cases

were laid before me by the still present sub- inspector. I think he knew that he was being observed and on probation. Since my first day in the precinct, he had been on exemplary behavior. I couldn't fire him for that, could I?

One thing that stood out in the reports was that there had been an accident just an hour before at the railway station where a vagrant had been run over by the express train passing through. She was sent to the trauma ER in the Medical College Hospital. I wondered who the victim was. The train was going too fast to stop, but the driver had immediately stopped at the next town and had confirmed that it was an accident over the telephone. The local police there was sending us the signed statement of the driver by courier.

Constable Shakir had just brought me the cup of tea that I was savoring when the phone rang. There is this feeling that I have when certain calls come in, as if they are important or ominous. This one definitely was. They were calling us from the hospital. Our train accident victim had succumbed to her injuries. We needed to go and get as much information as possible to see whether it really was an accident or foul play. My team was ready to go. I sent a few men ahead and told them to start working on the accident scene.

Getting statements from the treating doctors was important because it would help us if we were to ultimately investigate a murder. I had to go and see for myself what had occurred. Such cases were always the responsibility of the senior officer on duty. I preferred it this way. Maybe I had a mild case of obsessive-compulsive disorder, but I always liked to comb through the evidence myself.

I hadn't heard from Sarah for a while. I understood. Her studies were grueling and the few times I had seen her, she could hardly speak. She was so exhausted. Maybe she will have a bit of time to see me today? Hopefully she would be in a more upbeat frame of mind.

I parked my Jeep outside the ER and walked briskly in. As I entered the corridor that lead to the ER, I suddenly stopped in my tracks, which made the constable crash into my back. I was shocked at what I saw. Sarah was standing in the hall, leaning against the wall as if she was unable to hold herself straight. She had wound her arms tightly around herself and was crying quietly. I rushed over to her and engulfed her in a hug. She put her head on my shoulder and started to sob. Waiting for her to calm down, I led her to a bench nearby.

"What happened Sarah? Why are you upset?" I looked at her intently. Her white coat was soaked in blood. If I didn't know better, it seemed as if she had killed someone.

"It's Mai Bhagi!" she sobbed. "She was run over by the express train today. We tried everything possible, but she died a short while ago." I knew how much Sarah liked talking to the gypsy woman and that she had a soft spot for her. Her distress was understandable.

I agreed with her, but as a police official, I think that I had to develop a thicker skin. It was nice to see that a supposedly jaded medical student felt so deeply for the people around her. It was refreshing and further opened the door to my soul that had been shut very tight for a long time. I think I was falling in love with this woman who was beautiful inside and out.

"I am going to investigate her death, Sarah," I

promised. "We will try to prove that it was an accident and not foul play. We will get justice for her."

Reluctantly leaving a now much calmer Sarah, my team and I went to the railway station. After conferring with the stationmaster, we were reassured that for the next thirty minutes the tracks would be safe to inspect. That didn't give us a large window of time, so we had to hurry.

"Constable Shakir, please demarcate the area with police tape so that we can focus on exactly where the accident happened." I barked similar orders to the rest of my team, and we went over the area as meticulously as possible given the short time we had.

There wasn't much to see. There was a large blood stain that had soaked into the gravel of the tracks and was the most prominent sign that something untoward had happened there. Constable Shakir saw a small bit of cloth stuck in the groove where two rails were connected. It was firmly wedged in, so it took some effort to get it out. I put it in a small plastic bag and told the team to stop working on the tracks and start looking for relatives and friends of the deceased. I had to go to the hospital once more to see whether the bit of cloth we had found matched Mai Bhagi's clothes.

Sarah was still in the ER. Her instructor was making her fill out the relevant paperwork to release the body to the police. In usual circumstances that would have been all right, just routine, but in this case it was downright cruel on his part since he knew that Sarah was acquainted with the patient.

"Do you have to deal with this just now? Can't anyone

else do this paperwork for you?" I was concerned for her wellbeing and didn't want to seem overtly interfering.

"I know what you mean, Tanya, but this mundane task sort of gives me some closure. I do want to get her body properly settled before I head back to my dorm," she said sadly.

"My team is already looking for her next of kin. Hopefully, we can lay her to rest as soon as possible." I squeezed her shoulder in empathy. She seemed to get comfort from that small gesture and leaned into my hand.

Taking her aside, I showed her the piece of cloth we had found on the tracks. She recognized it straight away. It definitely was a piece torn off from Mai Bhagi's clothes. Just to be sure, we both inspected the pile of bloody clothes that were lying discarded in a bin. An orderly had put them there after they were cut off the patient when the doctors were working on her. Sure enough, there was a rip in the pants that matched the piece I had in my hand. Mai Bhagi's unfortunate death was due to a horrendous accident, one that could have been prevented if stricter safety protocols were implemented at the station.

There wasn't much that I could do there, so I reassured Sarah that we would do our best to find Mai Bhagi's next of kin and went back to join my team. But first I had to have a talk with the stationmaster about implementing stricter parameters for safety at the station. I did know that the law dictated the usual guidelines, but I suspected that the monitoring was lax due to the apathy of the police in the past.

As the days went by, we were not able to find a next of kin or even a friend of Mai Bhagi. Sarah and her friends tried to help as well. I shudder to think at the risks they took going to slum areas and gypsy camps. She wasn't aware that I had the foresight of having one of my men trail her. He would have stepped in to help the students in case there was any untoward incidence or problem. Thank God many people recognized the girls as those who cared for them and their ailments in the free teaching hospital, so they were treated with respect most of the time.

Unfortunately, Mai Bhagi was slotted into the unclaimed category and was sent over to the medical college to be included in the dissection hall. Sarah was upset, but I told her to look on the bright side—she wasn't a first-year student and didn't have to dissect her. Yes, I know it sounded callous, but I didn't know what else to say. Sarah, on the other hand, was sensitive and empathic. She said a special prayer for Mai Bhagi outside the dissection hall and then stoically walked away.

The stationmaster was fined for negligence and almost immediately implemented the prescribed safety parameters that were required by law at the railway station. It did not lessen the loss everyone felt. However, it did prevent future accidents to some extent. At least I hoped so.

CHAPTER 5

MURDER SO FOUL

"For life and death are one, even as the river and the sea are one." — Kahlil Gibran

Sarah

In our fourth year of medical college, we studied Medical Jurisprudence, which was a remarkably interesting subject. It is the branch of medicine involving the study and application of scientific and medical knowledge to legal problems. For example, inquests and autopsies. Modern medicine requires a medical practitioner to produce evidence and appear as an expert witness in cases where either malpractice is suspected or where a crime has been committed.

At times it hardly felt as if we were studying the subject. It was more like a Murder Mystery TV series come to life. Reading about the ways a person's life could be terminated, looking for forensic clues, and solving crimes through pathology and medical law was ghoulish but also fascinating. I am quite sure that many crime writers have researched their stories just by reading our textbooks.

One way to commit murder that did stick out was the use of a staff in martial arts. Apparently, it was quite popular with the farmers in the region, where conventional weapons were expensive.

While studying our Medical Jurisprudence textbooks, I was surprised to read how the innocuous staff could be used as a lethal weapon. Although many defensive techniques are taught as intended, a person could wield the staff with the intent to kill and definitely cause harm, not only by the traumatic conventional ways, but also by asphyxiating the victim with force over the trachea.

Since I found crime novels and films so interesting it was no surprise I excelled in the subject, but I missed getting top marks because I could not stomach the autopsies. I always tried to avoid being chosen to assist with them, but on that one fateful day, my professor singled me out.

"There is no slipping out today," said my professor throwing a pair of clean scrubs at me. "You need to attend at least one autopsy to get credits for your exams." He knew that I didn't have the stomach for autopsies and had tormented me many times, but he was right. I did need the credits. Therefore, I shrugged and caught the scrubs midair.

"Good, good, now go and get ready. We need to send the autopsy report to the police as soon as we can. They are getting impatient even though they just brought the bodies in this morning"

Bodies? Plural? It doesn't rain; it pours! I prayed that my stomach behaved through the ordeal.

I took the requisite papers from the policeman who had brought in the bodies and saw that we were supposed to examine a middle-aged woman and her teenage daughter, who had been brutally murdered in their sleep. After the heinous deed, their bodies had been hauled away by the murderer into the desert and carelessly thrown under the overhang of a boulder. Eventually they were found there five days later by a shepherd. Their rapidly decomposing bodies were already half eaten by scavengers and were barely identifiable. Since our hospital was the designated and nearest medicolegal and forensic center, we were given the distinct honor to perform the autopsies and gather any forensic information on these two victims of murder so foul.

The unfortunate victims looked wretched. While we did a superficial examination of them, the professor kept up a running commentary.

"As you can all see, the victims' faces are bloated. This is an indication of putrefaction. Most probably they have been decomposing for more than five days." He looked at me gleefully, knowing that I was on the verge of turning green.

"If you examine the back, you can see a large amount of pooled blood, probably post-mortem, which confirms that they have been lying on their backs all these days." *Well, so far so good.*

"Have a look at their abdomens," the professor

continued in his lecture mode. They were grotesquely swollen. "There has been a massive gas build up inside the bodies that has caused the intestine and other organs to swell up." I dreaded opening one of the bodies with the lethal looking knives and other instruments that the professor had almost lovingly set out on a tray.

One could just hope they had died instantaneously and hadn't suffered too much because it was heartrending just to look at them. The mother's cause of death was a single hard blow on the neck with a sharp axe. The person who did it must have been extremely strong, because just one blow had nearly severed the head from the body. The mere fact that her clothes were completely soaked in blood showed that there had been a large amount of bleeding from the major blood vessels.

The sixteen-year-old daughter had more than one wound around her neck and what one would call defensive wounds on her arms. It was possible that she hadn't been an intended victim, but she had woken up when her mother was attacked and therefore became collateral damage.

I was quite proud of myself that I hadn't (yet) turned green.

Taking the largest knife from the tray, and without warning, the professor sliced resolutely into the abdomen. As if they were straining to be free, the intestines ballooned rapidly out. Almost immediately, there was a horrible stench, much to the amusement of the professor, who kept smirking at me and waiting to see what I would do next. I didn't disappoint him.

I nearly fainted from the stench. I dropped the instruments and ran out into the courtyard. Believe me, my lunch was history! We had read about the process of decay but experiencing it firsthand was much more profound. I don't think there are enough words to describe the gut-wrenching stench, especially knowing it was coming from what was once a living, breathing human being.

While I was losing my lunch in the bushes behind the morgue, I felt eyes on me. I looked up and saw Inspector Tanya watching me with an amused smirk on her face.

"First time?" she asked me.

That is all I needed. A witness to my humiliation.

"Go take a long walk on a short plank," I mumbled, then adding some choice words that were not very polite and nice, which only set her off in gales of laughter. I was mortified. Seeing my discomfort, she changed her demeanor and in her kind way reassured me that it was quite normal.

"You really are feeling bad," she said. *Finally, some sympathy!* "I felt the same way when I had to attend a few autopsies while I was a rookie." She handed me some tissues and a cold bottle of water. "One never forgets their first murder victim. It's like a permanent nightmare."

"If these autopsies weren't part of the equation, it would actually be cool to study forensic medicine," I said. *There goes my glamorous career.*

Seriously, who would want to hurt a mother and a daughter in such a brutal manner? And then callously throw them at the mercy of the elements in the desert?

After I (halfway) recovered, Tanya and I made our way to the hospital cafeteria.

"Come along; let's go and get something cool to drink." She pulled me up to my wobbly feet. "I am sure your professor is not expecting you back any time soon. I saw that he has already pounced on another student victim to help him with the autopsy." Even though Tanya tried her best, she couldn't keep the amusement from her voice.

At the cafeteria, I sipped on fresh lemonade with mint to soothe my abused gastrointestinal system. Tanya had her usual cup of tea. Since she was assigned to the case, we started to discuss it while trying to piece together the very few clues and facts that we had on hand at the time.

After we were sure that enough time had lapsed for the professor to have completed his examination of the bodies, we went back to the morgue to get the final reports of the autopsies. The professor was still there and called me over.

"What will I do with you, Sarah?" He shook his head. "I know your theory is exceptionally good, but you do need credits for your practicals." He rubbed his forehead as if trying to work out a way to help me.

"I have a solution if you think that would work," said Tanya. "How about allowing Sarah and other students who haven't yet earned their Jurisprudence credits to follow our investigation for the two murders?"

To my delight, our professor thought that was a good idea and allowed a group of us to follow Tanya and her team's investigation for the requisite extra credits in Medical Jurisprudence in lieu of attending an autopsy. I guess he reconciled to the fact that I was absolutely useless there. And working with the police was an excellent way to correlate the medicolegal findings with the case to put it together with proper perspective.

Before we began the autopsy I had cut away the tattered clothes of the victims. We had observed that they were made out of pure silk and custom tailored. Both mother and daughter still wore their expensive gold jewelry, so evidently, they weren't victims of a robbery that had resulted in dire consequences. It was obvious that they were from a well to do family. We speculated that they could have been caught in the crossfire of one of the tribal feuds that were common in some of the rural areas.

While we were still discussing and theorizing, a constable came to our table and whispered something in Tanya's ear. She quietly nodded and told him that she would follow him in a short while. I was curious. Not that it was any of my business, and it could have been just routine police work, but there was something in our intrepid inspector's face that told me there was a breakthrough.

"What was that all about?" I asked her. "Was it related to the case? We are part of your team and would like to be kept in the loop." I said truculently when I saw her try to evade the issue.

Tanya pulled me aside from the group. No one thought it was strange that she did so since by now it was well known that we were friends. "I have to keep the information confidential for now," she said, "but I can tell you that this is a high-profile case. If we aren't discreet, it can get dangerous. And putting you and your friends in danger is the last thing I want to do." She looked worried, but I knew she would tell me whatever she knew once she was able to.

Sure enough, she visited our group a few days later with the files on the victims. We were not so naive to think that the police would disclose everything to us, but there was enough information there that made us think about the cases and speculate on the whys. We thought of ourselves as modern-day Dr. Watsons to Tanya's Sherlock Holmes. How exciting would it be if we were able to solve the case?

"Calm down," laughed Tanya. "You never know. However, do promise me that you all won't do anything without my help or consent. It could be dangerous for you."

"And it's not dangerous for you?" I argued.

"It's my profession. I have been trained to fight crime, but you haven't." I could see that her concern for me and my colleagues was tinged with irritation. "Just try and apply the medical jurisprudence perspective to the case. Promise me; otherwise, I shall tell your professor that the arrangement between us is not feasible and therefore null and void." She was nearly shouting by now. I realized she was concerned, so I looked at my colleagues and we silently nodded our acquiescence.

Satisfied that we wouldn't behave like reckless Nancy Drew wannabes, she told us what she knew about the case so far.

"The victims have been identified as the wife and daughter of a well-known and influential wadera of the district." We all gasped as that really was a high-profile case. "However," she went on, "it is very strange that no one has as yet reported them as missing or as the victims of a crime."

Investigating further, the police found out that one of the reasons that the crime might not have been reported was that the husband and brother of the victims weren't available in town. Both of them had been missing for the past few days, which was in itself peculiar. The husband usually travelled with a large entourage and his whereabouts were always known.

"We were able to bring the brother in for questioning. He had a solid alibi."

We were relieved. It would have been ghastly if he had murdered his mother and sister in cold blood.

"Our investigation team confirmed that he left home two weeks ago for his college in the neighboring town. We were able to contact him by telephone and the poor man was shocked when he heard the news." Tanya went on with her narrative. "He wasn't even aware of what had happened to his mother and sister." Evidently, he was quite grief-stricken and had immediately agreed to come back home as soon as he was able to.

Tanya said that the husband, on the other hand, could not be found for a long while. None of his family or employees knew where he was, therefore, he was the prime suspect on the list of suspects put together by the police. Oddly, it seemed he had just disappeared from the face of the earth.

"He was ultimately found after a few days, that too in a town over 1000 kilometers away," Tanya explained. "We observed that he was a tall mountain of a man who could have easily wielded the fatal axe, but we needed proof and could not randomly pin the crime on him with just circumstantial evidence or on the basis of his stature. Apparently, he had an alibi and witnesses to say that he had been visiting a friend for the past ten days. We think it is a bit too convenient."

We met Tanya the next day at the coroner's office after our classes and were anxious to know what new evidence or clues had been found. It was extremely exciting to be included in the investigative process and we felt quite important. I realized that any students who were interested in forensics would learn a lot with this liaison that we were lucky enough to have with the local police. I must say they were very tolerant and patiently answered our questions. I think they were happy to contribute to that part of our education.

Seeing our interest, our professor allocated a room in the forensics department of the college for us to brainstorm. Tanya had set up a copy of her story board here for our review. Whenever we could, we looked at it till we were cross-eyed and tried to make head or tail of the clues as well as the information collected so far. It was a bit sparse and the focus at the time was towards a beedi stub that had been recovered from the crime scene. We were constantly grasping at straws. We needed to review what we had very carefully, because the identity of the victims indicated that there were some powerful and influential people that could have been involved in the whole incident. Therefore, we needed to plan very carefully how we were going to go forward with our information and the subsequent development of the case.

"Let see what we have so far," said Tanya in her inspector mode, looking at the board while she spoke. "To summarize, this is the available information that we have compiled so far:

The name of the older victim, the mother, was Yasmeen, and she was the wife of Abdul Shakoor Shah, a wadera, a local feudal landlord." Shaking her head in disgust, she continued. "Witnesses have said that he was renowned for his decadent lifestyle and liked to smoke custom made beedis." The police investigators confirmed that a few beedi stubs found near Yasmeen's body were from the stash that belonged to her husband.

Tanya went on, her voice tinged with sadness and regret for the loss of such a young life. "The daughter, Nabila was just sixteen years old and a student at the local high school. She was normal and healthy. There was talk of her engagement to a family friend's son who was working in Dubai. The wedding was supposed to take place after she graduated from school. Poor kid having her life snuffed out so early was definitely a tragedy."

Abdul Shakoor Shah was a well-known politician, landowner, and basically a dangerous bully in the area. Therefore, the investigation hit a few roadblocks by the police, who were instructed by their senior officers to treat the evidence they had gathered so far only as circumstantial. They needed to tread with caution lest they offend anyone and cause political as well as personal backlash to the whole team. It was frustrating, but the police, under Tanya's leadership, were not discouraged and they tried their best to dig deeper.

We continued to collaborate with the police for weeks but were not getting ahead in any way. Our impatient digging for clues, formulating theories and speculating while trying to get ahead with the case were tolerantly smiled upon. We felt as if we were puppies that were occasionally thrown a treat to calm us down!

"We are hitting dead ends whenever we try out a new theory." I was frustrated and irritated with Tanya, who kept telling us that in cases like this, patience really was a virtue.

That night I had a dream, or I think I should say a nightmare. I relived Nabila's death in graphic detail. Her mother was already dead and lying on her bed. Nabila tried to fight bravely, but the cruel person who was attacking her didn't relent. She kept saying *"Abba! Abba!"* Now, anyone who has a bit of ESP will tell you that it's not an accurate science. We have to analyze the information we get from the signs we are shown. It can be frustrating in the best of times. Nabila's last words were calling for her father in horror. Was he the murderer? Or was she calling for help? As Tanya would say, without tangible proof there was nothing that we could do.

As the days coalesced into weeks and I thought we were not going to get any more clues to go further with the investigation, Tanya called our professor and told him that they had arrested a man who had confessed to the murders.

"He is the bodyguard of the wadera," she told him. "His co-workers have said that he is known to fly into a rage for no reason whatsoever. A perceived slight, or a look that he didn't like was enough to set him off. He said that he was enraged because the lady of the house didn't give him dinner; instead she gave him some money to go out to eat. A very flimsy excuse, I dare say. In his confession, he said he was very tired and just flew into a blind rage. Once he realized what he had done, he came forward and confessed to us."

"Isn't that a bit too convenient?" I asked. "Where is the proof? The reason seems so glib!"

Tanya shrugged and said the case was now a closed book. She was getting a lot of pressure from her senior colleagues to wrap up the case as soon as possible.

Knowing her, I was sure that she wasn't convinced that the real culprit had been caught… yet.

Tanya

The worst part of police work is when we see innocent murder victims. The two corpses that were found that morning could only affect a person who hadn't yet been hardened by gruesome or macabre death images. It was one of my duties to see that the victims were sent for their autopsies and to liaise with the medicolegal doctor, in this case the professor of jurisprudence at the medical college.

When I read the report I felt upset and depressed. One of the victims was just sixteen years old. How could anyone be so cruel to snuff out the life of one so young?

I saw my favorite medical student that day. She was definitely green around her gills. Autopsies are not for everyone. Even if they are studying medicine. I felt sorry for her, and her professor was about to tell her off because she wasn't getting enough credits for her jurisprudence practicals. I know it was reckless, but I felt sorry for her and the other students. Therefore, I jumped in and suggested that her group could follow the case with us for credits. It was a good idea at the time, but it sometimes became an effort to rein in the budding Nancy Drew wannabes.

"Would you like to visit the crime scene with us?" I asked the group. "Our Crime Scene Units have already gone over it once, but maybe you would find something with your fresh eyes?" They all whooped with pleasure, and even though I had suggested it, a small voice in the back of my mind said, "Tanya, what have you done now?"

The crime scene was as we had left it. Just the police tape and markers had been removed. Before we started, I lectured them how to handle a crime scene, then I showed the group how to sift through the sand to look for clues.

"Can you see that large dark spot in the sand?" I asked them. "That was where the bodies bled out. Don't touch that, but sift the sand around it and see whether you can find anything. Anything at all, no matter how inconsequential it might seem to you. It could be a life-saving clue."

The students were quite serious and thorough. It was a delight watching them sift the sand with sieves, hoping to find something that would help our investigation.

Suddenly, Sarah gave a shout and walked towards me as fast as she could even though her speed was hampered by her feet sinking in the soft desert sand.

"Look what I found!" She was excited. "A *beedi* stub. It seems to have been custom made. Look, it has an embossed, monogrammed gold band around it. I am not aware of the beedi brands, but I am sure a monogrammed one would be considered unique. What do you think?"

After putting on my latex gloves, I took the beedi stub from Sarah's sieve and sniffed it. It had a distinctive aroma. Marijuana! Contraband *and* custom made.

"I know where they make these," I said. Seeing Sarah's hopeful expression, I continued. "And no, you are not going with me. It's in an unsavory part of town. Because I am the law I can go there safely with my men. I would not put you or your friends in jeopardy."

"I understand," said Sarah wistfully. "Promise me that you will let us all know what you unearth there. Please!" she pleaded and made puppy eyes at me.

Laughing at her, because I could never resist that look, I said, "If it is not confidential, I will definitely tell you whatever is going on with this case." She had to be satisfied with that.

We brought Yasmeen's husband, Abdul Shakoor Shah, in for questioning, but whenever we tried to talk to him about the murders, his lawyer would stop us. It was a dead end. We were getting nowhere. My interrogators and I tried all sorts of ways to get the man to talk, but we weren't successful at all. It was extremely frustrating. Finally, we were told by our senior officers to stop "harassing" him because he was a political heavyweight. That definitely put a spanner in our investigation. I still remember how he tried to bully me when I first arrived. His triumphant smirk when he was released didn't help the disquiet I felt about him. Sarah had told me about her dream. While I would concur that he had something to do with the murders, we had no proof. We had to let him go.

Three days after the fateful autopsy, a tall muscular man walked into the precinct and confessed to both of the murders. He spoke in a monotone and would not look anyone in the eyes. I felt that he was covering up for someone and he definitely wasn't the murderer, but officially, he had signed a confession, and there was no other way—he had to be in the police lockup till his trial. Our senior officers congratulated us on doing a "good job," but I wasn't at all sure that we had the right man. My team and I were going to bide our time and keep an eye out for any clues or witnesses willing to come forward.

Politics, wealth… the bane of ethical police work. Probably a worldwide issue? Who knows?

Tanya

Sarah called me from the hospital. She sounded agitated and excited. It seems that she had a lead in the murder cases we had worked on a couple of months before. I tried telling her that the case was closed, but she was adamant that I meet her in the general surgical ward to hear the story of the man who had been convicted for the murders of Yasmeen and Nabila Shah.

It was clever of Sarah to arrange the meeting in the dressing room off the MRI laboratory. Nobody would see us talking to the prisoner, and we also made sure there was no one nearby to eavesdrop while we listened to his story.

To tell you the truth, I went to the hospital that day only because Sarah asked me to. I was quite nonchalant about the case. Before we met Sachal, we summarized the sequence of events that had been put together with the information we had garnered or received. Yasmeen was murdered in her sleep by someone who was big and strong enough to wield an axe that nearly took her head off with only one hard chop. Nabila was collateral damage because she apparently woke up when she heard the commotion and must have witnessed who was assaulting her mother.

Sachal explained in detail what actually happened on that fateful day.

He told us that he had been the bodyguard and general dogs body of his wadera and was with him on the day of the murder. After a long and tedious meeting with the tribe elders and neighboring politicians, they went home supposedly to rest, but his boss seemed tense and quite distracted. Sachal said that he thought it was probably due to what had been discussed in the meeting they had just left. He was not wrong.

"My assignment that day was to drive my boss to and from the meeting that he had with the council of the neighboring wadera. I believe things didn't go well in the meeting, but I didn't give my boss's foul mood much importance because he had a long-standing feud with the neighbors and it was normal for him to come away from the meetings with a bad temper."

He went on to say, "While I was still driving, my boss offered me some of his special beedis. That was really unusual." Even now, after so many days had passed by, he sounded surprised. "I was flattered because those beedis were only smoked by the wadera himself, and it was rare that he shared them with anyone, even his friends."

He thought he was being bestowed a favor and was even more thrilled when two extra beedis were tucked into his shirt pocket to smoke later on.

"Can you describe the beedis?" I asked.

"Yes, they have a distinctive gold band around them, and when I smoked one of them, I was quite surprised because I felt my brain had become like cotton wool. I also felt calm and maybe a bit sleepy."

Listening to his narrative, his open and sincere demeanor slowly convinced me that he was telling the truth, or at least there was some modicum of truth. However, the paucity of clues at the time and general lack of information had the police focused on the custom made beedis and they had obviously stopped the investigation once Sachal confessed.

"My boss's meeting was with another neighboring wadera with whom he had been feuding for years. Murder and mayhem were the norm between the two tribes, and the kidnapping and raping of their women was becoming intolerable. Therefore, a peace pact was agreed upon between them, but one of the conditions was that the pact had to be sealed by my wadera marrying his ex-enemy's daughter. A lot of money, land, and honor was at stake, and if he wanted the pact, the conditions had to be adhered to."

Shah, the wadera, knew that it was his wife who controlled the purse strings. Yasmeen was very wealthy in her own right and would never allow her property to be tacked on to someone else's with the new pact or the new impending marriage. Even if lives were at stake. She wouldn't permit him to marry a second time either, and he was sure she would make his and his new bride's lives miserable. If Yasmeen left him, she would take the deeds to her lands and her money with her. Since everyone thought he was the wealthy one in the family, that was something that couldn't be disclosed. He couldn't let that happen. He had to find a solution where he could save face and keep his wife's money and lands for himself.

"When we reached the main villa," Sachal explained, "I was told to wait outside the gates and ignore anything that I might hear. Where I was concerned, I had just escorted my boss home and was waiting for further orders in case he needed me for anything or wanted to go out once again." He became distressed as he continued and asked for a drink of water.

"While I waited by the car, I heard a muffled scream from inside the house. I was unsure what to do, so I stayed where I was, as ordered. In my defense, I thought that the husband and wife had an altercation as they had many times in the past."

Though the late hour and the request to wait weren't unusual, Sachal assured us that he had never killed anyone, and he didn't have any intention to do so in the near future, no matter what. He wanted his children to always remember him with pride, so he tried to live a clean life in spite of being the servant of a deviant wadera.

Twenty minutes after the first one, he heard another loud scream. Then there was silence. Sachal started to get an uneasy feeling. Yet he stayed where he was and waited for a word from his boss.

After what would have seemed a long time, though it could have been only a few minutes, he was curtly ordered into the house and was told that he had a special covert assignment. On entering the courtyard, the first thing he saw was a large amount of blood spattered all over the walls, the floor, and even the ceiling.

"You are to keep your mouth shut. If you say anything to anyone about what you have seen here today, not only will you be killed, but also your wife and three children won't see the light of another day." His boss was angry and agitated and kept on hurling threats at him while instructing him what to do about the grisly situation.

To his consternation, Sachal was also instructed to get rid of the two bodies. He recognized them as Yasmeen and Nabila. He was shocked and sad because they had always been kind to him.

"After you have disposed of the bodies, come back to the house and clean up the place as much as you can. Use bleach to get rid of the traces of blood," he was ordered.

Sachal did as he was told, but he thought that was futile, since the bodies were later identified as the wadera's wife and daughter. The biggest mistake was that one of them had smoked a beedi and thrown the stub into the sand next to the bodies. Was it a deliberate ploy to implicate Sachal? The likelihood was definitely plausible.

Sachal went on to say that things were relatively quiet at the villa for a few days. The wadera left for the next town and was not reachable. Everyone was told that Yasmeen and Nabila were visiting relatives in the next village, but when they realized that the police were closing in with their investigation, Sachal was compelled to confess to the murder.

Actually, that wasn't unusual for most of the waderas in Sindh. They would commit the crimes and have their loyal servants take the fall for them. The issue with Sachal was that four generations of his family had worked for Shah and his household. His family's loyalty to them was infinite. It went against the grain of their upbringing and beliefs to betray their boss. They wouldn't give him up for anything. What ultimately caused Sachal to turn against him was the way he was abandoned and his wife and children neglected, even though he was promised that they would be taken care of. Added to that, the daily threats of the other henchmen raping his wife caused him to be frantic with worry. He was willing to sacrifice a few years in jail in exchange of a better life for his wife and children, but they had been betrayed as if they were expendable and discarded like garbage.

I was aware that feudal landlords controlled the areas like Mafia godfathers. Everyone had their own designated area, land, indentured servants, and loyal sidekicks who would take the fall for their waderas whenever he needed them to. The problem was that the waderas thought they were omnipotent and many times reneged on their promises to look after the families left behind. Therefore, the evident poverty and squalor were pitiful.

I would not like anyone to think that these people are representative of the region. Waderas are a small minority in Sindh and in no way typical of the colorful and extremely hospitable folk. Sindhis are dreamers, the original Sufis, and if they could, they would be communing with nature the whole day.

Sachal, who was now the key witness to the terrible crime, worked out a deal with me and my chief. We would arrange asylum for him in a friendly neighboring country with his wife and children if he testified in court. Till such time they would all be incorporated into the witness protection program and his family would be quietly spirited away. They would be waiting for him at an undisclosed location once the hoopla of the trial was over.

I hoped we could finally lay the memories and souls of Yasmeen and Nabila to rest.

. . .

Sarah

We all were relieved that the crime had finally been solved, but I was still worried for Sachal. There was this heavy feeling in the pit of my stomach whenever I looked at him. I felt that by extracting a confession from him and asking him to testify, we had helped to sign his death warrant. I just saw dark clouds hovering over him and I felt very afraid. Even though it was the middle of summer, my teeth chattered and I just couldn't settle down.

"Tanya, please hurry up with the relocation procedures for Sachal. He has to be taken immediately away, since the hospital ward is too open for proper security and his safety. I am afraid for him."

Tanya was by now aware of my premonitions and intuitive feelings, so she agreed with me and arranged for Sachal's transfer as soon as she could. She said that she would personally take responsibility for his safety. As she led him away, he asked to speak to me before they left. He quietly stood in front of me. I looked up and saw tears quietly running down the cheeks of this strong man, who had put his life in danger for the love of his family. Slowly and deliberately, he took his cap off, kneeled down and placed it at my feet.

"I don't have anything of value, but please, take this cap as thanks for all you have done. My family and I will always pray for you. We will never forget you."

I was touched by his gesture in trying to honor me. It

was poignant, and yet I felt flustered and hoped I could handle the situation gracefully. "Keep the cap, Sachal. It was made with love for you by your wife. Besides, you probably will need the money wherever you are going."

After arguing a short while, I was able to persuade him to keep it, but his gesture touched me and I still feel the respect and gratitude he was trying to convey to me that day.

Unfortunately, like in many other countries in the world, the police were entangled in bureaucracy and paperwork, and I suspect that they were either frightened or even bribed by Shah to prevent Sachal from being transferred immediately. I had faith in Tanya's integrity, but one can never rely on the working of a system. She would be as helpless as anyone else if senior officials were involved.

After untangling a lot of red tape and paperwork, when he was finally able to leave, I gazed after him with dread in my heart. For some odd reason, I did not feel the exhilaration that should have been there. He was flanked by Tanya and her constable as they walked out. I wanted to shout after them. Tell them not to go. Not just then. And yet they had to. Why was I feeling this way?

Just as he stepped out of the hospital, hoping that he was a free man, I heard a car gunning its engines and tires screeching. All of a sudden, there was the sound of rapid gunfire. Running in panic towards the exit where Tanya and Sachal might have been, I came across a terrifying scene. He had been ruthlessly gunned down just in front of the main entrance by an unmarked black car that rapidly drove by. I was lucky that I had opted to stay back or I would have also been injured or worse. Tanya wasn't so lucky—she had a bullet wound that was bleeding profusely on her upper arm. Luckily, the ER was nearby and both of them were immediately scooped up on gurneys and taken there.

Sachal breathed his last on the examination table. He didn't say a word, but before he died, he looked at me with a plea in his eyes. I slowly nodded, knowing what he wanted. His last thought was of his family. Finally, in spite of the doctors' efforts, he heaved a sigh and slowly slipped away.

I was torn between Sachal and Tanya, but I saw that she was taken care by the ER doctors and it was important for me to be there for Sachal. Tanya had a minor injury caused by a stray bullet, thankfully a flesh wound. When she came looking for me with her arm in a sling, I just stared at her and couldn't stop crying. I had lost my patient, but most important, I almost lost my dearest friend. My grief boiled over like a volcano waiting to erupt. I cried for Sachal and his family, and also out of relief that Tanya was alright. I clung to her and sobbed piteously. She was still in her uniform and I am sure she was embarrassed at my waterworks because she just awkwardly patted my back.

From that point on, I kept pestering Tanya because I wanted her to act as quickly as possible to take Sachal's wife and children into protective custody. We were all worried that there would also be some backlash on the grieving family. Thankfully, the police were able to reach them before anyone else could and they were immediately spirited out of the country.

The fact that the murderers were still out there living a normal life was outrageous, but there were no witnesses and no solid clues pointing to the guilt of Abdul Shakoor Shah. We got to know that he eventually got married again, and the two *waderas* had stopped their bloody feuds as agreed. But at what cost? Three lives were lost to achieve a shaky truce. With their phenomenal egos and thin skins, one would never know when they would start once again.

Though it was confidential where Sachal's family ultimately landed, we were told that they were well taken care of and comfortable. A few years later, Tanya told me that Sachal's son had grown up to be a fine upstanding young man and was studying to be a lawyer in a prestigious university abroad. He made it his life's goal to bring his father's murderers to justice. I fervently hope that one day he is successful. Sachal, Yasmeen, and Nabeela deserve justice.

CHAPTER 6

A BEAUTIFUL HEART

"That it will never come again is what makes life so sweet." — Emily Dickinson

Sarah

My friend Sohaila and I liked to sit on a bench outside the Out-Patients Department (OPD) after our clinical rounds and chat for a bit before we went to our dorms. It was here that we would get to know if there were any unusual cases admitted, and we would jump up and dash over to the hospital or morgue to have a look. Studying to be a doctor is an obsession, a calling, so unusual cases for medical students with voracious appetites for learning were like the Beatles mania of the sixties. The stampede and rush to see the cases, and to be involved in the diagnosis and treatment, was as much fun and as satisfying as attending a rave!

One day, while we were chatting and winding down from our hectic day, we were pulled out of our mellow mood by the ward boy, who told us that there was an emergency autopsy and our Jurisprudence professor wanted us to attend it for extra credits. Once we knew who the victim was, the shock was palpable.

Sohaila was appalled because it turned out that she knew the victim. She became upset and even shed a few tears. When she calmed down, she told me the story about her short life.

"Nargis was a beautiful young woman," she said. "Her life was just as tragic as her death, and her end will cause emotional repercussions for many people because she was well known and had a reputation of being kind." She paused and took a deep breath. "She was just sixteen years old when her parents were killed in an accident that left her to take care of her younger brother and sister. Her father was an officer in a well-known construction company. He had told her many times that his firm had good life insurance and pension plans in place, and she shouldn't worry in case anything happened to him. Since he worked in a dangerous environment, he wanted to be prepared in any eventuality. It's as if he had had a premonition. He showed Nargis and her mother where all the relevant papers were kept and who to contact in case of an emergency."

Sohaila went on to tell me that Nargis was devastated when the accident occurred, especially since she had to take care of her six-year-old and ten-year-old siblings. She was a child herself and could not even imagine how to go forward with their life. Unfortunately, the house they lived in belonged to the company her father worked for, and though they were allowed three months grace, they were firmly told that they had to look for other accommodations as soon as possible. The company needed the house for her father's replacement.

As instructed by her father, Nargis went to see his boss and inquired about the insurance money and his pension.

"I am sorry, but our company insurance policy clearly states that compensation is only applicable if your father had died while at work. Additionally, as per the company guidelines, he hadn't worked enough years in the firm to warrant a pension. While we are sympathetic to your plight, I am sorry I can't do much for you." Her father's boss, though concerned, was unhelpful. He offered some funds on humanitarian grounds, but they were not enough and didn't last long.

Three children were homeless and destitute. Nargis was at her wits' end. How would she feed her brother and sister? Send them to school? Or even continue to go to school herself? Since she had no one to advise her, she took things as they came and rented a small adobe house in one of the less than savory areas of town. She didn't like that at all, but with the pittance she had received from her father's company, it was all she could afford. On a positive note, she was able to pay the rent for a year, so at least for that time period she didn't have to worry about where they were going to live.

The next step was to get a job. She had decided to drop out of school, but she still needed to feed the children and send them to school. Since she was basically a child herself and wasn't trained or skilled in any profession, she was fortunate to get a job as a sweeper in the upscale neighborhood where she used to live with her parents. But to her dismay, the male members of the family where she worked started harassing her and she was nearly raped. Luckily, someone heard her frantic cries and they were interrupted. Her beauty was blamed by the family, and she was asked by the irate lady of the house not to come to work anymore. The story of her unprecedented reputation spread like wildfire and getting another similar job became exceedingly difficult.

Nargis's unemployment added to her stress because of the mounting expenses along with the rapidly dwindling funds. Whenever she was stressed, she used to sing to calm herself down. She had an amazing singing voice and used to lose herself in the rhythm and beat of the music whenever she sang and danced. Her father was quite progressive and had encouraged her passion by letting her attend singing and classical dancing classes after school.

One day, while hanging up the laundry in her courtyard, she started to move and dance to the loud music coming from the radio playing in the neighbors' house. Just at that time, a friend walked in and was mesmerized as she watched her dance gracefully. When the music stopped, Nargis looked around in a daze and realized she was not alone. Her friend started to clap enthusiastically.

"With your looks and your graceful dance moves, you could become a successful dancer or entertainer. Maybe even a film star!" Her friend was impressed with her talent and encouraged her to look for jobs in the entertainment industry.

In that small rural town, being a dancer was not considered a very reputable profession because they were judged to be just a step above a courtesan, but she was told that the pay was good and the tips fantastic. After debating the pros and cons with her inner voice, she realized that she was desperate enough to go to the red-light area and talk to one of the leading madams about a job. She was asked to audition for the woman, and her grace and good looks helped her to get a job almost immediately.

Well, to cut a long story short, she became quite popular; as a matter of fact, she even danced on stage at the inauguration of our college. We got to know her quite well because we used to see her very often when she visited our teaching hospital and clinics for her siblings' vaccinations and minor ailments. We also treated her a few times in the Out-Patients Department. Whenever we met her, she had a friendly demeanor and used to chat with us if we had time. So, when we were called that sultry afternoon to attend the autopsy of a murder, it was an unpleasant shock to see Nargis lying there.

She was beautiful, even in death. She seemed to be fast asleep. The only thing that seemed incongruous was the small bullet hole in the middle of her chest. It was almost a sacrilege to perform her autopsy, but we had to do our job because we had to retrieve the fatal bullet that caused her death and we needed to know the extent of the damage occurred.

She was just twenty-six years old when she died. Ten years of strife and hardship just to care unselfishly for her siblings were all gone with the force of just one small bullet.

As we were busy putting together the summary of our findings, Tanya walked in to get the autopsy report. As always, it was nice to see her, although I wish it would have been in better circumstances. Our professor once again asked me to coordinate with her to piece together the evidence and autopsy findings and try and solve the case.

"Since you have worked together before, why don't you and Inspector Tanya put together the forensic evidence gathered so far and let us know how the case progresses?" He said enthusiastically.

Little did he know that Tanya had already investigated the case and a suspect was already in their custody. She knew that I would pester her with questions, so she started to tell me the interesting sequence of events. I made it a point to listen very attentively.

Tanya

We sat down in the cafeteria and ordered lunch. That was our meeting place. We were always discussing our cases or meeting for coffee as much as our time allowed us. Once we were comfortable, I started telling Sarah what the police knew and what information we had collected so far.

Nargis had made quite a name for herself in her chosen career. She was well known to the police because she was sometimes a confidential informant for them. Working hard, and in not so palatable conditions for ten years, she was able to send her siblings to school, and then on to college. It was heartening to know that her sister was now studying at the University of Sindh and was on her way to becoming a clinical psychologist.

"When I last saw Nargis, she was elated because her sister had met a young man at the university and they wanted to get married after they earned their degrees." Sarah leaned forward, intent on listening to what I had to say.

"Nargis was very happy and immediately started to collect jewelry and other things to give to her sister for her dowry. As a matter of fact, she had put together quite a large collection of jewelry."

I went on to tell Sarah that the day she died, Nargis was sitting in her courtyard (quite reckless if I may say so) sorting and arranging the pieces of jewelry in velvet custom made boxes so that her sister could conveniently store them with the other items she had put aside for her dowry in the traditional bridal chest. Little did she know that she was being observed from the neighbors' roof by the eldest son of the family, Mansoor, who was a known rake and a compulsive gambler. Whenever he was mentioned by anyone, it was in conjunction with either being in debt or high on drugs. He was not liked by anyone in the neighborhood because of his bad habits and the unsavory company he kept. In addition to that, he was peeved with Nargis because she would spurn his advances every time he tried to get close to her.

That night, he stealthily entered Nargis's house via the roof top—the houses were close together, so jumping from one roof to the other was quite easy. As he was about to open the cupboard where he knew the jewelry was kept, he was disturbed by Nargis herself.

"What are you doing in my house?" shouted Nargis. "Are you trying to steal my jewelry? Help! Help! Thief!"

Nargis was angry and she looked around to see whether there was something to defend herself with. Just as she spied her brother's cricket bat in the corner of the room, she realized that Mansoor had become agitated, and in his nervousness, fumbled and accidentally fired the gun that he had in his hand. The bullet went straight to Nargis's heart and her death was instantaneous. Mansoor foolishly ran off with the jewelry, which he stashed at a friend's house. Then, to add insult to injury, he got high on marijuana. He crept back home before dawn to fall asleep and gave the impression that he had been there the whole night. His friend was just as corrupt as he was and promised to back up his alibi, but he was unaware that Nargis's brother, who had arrived unannounced from the university that day, had seen him, and he was able to positively identify him from a police lineup.

"That is the man who killed my sister!" he said when the men were paraded in front of him behind a one-way mirror. He was beside himself with grief. If there hadn't been a barrier between him and the suspect, he would have tried to beat him to a pulp. He did try to get his hands on him but was held back by his friends. Mansoor was not worth the bother to ruin even another life.

The bullet that we had retrieved from the autopsy also matched the gun that was stashed at Mansoor's friend's house. The GSR (Gun Shot Residue) test showed that he had fired the gun. He did not last long when we interrogated him—he confessed almost immediately. He wasn't very brave and the police terrified him.

"I didn't want to hurt Nargis. I was in love with her! I just wanted to steal her jewelry to pay for my gambling debts. My creditors were closing in and they are very dangerous people." He broke down and cried. "I had no intention of firing the gun since I didn't even know how to use it. I wasn't even aware that it was loaded!"

Apparently, he didn't know that the safety of the gun was off. He insisted that the gun was fired by mistake when he became agitated and nervous at being caught by Nargis. With the testimony of the brother, his confession, and the positive GSR, the jury didn't deliberate and he was immediately found guilty of murder. Mansoor the gambler, thief and thwarted lover was now serving a life sentence in a high security jail.

The police returned the jewelry to its rightful owners. But a life was lost. After all she had to suffer and go through, Nargis died a violent death due to inherent stupidity and greed.

After a few of months, Sarah and I had one of our usual hurried rendezvous in the cafeteria. I have always thought that our friendship was turbo charged. There were days when we would meet whenever we could, and then long periods of time when either Sarah or I were extremely busy. But we always tried to make a bit of time for each other. If only just to share a pot of tea with each other. Anyway, when we met that day we started to talk about Nargis and I wondered what had happened to the siblings.

"I am glad to report something positive." Sarah smiled. "I have been in touch with Nargis's sister, who finally married her fiancé in a simple ceremony after a brief mourning period. The lavish wedding that they had planned was cancelled to respect her sister's passing."

Sarah was invited to the wedding, but she wasn't able to go due to her exams.

"Soon after, the newlywed couple migrated to

Australia," she went on. "I believe they are doing quite well there. And Nargis's brother finished his studies at the university and became a civil engineer. He also married one of his colleagues, and now works in Dubai." Sarah said that they didn't want to stay here in town anymore. "For them this is a depressing place with memories that hurt them deeply. They miss their sister too much to be comfortable living in the town where she died."

Rest in peace, Nargis. You will be remembered by everyone who knew your kindness and your inner beauty.

CHAPTER 7

CHILLING DREAMSCAPE

"When God sends a message of warning through dreams and visions, he is not sending them to instill fear in your heart. He wants to avert the evil that could have happened and soothe your heart with profound peace." — Michael Bassey Johnson

Sarah

As the years passed and we continued up the promotion scales towards finishing our basic medical education, we became more comfortable with our surroundings. We were thriving by just doing what we were supposed to do at the time.

But the best part of my journey was my friendship with Tanya. It was wonderful to have a friend who understood me and was there for me whenever I had my highs or lows.

It had become a routine by now that we would meet for an evening cup of tea or a snack at the cafeteria no matter how busy we were. People started to call us inseparable and many hinted that we might be in a relationship. *Wait! What? A relationship? With a woman? No, no!* I didn't want to spoil a beautiful friendship by having others make it into something not acceptable by our society.

That said, I looked at her. Really looked. She was so stunning in her uniform. She could carry off her authority and polish so well. And yes, I blatantly admired her for it. Her confidence made others respect her, while I went weak in the knees.

Oh, God! I was in love with Tanya! But I didn't want to say or do anything to jeopardize her career. She had worked so hard to pull herself up the ranks in a male-oriented career. Just one slip could harm her. I decided I wouldn't say anything to her at all. One can love a person from afar… can't they?

I thought the visceral feeling that I got when I was near her should be enough for me. I wasn't only thinking of how the implications of a relationship would affect her; I was also sure that the stigma of being gay would be devastating in our very inclusive medical college society. Maybe we would be able to be ourselves once we were away from there? That was wishful thinking, a dream. I looked forward to the day when I finished school and we could go away. I had often rehearsed what I would say to her, but my friendship with Tanya was my all-round support. I am not ashamed to say it was my crutch in the time of grief and I woke up in the morning happy because I had her in my life. I couldn't jeopardize my friendship, and I couldn't take the risk of her not feeling the way I did.

"The summer holidays are in a week's time," I said to Tanya over a plate of pakoras and cups of hot tea while the monsoon torrents beat a heavy tattoo on the corrugated iron roof of the hospital cafeteria. "I will miss you so much." She looked startled. Because I had never been sentimental. I tried to keep my attraction at bay by being even more matter of fact than was required. But oh, those eyes, those eyes! They were my undoing. Surely, she would see what I was feeling if she looked closely?

"Yes, I will miss you too." She smiled. "I have to visit my uncle next week, but I will be here most of the time. I don't have the luxury of a holiday like you spoiled students." She grinned as she ducked the pakora I threw at her. "Seriously, anytime you need me you know where to find me."

I was touched because I knew that she really meant it.

However, despite being comfortable and at peace with the world, I felt off kilter. The world was turning as it was supposed to, I attended my lectures, did hospital / ward rotations, ate, slept… and yet, there was a feeling of anticipation, of impending doom. I couldn't call it déjà vu because it had never happened before, but I sort of felt discombobulated and looked at the world as if from another dimension or plane. Those feelings had happened time and again to me, and when they did, I was extremely disturbed for days, but one incident shook me to my core and, to this day, I can't shake off the enormity of the events that happened then.

Springtime in Nawabshah was spectacular. I woke up

before dawn with an extremely uneasy feeling in my gut and decided to take a walk in the gardens to rid myself of it. The grounds at that time of the day, when the sun had just started to rise, were exceptionally beautiful. The spring flowers were blooming and they still had a sprinkling of dew on them that gave them an almost magical appearance. A few almond trees were covered with white blossoms that had a light pink blush on them. Their falling petals fluttered in the morning breeze, looking just like falling snow. A small fragrant carpet of the white petals had already collected under the trees and they made the garden look even more magical. In spite of the idyllic surroundings, my feeling of dread refused to go away. It was especially strange since I had been feeling quite comfortable in my own skin for quite a while, but there was a restlessness that was building inside me that day and I needed to address it before it erupted like a volcano. I didn't have a clue what it was.

Thankfully, it was the weekend and we were able to get permission slips to go home for the next two days. I missed my parents very much, so hoping to see them, I phoned home, but I couldn't reach them. I did manage to talk to my brother Azan, who was also home for the weekend.

"They have gone to Larkana for some of Baba's work. Amma has gone along for the outing. They are installing a new manufacturing system there and he has to oversee it and talk with the people installing it." Azan went on to tell me that they were staying with a family friend.

"I just miss them," I said when he started to make fun of me and call me a baby. Brothers! Since I wasn't able to contact them directly (no cell phones in those days), I decided to travel where they were supposed to be with a junior colleague who happened to be the daughter of my father's friend.

The route we travelled was in the opposite direction to the one I usually took. We lived in the south, in Karachi, but Larkana was in the north, near the borders of Baluchistan and Punjab. It was an old and historically renowned city which used to be the hunting place for the Soomro Kings of Sindh and then became an important trading town on the river Indus. I knew people who had bought exquisite antiques for their homes there. Since I love antiques and history, I was looking forward to a change of scenery with new and old sights and sounds. Anything to make that strange feeling to go away!

The four-hour train journey was entertaining because we were travelling with twenty-four other people who were also going home for the weekend. As was typical of students, we sang songs and spoke to each other at the top of our voices so we could be heard above the clackety clack of the train's wheels on the tracks.

"Tea! Get your hot tea here!" The vendors would yell when the train pulled into the stations.

"Cold drinks! Ice cold!" Boys with buckets of iced drinks would create this irritating cacophony when dragging their bottle openers over the bottles. It was a bustling, even frantic atmosphere.

The camaraderie during the journey was a stress reliever for a short while, but once we reached our destination, the cloak of anxiety plagued me once more and caused me to briefly question my sanity.

We were welcomed with the warm Sindhi hospitality

that was unique to the indigenous people living there. The genuine affection and care showered on me was heartening and a balm to my restlessness, but, to my dismay, my parents had left just that morning and were travelling towards Baluchistan.

"Your father has been unexpectedly called to Quetta to troubleshoot an urgent matter in the factory there," said my benevolent host. "You are most welcome to stay here with us as long as you wish."

Darn! Since they were once again enroute, I wasn't able to contact them. However, my hosts were genuinely nice and made me feel extremely comfortable. They heaped me with abundant fragrant and delicious Sindhi food, along with the famous sweet and sour mango pickles that are very well known in the region. I told the hostess that my friend Tanya would love the pickles, and there appeared a jar just for me to take back. I knew she would love it, and I would love to see her delight when she ate the pickles… I would love… hold it! I missed her!

That night I had a dream, or rather a nightmare, which increased my disquiet a hundredfold. I dreamed that I had traveled back to the college, and as I walked in, I saw that the resident students were having a party. The mood was festive and exuberant. As I walked down the tree lined path towards the crowd to join them, a junior student ran up to me and asked me to come to the morgue immediately. There had been a traffic accident and there were two female victims that had been brought there for identification. One of them had exceptionally long hair and the other had light brown, nearly blonde hair.

I shuddered with fear in my sleep, but I couldn't wake up. I started to panic! My mother was blonde and she was travelling on the treacherous Baluchistan Highway, so I immediately thought of her. What if she had been in the accident? Was that the last time I would see her? It was a dreadful nightmare, and yet, no matter how hard I tried, I couldn't wake up. In my dream, I ran in terror towards the morgue, but wasn't allowed to enter. I looked in and saw the long hair of one of the victims hanging over the side of the table and the lighter hair of the other victim. I struggled to identify them, but I couldn't see their faces or the bodies themselves.

After a seemingly long while, I woke up with a painful jerk, covered in sweat. My heart was beating so loud I was sure everyone in the house could hear it. I wasn't going back to sleep anymore, so I spent my time making plans to leave as soon as the household woke up. I started to pray for the safety and well-being of my parents as well as anyone else who might have been a victim of a horrendous accident.

I didn't want to offend my hosts, who had shown nothing but kindness to me, and I tried to think of a way to explain my desire to leave.

"Majeed has to go to Karachi this morning," said my hostess while bustling in the kitchen to get breakfast ready for the large family. "I am sure they won't mind dropping you off at your college. You will save the train fare going back."

That was such a great relief—my dilemma was solved without offending anyone. I immediately prepared myself for the journey back and we were on our way after a substantial breakfast of *parathas*, strong milky tea, and fried eggs.

As we drove along the highway, I found it quite disconcerting that I would flinch whenever a car or a truck would pass our vehicle. I had travelled on those roads many times, and this had never happened before. I was sure it had to do with my nightmare.

When we reached the college, the feeling of déjà vu strongly kicked in. Just like in my dream, I walked as if in a daze through the gates and up the tree-lined path, and there they were. The signs of a party. But, unlike in my dream, all the revelers had disappeared. The tables, the chairs, and the food were there, but no guests were around.

I saw a gardener working near the flower beds. I tried beckoning him, but he had his head bowed and was attacking the weeds with a vengeance. I walked over to him.

"Where is everyone, Mali?" I asked in a small voice, fearful of what the answer would be. He lifted his head and looked at me with concern in his eyes. His expression made me hitch my breath.

"Everyone has gone to see the two accident victims who have been brought in this morning. They are at the morgue. They have been asked to identify them there."

I felt as if my heart would burst into a million pieces with the intense pain that shot through me. I bent over with agony and tried to compose myself. I had to go to the morgue and see who the accident victims were. *Please, please, God, not my parents!*

I ran towards the morgue and saw that a large crowd had already gathered. They were speaking in hushed tones with each other. Just like in my dream, I wasn't allowed into the morgue, which was quite reasonable because it wasn't supposed to be a peep show or some form of entertainment. As I was led away by my friends, I could get a glimpse of the long hair of one of the victims as it spilled off the side of the table she was lying on.

Quite a few of my colleagues looked shocked, and many were crying or supporting each other.

"What happened?" I finally found my voice to ask my friend Sumera, who was standing nearby. "Anya and Tahira decided on the spur of the moment to go home for the weekend this morning." Sumera was sobbing so hard it was difficult to understand her. Taking a deep breath, she composed herself and went on.

"They had tickets for the express bus because it didn't stop at any town or village on the way. They were very happy when they went off because they were able to get seats right in front, away from the crowd. Their plan was to just stay one day in Karachi, buy some much needed study equipment and books, and then come back to the college the next day." Sumera used the tissue I handed her to wipe away her tears and blow her nose.

"On the way to Karachi, their bus had a tragic accident —a head on collision with another bus coming on the wrong side from the other direction. It seems that bus driver was trying to overtake a lorry and didn't see the bus in which Anya and Tahira were travelling. The driver escaped with just a broken arm and a leg, but our friends caught the brunt of the collision and died immediately on impact. They were the only casualties." I hugged Sumera and made her sit down.

To identify our friends, the police at the accident site had searched their bags and found their college identity cards. Tanya had been contacted, and she immediately took charge and escorted their bodies back to the college.

Through the haze of my grief and confusion, I spied her on the other side of the corridor and made my way towards her. Without giving a thought to what people would say or to the fact that she was there in an official capacity, I hugged her and started to cry on her shoulder.

Once I had calmed down, she took me aside and made me drink a bottle of water.

"Well, that was intense." She smiled to try to defuse the tense situation. "I am so sorry, Sarah. This accident is an irreparable loss not only to the family, but also to all of you who were their friends." She rubbed my back while she spoke, trying to comfort me in my grief.

"I had to restrict access to the morgue," she added. "There were a lot of unnecessary spectators and I didn't want the girls to be disrespected. However, I did allow the victims' roommates identify them."

Anya had very long hair. We used to admire its thickness and length when she dried it in the sun. She was just five feet tall, and the ends of her well-kept hair used to brush her calves. I saw that hair, which was her particular feature, in my dream… and also saw it spill over the table where she lay when I glanced into the morgue The other class fellow who died that day, Tahira, had lighter hair, nearly blonde. Both of them were well liked and were undoubtedly beautiful souls. That day, a multitude of prayers were said for them, collectively and individually. A well-attended funeral service with eulogies spoken by her friends and teachers was a tribute to their kindness and inner beauty.

It was extremely sad that we lost our friends to such violent deaths, and we mourned them for a long time. Many of us stopped travelling home by bus. Trains, and later the airlines, became the preferred mode of transportation. Their deaths had a profound effect on all of us, but I am sure none of the other students had the precognition of the impending gloom and the perception of the dark aura of their deaths as I did. It was extremely disturbing for me.

My feelings were taking a toll on me that day. I was not present mentally and kept thinking about the wherefore and what ifs. Realizing my distress and intense fatigue, Tanya took me home with her and the next thing I knew was that I was falling asleep in her comfortable bed.

When I woke up refreshed the next day, I still felt irrationally guilty that I hadn't spoken up and warned them, but then, what could I have done? Would anyone have listened to me? I wasn't even sure who the victims would be. I was also feeling guilty because I was relieved that my parents were safe. That is human nature, isn't it?

Tanya

It was one of those days when I woke up with a feeling of dread. Had I forgotten something? Was there some paperwork pending? I had to be on my toes all the time. Being a senior police officer made me more visible and mistakes made by my male colleagues would more often than not be overlooked but made into a serious issue if I made them.

Sarah was off to see if she could catch her parents at Larkana. She seemed pre-occupied, as if she was in a different world. She tended to do that when she had one of her "feelings." I respected that she could help people with her intuition, but unfortunately, I still needed tangible proof when things happened.

I thought maybe she was also disturbed about us. Our friendship meant a lot to me, and I knew it did to her as well. It was clear that I had been slowly falling in love with her. Our daily cups of tea at the cafeteria showed me what a kind and compassionate person she is. She was a bit naïve in the ways of the world, but then, who wouldn't be after such a cloistered existence? First the convent school, and then a medical college exclusively for girls.

I didn't think she had noticed that I always tried to touch her when we spoke. She took it in her stride because she thought that was my way, to touch people I talked to. But I didn't unless that person was Sarah. I grinned at the thought.

I didn't want to spoil our friendship. I treasured it too much to jeopardize it. I wondered what would happen to my career if I came out. I knew even covert whispers would be detrimental for my advancement. "What should *we* do?" I thought. "Do I wait till she graduates, and we meet on a more open ground?"

She must have noticed the way I looked at her. I had also seen her sneak discreet looks at me. I wanted to believe that maybe she felt the same way, but I could be mistaking friendly affection for something more.

I always knew that I preferred women. Men never attracted me in any way. My drive to excel in my chosen profession kept me so busy that casual dating or even a relationship was never on the cards, but I knew if there was a person that I would like to spend the rest of my life with, that would definitely be Sarah. I knew she would enrich my existence.

She had done it again. Her premonition of doom and gloom did bring a tragedy to the college. I felt fortunate that I was the one who had to go there in an official capacity because Sarah was devastated. She needed a bit of hand holding, of that I was absolutely sure.

The police from the next town reported the accident to my precinct. Since the passengers were predominantly from this area, they were obliged to inform us. The medicolegal procedures had to also be complied with. Of all places at the medical college.

The men had walked into my office with their hands covered in blood. They held two mysterious looking bundles covered in cloth.

"How can I help you, gentlemen?" I looked curiously at the blood-soaked bundles. "What happened?"

"There was a fatal accident on the main highway near Mithi. Two buses collided head on with each other. Though there were many injured, there were only two fatalities." The man sounded upset.

"Isn't that in your precinct's jurisdiction?" I asked while still eyeing the bundles.

"Yes, it is, but we believe the victims are connected to the medical college, so we are handing the case over to you." He spread a newspaper on my desk and put the bloody bundles on it. They turned out to be ladies' handbags.

We put on some latex gloves and fished out the student IDs from the front pockets of the bags. They were definitely medical students. I had to go and see that the bodies were immediately transported to the morgue. I didn't want anyone to gawk at them. They deserved respect.

I walked into the college and made my way to the principal's office. There was a party of some sort on the larger lawn. It was unsettling to know that the festivities would be abruptly halted due to the tragedy. For now, everyone was blissfully unaware of what had happened. The fact that they didn't even bat an eyelid when I walked in wearing my uniform showed that I was a frequent visitor there and they had become used to my visits. It would have been amusing if it just weren't so tragic that day.

I knocked on the principal's door and pushed it open. There was a staff meeting going on, and the principal signaled that I was to wait outside till the meeting was over.

"I apologize for the intrusion," I said standing my ground. "I need to talk to you immediately regarding two of your students." I didn't want to just pounce on him with the news, but if he was being funny about it, I would just have to be blunt.

"I told you to wait outside. Can't you see we are in a very important meeting?" he growled at me.

I stood up straight and gave him a stern look. His arrogance was well known, but this was just too much.

"I am here on police business, sir! I wanted to be discreet, but you give me no choice but to tell you that two of your students have died in a traffic accident. I have accompanied their bodies here so that they are put in the morgue. If you still think it is not important, I shall go to the morgue without your permission and with the help of a court order." I was now fed up with this little man who was at least six inches shorter than I was but acted as if he was taller than a basketball player.

The teachers and the now subdued principal became pale and looked shocked. I wasn't concerned about that. I just wanted to do my job and then see whether Sarah was all right. I took the relevant papers from a leather folder that I had brought with me and made the principal sign them in triplicate. Turning toward the door, I tried to leave silently, but I was more or less mobbed by the teachers, who had by now snapped out of their stupor.

"What happened?"

"Who are the victims?"

"Have they been identified?"

The questions went on and on. I looked at the principal, indicating the copies of the papers he had signed. "Everything is written in the report. I need to go and get the bodies settled. It is very hot today and I don't want them to be affected by the high temperatures. In the meantime, if you or anyone else have any relevant questions, my men or I will be happy to answer them for you." I resolutely set my hat on my head and stalked out of the room. Before I left the building, I gave my visiting card to the secretary of the principal. She had always been cooperative in the past, so I trusted that she would let me know if anything further was to be done according to the college's policies and procedures.

"Natasha, could you please let me know when the

parents of the victims get here? They might want to talk to me. My men have the release papers ready and will help to expedite taking them back home as soon as possible."

Natasha sniffled. She knew the girls and was understandably sad, but I knew she would handle the paperwork and processes efficiently.

Once I was outside the main administrative building, I walked toward the morgue. They had just brought the bodies in and had set them on stainless steel tables. The students had gathered round and wanted to see what was going on. There was a lot of outright howling, but many sat huddled in corners either crying or talking quietly. I didn't want the victims to be made into a freak show, so I told my men to close the doors of the morgue and not let anyone inside.

"Who are Anya's and Tahira's roommates?" I had to shout over the din. Two students came forward. "Please, go inside and give me a positive identification so that we can inform the families and do the needful for them." They didn't want to go in, but then they held each other's hands and quietly crept in, only to rush out crying and retching.

"Yes, those are Anya and Tahira," said one of them sobbing. "They were my friends! How can I live with that last impression of them! I will remember it my whole life!"

Just as I turned to go, I saw Sarah running towards me with an anguished look on her face. Before I could stop her, she flung herself into my arms and started to sob wretchedly. Her grief was so overwhelming that I am sure she wasn't even aware that she was hugging me tightly. Not that I was complaining, but I was in uniform. I needed to maintain a sense of decorum while I was on duty.

"I am so sorry for your loss," I whispered in her ear. I kept patting her back and finally she stopped crying. I realized that she was overwrought so I sat her down and gave her some water to drink. After taking permission from the hostel warden, I took her to my house. She was absolutely limp with fatigue which was more mental than physical.

"Why don't you have a nap and we can talk later if you like?" I led her to my bed, where she curled up on her side like a small child and promptly went to sleep. Poor girl, the last twenty-four hours had taken a toll on her.

A cool shower sounded like heaven. So, while Sarah slept, I indulged in the luxury of my apricot scented shower gel. That always cheered me up.

My stomach started to growl. I remembered that I hadn't had anything to eat since breakfast, and it was nearly evening now. I picked up the phone and ordered some Chinese food. I knew that Sarah would wake up as soon as she smelled the savory aromas. The restaurant said they had a backlog of delivery orders, so the food would be delivered within ninety minutes. Just enough time for a nap.

I lay down gingerly on the king-sized bed next to Sarah, making sure I kept my distance. First of all, I didn't want to disturb her, and I also wasn't very sure what I would do now that she was finally in my bed. Albeit for altruistic reasons.

Sarah probably sensed that I was there, and even though she was fast asleep, she turned to me and wrapped her arm across my abdomen. The small frissons of electricity all over my body that her touch was eliciting was something I had never felt before. I was older than Sarah and I had had girlfriends before, but I had never felt like this. It was new, terrifying, and absolutely amazing.

I looked down as she slept and gently stroked her cheek. "I really do love you, my little one." I didn't realize that I had said that out loud. I looked in shock at Sarah hoping that she hadn't heard, but she murmured softly in her sleep as she snuggled even closer. I could just make out her words as she said, "I love you too, my trooper."

CHAPTER 8

THE RIGHT ARM

"Though the doctors treated him, let his blood, and gave him medications to drink, he nevertheless recovered."
— Leo Tolstoy, War and Peace

Sarah

Nowadays, if one has a medical query, they browse the internet and get their answers. If the information is used intelligently, then one can be somewhat satisfied, or one could even end up being more confused. When I was in college, the internet was more of a dream than the modern fact as we know today. Medical information was limited to what your doctor told you. It is alarming when one is presented with a *fait accompli* as a diagnosis, so it is understandable that many patients get a second, third and even fourth opinion. Especially if the conditions are serious. Particularly if one were about to lose a limb, the right arm no less. But one thing a physician or a physician-to-be needs to know is that there a couple of major things that are important when dealing with patients, one of which is continuously drummed into us.

"Every patient needs a proper detailed history followed by a thorough physical examination."

We need to know that one without the other cannot be considered. If either of them is not properly done or ignored, it could lead to serious misdiagnosis.

It so happened that one hot summer day, during one of our ward rotations, as we were discussing the differential diagnoses of a medley of patients with a senior doctor, Dr. Murad, a disheveled and anxious young man unexpectedly ran into the classroom and thrust an x-ray film at the doctor.

"Dr. Murad! You have to help my brother! Please, please, look at the x-ray and tell me whether he needs surgery. They want to cut his arm off! His right arm!!" You could hear the panic in his voice. He was nearly hysterical.

He was so out of breath that he could hardly speak. We had to make him sit down and drink a glass of ice-cold water. Once he calmed down, he said his name was Nasir and asked the doctor once again to look at the x-ray because his brother was on his way to have surgery and about to have his right arm amputated.

Dr. Murad was one of those people who were single minded in their work, and multi-tasking was not a forte with him. Therefore, quite irritated at having his class interrupted so rudely, he just gave a perfunctory look at the film and flipped it dismissively on the table in front of him.

"According to the x-ray, there is a clean break of the *humerus*, and there is absolutely no need whatsoever to have the arm amputated," he said arrogantly.

Dr. Murad hadn't examined the patient, but his words still created serious doubt in the brother's mind. He became even more resolute and combatant to prevent his brother's amputation. After all, as he kept repeating, it was his right arm.

In the meantime, Dr. Murad singled me out.

"Sarah, take the young man to the operation theater to find out what the hullabaloo is all about. And tell the ward boy not to let anyone into the ward when we are doing our rounds." He snapped his mouth shut and moved to the next bed to examine the patient there.

Nasir and I literally ran to the surgical block next door where the operation theater was situated. I used my student privilege card to walk into the sterile area, and luckily, was able to catch the surgeon just as he was about to scrub up and walk into the operating area to start the surgery. The surgeon was a nice man and listened to me while I explained Nasir's concern about the impending amputation.

As I anxiously spoke to him, he stopped me in mid-sentence and said, "Before I tell you about the reason why I am amputating this young man's arm, please go and examine him yourself." He went on to say that he would wait for me in his office. "His name is Obaid. I would like you to tell me your opinion and what you would suggest about the treatment and the ultimate prognosis of the patient. Once you have formed an opinion of your own, I will be happy to answer any questions and discuss the case with you."

I walked over to the young boy lying on the operation table. I guessed he was about sixteen years old. He hadn't yet started to shave, and the light fuzz on his face gave him an innocent, nearly vulnerable look.

He was already mildly sedated, but he could understand and respond to me when I talked to him.

"Obaid, my name is Sarah. I am a medical student here. May I examine your injured arm?" When he sleepily nodded, I moved nearer. I noticed a rotten smell and saw that his arm was fulminating and gangrenous. It lay limp and lifeless by his side and was a deep black in color. Just so that I could reassure Nasir and tell him my findings, I palpated Obaid's arm, but there was no pulse. If the dead limb was not removed immediately, the results would be fatal.

I ran back to the surgeon, who was talking with Nasir. He gave me a terse nod when he realized by my expression that I knew the diagnosis and the necessity for the surgery.

"I have examined Obaid myself," I told Nasir. "I do agree with the surgeon that the surgery will save his life. The limb is dead and the toxins have already started to spread."

Both of us tried to explain the danger of his condition to Nasir. It was an exceedingly difficult decision for him, as neither he nor his other relatives who had started to congregate in the hallway were in any mood to listen or understand what we had to say. After all, losing a limb was not something to be taken lightly. As opinions and suggestions were voiced by the relatives, the commotion became louder and louder, so much so that we thought that there might be fisticuffs to contend with.

"These people use our patients as experiments to teach the students!"

"They don't care for our lives because the hospital is free!"

"They just want to cut off the limbs to make specimens for the anatomy museum!"

"We don't want our children to be guinea pigs!"

The shouts reverberated in the corridors, and I started to pray that Tanya would swoop in and save the day. It was evident that the doctors and students were not able to control the rowdy crowd anymore.

I quietly signaled to the nurse to call hospital security and the police. We had tried our best to explain Obaid's condition to his family. We even took his father into the operation theater to show him the signs of gangrene, but again, our efforts were futile. If he could, the surgeon would have gone ahead with the surgery on the premise to save the boy's life, but the main legal issue was that Obaid was a minor, and an informed consent form had to be signed by his parents before the doctor could start the procedure.

Unfortunately, Dr. Murad, who had unwittingly instigated the riot, had already left the hospital and was nowhere to be found. That was frustrating because I felt that he had to take responsibility since it was because of his assurances that they were refusing to go ahead with the amputation. After a long winded and heated debate, Obaid's father angrily signed the requisite release papers and left the hospital against medical advice. We saw how ill Obaid looked, and it was evident that his condition was deteriorating further.

Tanya arrived just in time with her team and tried to help us. I was so happy to see my guardian angel. Even though the crowd dispersed once the police arrived, the relatives were still abusive and one of them grabbed the back of my coat as I tried to walk away. I felt my coat tear and I tripped and fell down on my back, hitting my head on the floor with a resounding thwack. Tanya immediately stepped in and rapped the man's knuckles with her night stick. Otherwise, he would have dragged me across the floor. He was inexplicably blind with rage. I felt that he wanted to hurt someone in the heat of the moment, and that it wasn't about Obaid anymore.

I looked up at Tanya, scared at what I might see there in her eyes. I realized that she was angry because she was worried I had been hurt, but she was being very professional and controlled herself. Once her men pulled the man aside and arrested him for assault, she helped me stand up. I was disheveled but unharmed. There was just a small bump at the back of my head.

"Are you alright?" She ran her hands over my shoulders and head to see whether I was hurt. I knew she wanted to tell me to go to a safer place, but she couldn't because I had to be there for Obaid. Nevertheless, I was confident that she wouldn't let anything bad happen to me while she was there.

Till the last moment I tried pleading with Obaid's parents to stay and let us treat him, but no one wanted to take the responsibility of the final decision. In the end, I was able to persuade them to *at least* go to one of the private hospitals nearby and hoped against hope that they would reach there in time.

A week later, I received a pleasant surprise when Nasir came to visit me in the hospital. He said that he wanted to see me because he had seen how much I had fought for his brother's proper treatment.

"The surgery was a success," he said. "Dr. Haldi Ram from the Indus Clinic agreed with your diagnosis. The only unfortunate fact was that the amputation was much more extensive than was initially decided because the operation was delayed and the gangrene had spread. I wish that we had listened to you."

I guess his visit to me was in a way an olive branch.

We kept in touch, and I was told that as soon as Obaid healed, he was fitted with a prosthesis and, with the help of extensive physiotherapy, he was able to resume his studies and go on to be a high school teacher.

Such patients always leave a sore mark in one's heart. Indubitably, as doctors we learn the important and valuable lesson that we need to see for ourselves and personally examine the patient before giving a diagnosis. Especially if a second opinion is sought. Just one misplaced word or sentence could be the fragile balance between life and death.

But the question always hangs in the air… what could we have done better?

Tanya

It was a tiring day. Raiding a so called "pharmaceutical company" that manufactured fake medicine in plastic buckets in a garage was not my idea of fun. It was exceedingly hot that day and my whole team was tired. I didn't blame them because there was a lot of running and fighting involved as well, but the positive note was that we were able to arrest the goons who were profiting by playing with people's lives and their health.

I was ready for a rejuvenating cup of tea.

Just as I took my first sip, a constable knocked on the door, walked in, and saluted.

"What is it?" I was irritated and tired and didn't want any drama so near the time to go home. But that was police work. No proper timings whatsoever.

"There is a riot at the hospital, sir," he said cautiously. 'Shall I take a unit and see what's going on?"

"Now what has Sarah got herself into again?" I thought. Smiling at the idea of seeing her, I got up, straightened my hat, and picked up my night stick.

"I am coming along with you," I told him.

"I thought you would say so," he smirked. "Since your friend seems to also be involved."

I groaned inwardly and signaled him that we should go.

We reached the hospital and saw there was quite a crowd. Thankfully, most of the people scurried away when they saw us. However, there were some who still were trying to create mayhem.

I spied Sarah her a few meters away and was about to call out to her when I saw an overweight, grubby man lunge towards her and pull her to the ground. He hung on to her coat and it seemed as if he was going to drag her along. I was furious! How dare he hurt her! I reacted instinctively and gave him a hard rap on his knuckles with my night stick.

"Unhand her immediately! You are under arrest for instigating a riot in a government institution and assault on one of its employees!" I had to shout over the din in the corridor. My men promptly cuffed the rioter and took him away.

Looking at Sarah, I was relieved to see that she seemed unhurt, but when I saw her lying there and when I heard her head bang loudly against the floor, I nearly had a heart attack myself. I couldn't bear it if anything happened to her.

"I am so glad that you are not hurt," I said keeping a strict control over my emotions since I was still on duty. I still did give her a hug before I let her go back to her classes.

As I watched her retreating back, I realized how much it would have upset me if she had been a casualty that day. And yet I hadn't told her how I felt about her. Telling her while she was fast asleep was the coward's way out. I was scared. So darn scared. Of losing our friendship if I was wrong about her feelings for me, of losing my position on the police force, and of the stigma that society in all their hypocritical holier than thou attitudes inflict on people who love each other without the discrimination of gender.

I knew she loved me. She had said so that night while half asleep. Then, why was I baulking? I asked God for strength, but I wanted a life with Sarah, an equal partnership. *Please, God, give me courage to live a life of happiness with her.*

CHAPTER 9

DYING TO CELEBRATE

"You have started to wear off my heart,
Like the henna dying on my hands,
An ugly remembrance of what was once breathtaking." —
The Blossoming Chrysalis

Sarah

While we ran off home whenever holidays were announced or when we had a weekend free, there were many times that we opted to stay back in the college. This would usually happen when the dates of the exams were looming painfully near. Let's face it, there were too many distractions at home. The intense study regimen that was required would be peppered with interruptions, whether it was trips to the market or a day out on the beach, but then, who could blame a person starved for entertainment after being cloistered in an all-girls' medical college?

My parents were quite popular and entertained a lot, and as the only daughter, I was recruited to help out whenever I was at home. It's not that my parents didn't want me to study; after all, they were paying for my expensive education, but they did not realize that my visits home were supposed to be to revise and study. That's why it was called "Study Leave." And of course, in all fairness, I actually wanted to be distracted, especially when I was recruited to be the DJ of the night's soiree.

As the years went by and the final spate of exams inched nearer, a lot of us opted to stay in the college during the holidays. The peace was phenomenal and we could study at our own pace in the library or in the wards without the stress of timetables and assignments. I also had an ulterior motive. Oh, I was focused on my exams and I wanted to excel as much as possible, but I had a distraction that made staying back worthwhile. Tanya. I couldn't bear staying away from her for long periods of time, but I didn't tell her. The coward in me sealed my lips whenever I wanted to say something. I tried to show her by being caring and considerate, but that was what good friends did as well. The warm and fuzzy feeling that I got from her is that she wanted to spend as much time with me as I did with her. And that was definitely worth staying.

Usually, the students were given the option to go home for Ramadan, the holy month of fasting for Muslims. Many decided to take advantage of the peaceful ambience to stay back and study for the upcoming exams while using the facilities offered by the hospital and the library. It was quite pleasant. The rituals of fasting and the informal camaraderie caused friends to become as close as families.

We never needed alarm clocks for the morning pre-fasting preparations because our mess staff would come long before dawn and bang on our doors to let us know that our breakfast was ready. The banging would start on the first door in the corridor, and the rat-a-tat continued until every door in the dorm had been thoroughly drummed upon. They created such a ruckus to wake us up that I am sure many had the same idea I did—to throw the blighter over the balcony railings! "Shut up!!!!"

Tanya often came and shared our evening meals during Ramadan. No one thought it was unusual since hospitality is kicked up a few notches in the holy month. Breaking our fast at sunset was enjoyable because we could go for the mundane menus in the cafeteria or we could order something from the restaurants in town instead. The snacks that Tanya nearly always brought for us were very welcome.

"What are we going to eat for dinner today?" asked Tanya while lounging on the bean bag in my room. She looked pale and tired, but then she didn't have the luxury of staying in while she fasted. Her duties took her all over the city, sometimes to places where it was very hot and there was very little shade.

"Let us order some Chinese food," piped up Shagufta, one of my roommates that year.

"Yes, we haven't had that for a while and I do feel like eating something other than cafeteria food today," mused my other roommate, Yasmin. "I crave for something sweet and sour."

"Will Tasneem be paying her share today?" Yasmin started to giggle and we all joined in.

We were quite honest with dividing the bill equally, but one of our roommates refused to pay her share. Tasneem's excuse was that she didn't like what we usually ordered since she was watching her figure. She always said that she would be going to eat at the college cafeteria, but when the final siren blasted noisily indicating at the end of the day that we could break our fasts, she would loiter and hang around until we asked her to join in.

"Come on, girls, don't be mean," I said while continuing to giggle. We couldn't have made her go away. We were too polite and it went against the sanctity and the hospitality of Ramadan, didn't it?

After the requisite twenty-nine or thirty days of fasting (that was decided by the sighting of the new moon), many students finally went home for Eid, the celebration that marked the end of Ramadan. It is known as "*The Sweet Eid*" because sweets are distributed to friends and family to herald the end of a difficult but holy month where prayers are answered, and souls are supposedly cleansed.

That year, a group of us decided to stay for Eid since regular college was recommencing just after three days. It wasn't sensible to make the long journey home and back when we could still spend as much time as we wanted in the library and the wards.

We were not constipated nerds. Just occasional nerds. We knew how to have fun and we did celebrate Eid in our own way. The night before Eid is called "*Chand Raat,*" or the night of the moon sighting. We got permission to go to town and had a lot of fun in the hustle and bustle of the busy bazaar.

"Just be back before the official curfew!" Our hostel warden yelled after us as we sped away in Tanya's jeep. She wasn't restricted by parking parameters, so she could take us right to the middle of the bazaar. What a kaleidoscope of color there was! And it was so much fun to mingle with mostly women and children who were last minute shopping before the big day. Having Tanya with us was a plus point because, thanks to her uniform, the crowd melted before us and we could shop unencumbered. We would watch shawls and veils being dyed to match the new Eid suits and dresses, and we'd try glass bangles and costume jewelry that matched with our outfits. Since there was such a crowd, no one thought it was unusual that Tanya held my hand most of the time. She was worried that she would lose me in the throng.

"I need a pink shawl," yelled Tasneem over the noise. "I will meet you at the samosa booth when I am done."

I nudged Tanya in the ribs and told her to look at the bangle vendors. "See how they are measuring the young girls' hands?" Tasneem and Shagufta heard me and turned their heads in the vendor's direction and burst out laughing. The vendor would "measure" the girls' hands by squeezing their wrists to gauge what size they wore. It was blatantly obvious that it was all a ploy to hold the hands of young women and girls without any recriminations from their eagle-eyed chaperones. I am sure that they were enjoying themselves thoroughly, but if they went too far, Tanya would put a stop to it just by clearing her throat pointedly.

I wanted to buy some bangles as well, but Tanya didn't

let the vendor help me put them on. She held my hand and slowly slid on a dozen of glass bangles without breaking any of them. She discreetly caressed my wrist with her thumb before letting go. I felt that all the way to my toes. My love for her was growing day by day. How could I keep it inside? I felt like I was going to burst!

The highlight of the evening was when we discovered the little makeshift kiosks that the local women had set up all over the bazaar to apply intricate henna tattoos on the hands and feet of whoever was willing to pay their nominal fee.

"I want henna on both of my hands," I said.

"Just remember your curfew time," Tanya replied. The spoilsport. "Hey! Don't make a face like that, Sarah! I told your hostel warden that I'd bring you all back in time. She might not allow you out with me the next time if we are late."

Though we nearly didn't get back in time, we all made sure that either our hands or feet were decorated to some extent with the clever floral designs. This little ritual was important to us because we needed to feel part of the celebrations, since some of us were missing home at this time when families celebrated together. We tried to get Tanya to decorate her hands as well, but she declined—she was in uniform and that went against protocol.

One of the traditional sweets distributed on Sweet Eid is a dessert called Sevian. It is a simple but sweet milk pudding made with roasted vermicelli and cooked until it has a soft custard-like consistency. What I like about it is the added dried dates, raisins, pistachios, and almonds, and

I love that it's flavored with cardamum and a dash of rose water.

One of the reasons why we decided to go into town was to get the ingredients for Sevian. There was a whole ritual in preparing it. We sat together late into the night telling each other Eid stories while cutting the various nuts into small slivers and slicing the dried dates after they had been soaked in warm water.

Tanya had promised to cook Sevian for us using her grandmother's recipe. It was a bit difficult because we could only cook in our room on a small hot plate, but it did turn out well. Who knew that my beloved policewoman was such a great cook? We also invited our dorm neighbors to join us for breakfast. Everyone brought something to contribute to the breakfast feast and our meal turned out to be quite a smorgasbord—fresh bread, boiled eggs, fruit, butter, and jam.

Everyone was wearing their new Eid clothes and matching glass bangles. Tanya didn't want to get spatters on her clothes when she cooked, so she went to get changed while we laughingly examined each other's henna tattoos to see how dark the skin was dyed by the herbal mixture and how prominent the designs were on the palms of our hands. According to the legends, if the henna dye leaves a dark stain on the skin, the girl's future husband and mother in-law will be very nice to her as a future bride. The joking and teasing were actually part of the fun and the mood of the occasion.

Tanya stepped out of my room into the corridor and I looked up in wonder. She was in her uniform most of the time, and I had seen her wear jeans when she was off duty, but that day she was this beautiful, sophisticated woman. She was wearing a stylish cream-colored outfit that was lightly shot through with gold thread. It was custom tailored and fitted her well. Her small waist was accentuated by the fine darts and pleats that were part of the design. The top had a sweetheart neckline that showed just a hint of cleavage, but it was enough to make my mouth run dry. The matching gold sandals and bangles just added to the elegance of the whole outfit. Her hair was loosely braided, not the way she did it for work, but in a softer style and the braid was interwoven with a garland of fragrant jasmine flowers. Oh, my! If I hadn't been in love with her before then, I would surely have fallen for her right at that moment. I knew I would always correlate the sweet smell of jasmine with Tanya after that day. She noticed I was blatantly staring at her and looked down at her feet. She was shy!

Later, after a pleasant day of festivities, Tanya had to go back to the precinct in the evening. A group of friends and I decided to go trolling for cases at the hospital. We hadn't studied much that day and we were feeling a bit guilty, so we wanted to at least practice some of our Basic Life Sciences (BLS) skills and tried to find an available intern to time us. Actually, it was as if something was compelling me to go to the ER, A feeling of uneasiness that I had succinctly translated into guilt. Much to our surprise, when we reached the hospital, there was a loud ruckus going on in the Emergency Room. We found a young woman in one of the examination cubicles wretchedly crying out in pain as she waited for the extremely busy ER doctor to attend to her. Like typical students, we stood there, wondering what to do and scratching our heads, when we were sharply told to make ourselves useful and at least take her history. That would help to expedite her diagnosis and then her treatment.

We didn't want to stress the woman any more than she already was by crowding curiously around her, so two of us volunteered to talk to her.

She was a beautiful young woman, all dressed up in a yellow silk outfit that was the traditional color before a wedding. The friends who had accompanied her were also wearing the same color. The pretty tableau was marred by the fact that her hands were wrapped in moist blood-stained cotton gauze and she held them stiffly up and away from her body as if she were in excruciating pain.

While taking her detailed history with the help of her sister, we found out that her name was Sakina. She was to be married in two days and had been getting ready for her Night of Henna celebrations. As was the custom in her family, her in-laws had sent her a hamper with cosmetics, clothes, henna, and bath accessories to get prepared for the party. Sakina and her sisters were surprised that the henna was not in the usual distilled or dried powder form typical of those days. It was presented in one of the new-fangled "modern" cones that were created to facilitate the application of the more intricate designs, much like the way one would apply icing to a cake.

We were told that the henna was applied to her hands that afternoon by a henna artist with intricate traditional lacy patterns. After an hour or so, Sakina started to complain that her hands were itching exactly where the henna had been applied. Slowly and gradually, the itching became more intense until her hands started to burn as if on fire. Then the skin of her hands swelled up and even started to blister. Sakina had already washed the tattooed areas with cold running water the moment the burning started, but that didn't seem to help much. Her mother wrapped her hands in moist gauze and the family brought her immediately to our ER. Sakina's sister, who was loudly abusing all and sundry (especially the poor groom, who was beside himself with worry) regarding Sakina's predicament, had the foresight to bring the used cone along with her. She made a face of sheer disgust when she showed it to us.

I put on latex gloves and picked it up gingerly. On examining it closely, my colleagues and I noticed that the consistency of the brown paste within was quite un-henna like. It was darker than normal and had a smoother consistency. Moreover, it smelt nothing like henna should —there was a distinctive but as yet unidentified chemical smell that was extremely pungent. I had the foresight to seal it in an evidence bag in case it was needed later.

This was no doubt a case of criminal negligence and dangerous adultery of a consumer product. After discussing the matter with the ER doctor, we called Tanya and asked her to come to the hospital.

With the permission of our seniors and the consent of the patient, I scrubbed my hands thoroughly and put on a fresh pair of sterile gloves. I started to remove the gauze from Sakina's hands layer by layer as gently as I could.

I just stared at the devastation I saw. I was flabbergasted. I think that's the only word I could think of that could convey the horror as well as the empathy I felt for the poor bride who was supposed to be married in a couple of days.

Her hands had certainly been painted with henna in an intricate pattern that covered most of her palms, the back of her hand, and her wrists. Red angry looking welts and blisters followed the designs. This was a disaster, both medically and psychologically, for Sakina.

We transferred her to a sterile operation theater and ensured that she was properly sedated, not only because the procedure would otherwise have been excruciatingly painful, but also because she was quite distressed and we didn't want to cause further damage to her injuries.

Unless she was an abnormally fast healer, there was no possible way for her to get married on the date she and her fiancé had set. Monitoring her for the first twenty-four hours was crucial, especially as we wanted to prevent any superadded infection. She also needed intravenous plasma and fluids. Since some of the injuries were also third-degree burns, thus deeper and more serious than superficial burns, she would get nutrients, antibiotics, and painkillers as well. Therefore, in spite of her vehement protests, we had to admit her into the sterile burn's unit. At least for a short while.

I left the operation theater once Sakina was settled and sought out her sister, who had appointed herself as the family spokesperson.

"I am sorry," I started to say.

"How is Sakina?'

"When can we take her home?"

"Why is it taking so long?"

"We need to take her home immediately; the house is

full of guests. What will they say if the festivities won't continue?"

The questions bombarded me from all sides. I was trapped within the ever-growing crowd of relatives that wanted to just go home and continue what they were doing. In their minds the situation was not grave and they thought that after applying a band aid or two, we would release the hapless bride to be.

Though I stood there stoically, I started to panic when they pressed closer and closer. I suddenly heard the shrill sound of a police whistle, and Tanya strode in while her team of constables dispersed the crowd. She had rescued me once again!

"Listen to what Ms. Sarah has to say. She will only say it once, and then I expect all of you to disperse and go home. Only one attendant may stay with the patient as per hospital regulations!"

There were howls of protest, but Tanya gave them all a stern look and her men took a few steps forward, their night sticks primed for trouble.

Tanya pulled a sturdy stool forward and signaled that I should stand on it.

Clearing my throat, I began to speak. "You will all have to understand that Sakina's wedding plans are temporarily postponed. Considering the gravity of her injuries, the surgeons have tried their best to clean and manage her wounds. Additionally, her physiotherapists have to perform ongoing assessments that are to be in line with her rehabilitation goals."

"What do you mean by that?" said Sakina's sister resentfully.

"It means that Sakina has very grave injuries and she needs special care. If her treatment is neglected, she can get severe contractures. Her treatment goals would obviously include to ensure the best possible range of motion of her affected joints along with their functional abilities."

I went on to explain to the hostile crowd that as soon as the acute scare was over, her rehabilitation had to be started seriously if we wanted to prevent disabilities that commonly occur after severe burns.

After escorting Sakina to the burn's unit, I was relieved that Tanya had arrived just in time. She was back in her uniform, which was a shame because she had really looked stylish before.

I gave her a short summary of what had happened to Sakina. We went back to the ER and talked to Sakina's immediate family. Thankfully, the rest of the crowd had already dispersed, but I was still grateful for Tanya's reassuring presence.

"You have to postpone the wedding for now," I told them firmly. "What has happened to Sakina is serious and we need to keep her in the hospital for at least one week."

Some relatives were a bit argumentative and kept bringing up the expenses of the wedding and that the "evil eye" was the cause of this catastrophe, etc. Some even blamed the mother-in-law for deliberately trying to harm the bride. In the end, we managed to convince the family that Sakina's well-being and recovery was more important than any social faux pas. They went home, albeit grumbling and not very happy with the situation. But then, who would be?

"I am so sorry for disturbing your Eid, Inspector," said

the ER in charge apologetically. "As you can see, even though there is no overt foul play, we needed you to be aware of the adulterated henna that is being sold in the city. There could be many more victims and we need to stop whoever is trying to profit illegally, especially during Eid and with the wedding season around the corner."

"Oh, that's perfectly all right," Tanya said brushing off the apologies. "This case has to be publicized so that people are aware of the dangers of the chemicals in the henna cones. I shall ask my contacts in the press to also investigate and write about it."

The investigation revealed that the unjustly maligned in-laws were actually innocent. They had bought the henna because they wanted to be perceived as "modern and moving with the times." Also, the packaging of the cone was colorful and looked elegant when they decorated the bridal hamper.

Our intrepid police force was able to catch the culprits and bring them to justice.

Exactly six months later, we had a surprise visitor. Sakina walked in to the OPD accompanied by her sister with a big smile on her face. Her hands had healed quite well even though they showed some red, flower-shaped scars. Not all would fade with time, as some of the burns were quite deep, but due to our timely intervention and her almost dogged adherence to the prescribed and proper rehabilitation, she didn't have any contractures. The full range of movement of her hands was nothing short of miraculous.

The reason for her impromptu visit was that she wanted to extend an invitation to her wedding, which was finally going to take place on the coming weekend. We were incredibly pleased for her. She even gave me an invitation card to pass on to Tanya. I hoped she'd wear her Eid clothes again…

That was one wedding we were all happy to attend. On the Night of Henna, we got caught up in the festivities and danced enthusiastically to Sindhi folk songs. Everything was a veritable buffet for the senses—the sights, the sounds, and even the smells, especially the sultry fragrance of the garlands of roses and jasmine that the hosts had placed around the necks or wrists of every guest. We took our cue from the beautifully dressed and bejeweled Sakina, who enthusiastically joined in. There was a rainbow of colors projected by the gracefully twirling dresses of the dancers that created the impression of flamboyant flowers in a garden lit by fireflies and fairy lights.

I saw Tanya looking at me with a strange expression in her eyes, as if she wanted to say something but was too afraid to do so. My Tanya? Afraid? Unbelievable... but I dare say she looked just as beautiful at the wedding as she had on that Eid day a few weeks before.

The second day of the wedding hosted by the bride's family was a more formal occasion. The alcove where the bride and groom were to sit and receive their guests was fashioned into a faux gazebo that was shaped with long garlands of roses, jasmine, and marigold. The intricate lattice work created with the flowers was a work of art.

The smell of kebabs being barbecued wafted from the cooking areas behind the marquee, and it mingled with the fragrance of freshly baked naans that were being made in portable clay ovens. It was enough to make our mouths water in anticipation. The tables were already set and they beckoned us with their gourmet siren song.

However, that evening was to celebrate the bride's recovery. We were all pleased to see Sakina and her handsome groom, who were radiant and literally infecting everyone with their happiness.

Tanya

Ramadan was fun that year, most of all because I didn't miss home as desperately as I used to. Celebrating with Sarah and her friends was almost like being at home. For the first time after a long time, I felt loved and accepted.

Coming out to my family and being shunned by them was the most painful incident in my life. I could understand my father, the super masculine Air Force officer, being disappointed in me, but my mother? She had always been there for me. She was my strength, my rock, but I think she felt she had to side with her husband.

At least she didn't cut me loose without any support. Before I left home when I was sixteen, she directed me to her brother, Jamal. The day I was to leave, she took me aside and told me that I had to make my own way in the world, but my strengths would always be getting a good education and a career. Crying bitterly, she shoved a bundle in my hand and turned away from me. Her retreating back and her sobs were the last I ever saw or heard of her. I didn't open the bundle for months. I just couldn't, but three years later I found it stuffed at the back of the top shelf in my cupboard. It was time to open it. What I saw nearly blew my mind. It contained the jewelry my mother had collected for my dowry, which, being the only girl in the family, was quite substantial. There were also five thousand US dollars and some prize bonds. I was surprised to realize that I had the equivalent of a hundred thousand US dollars. I was well off! Opening a dollar fixed deposit account was now necessary, and I had to rent a safety deposit box at the bank. To think I had been so careless with the bundle…

Uncle Jamal took me in and, with funds that I suspected were secretly provided by my mother, he saw to it that I finished my master's degree in criminology and helped me apply to join the police force.

I found out much later that my uncle was also gay, and I always felt comfortable living with him. On the day that I was leaving for the police academy, he sat me down and said there was something he needed to talk to me about.

"Tanya, please, promise me one thing." He looked worried, as if he expected me to be upset at what he was going to ask me. "We are good persons, inside and out."

"I think so, Uncle Jamal," I said. I was confused.

"No matter what, the world, and especially the political atmosphere of the country, is not geared to accept people like us. It will already be an uphill task for you, choosing a career in a male oriented profession."

"I understand. You don't want me to be overtly gay." I smiled my reassurance at him. I was already aware of the implications, but I was touched that he cared enough to talk to me about it.

Uncle Jamal hugged me. "I will always keep you in my prayers. I love you, Tanya. You are the daughter I never had. You will always have a home with me."

I was pulled out of my journey to the past by the shrill ring of the telephone on my bedside. Did Sarah miss me already? I laughed to myself.

It wasn't Sarah, but it was the hospital calling. They needed me there… a policewoman's work is never done. Even on Eid.

I walked into the ER. and saw a crowd of people creating a ruckus as they were wont to do when they didn't agree with the doctors. I wished they wouldn't do that. The doctors worked hard enough and they didn't deserve that added stress. Sarah told me she didn't mind because it helped to hone her people-skills, but one never knew when a crowd could become violent.

Sure enough, who did I find in the middle of the raucous melee? Sarah seemed to be on the verge of losing her cool. To give her credit, she was trying her best. Here was where my team became helpful. I signaled my constable and he blew a few blasts from his whistle. I could never get used to that shrill sound, but it did get rid of those who were afraid of getting arrested. It always amused me.

I helped Sarah stand on a stool in the middle of the crowd so she could talk to the many relatives of the patient. What I heard her say gave even a seasoned lawmaker like me goosebumps. I knew then why the ER chief had called me. There are despicable people in this world who sell poison for profit. They don't care who they hurt.

Sarah gave me the used cone and we sent it to the police laboratory. They isolated high amounts of para-phenylenediamine, or PPD, which would have worked if the amounts had been small, but the indiscriminate addition of the chemical to the henna created a violent reaction in Sakina.

We traced the manufacturers to an abandoned house. My team was able to track and sneak upon a group of men who were mixing the chemicals and henna in unhygienic and unsavory looking plastic tubs and were packing the concoction by hand into cone shaped plastic envelopes. Apparently, they thought they would make a profit during the Eid holidays, when henna was very much in demand. Their limited knowledge of chemistry made them overdo the addition of PPD, which in turn caused the devastating burns on Sakina's hands. We also found out that there were many cases reported of sensitivity connected with this gang's henna concoction, causing various degrees of injuries ranging from mild rashes to severe burns.

The culprits were jailed for a few months and heavily fined. Their brand of henna wasn't seen in the market anymore. The press was told of the case and a journalist interviewed the doctors as well as our team. With Sakina's consent, we gave the journalist a few photographs of her injuries. We wanted to spread the information and to let the public know that there were racketeers who would stoop extremely low just to get a quick profit. Because that's what the culprits were… profiteers! They jeopardized young women and children with their adulteration of the henna cones. The newspaper article got national acclaim, and as a result, the government decided that in the future henna and its products were to pass an inspection before they could be marketed. That was quite a victory for us.

As I lay down in bed that night, my thoughts went back to Sarah. She had been amazed when she saw me in my Eid clothes, but there was something else in her eyes. Was that desire? Love? Did I have a chance with her? Could we make a life with her together? I had to put together solid options before I talked to her about my feelings. One thing was absolutely certain—if we were to be together, it would not be here. We would have to think about leaving, and I wasn't sure if she would be willing to do that.

CHAPTER 10

WHEREFORE ART THOU?

"Life is full of confusion. Confusion of love, passion, and romance. Confusion of family and friends. Confusion with life itself. What path we take, what turns we make. How we roll our dice." — Matthew Underwood

Sarah

When we were in college, the era of mobile telephones hadn't yet encroached on our times. Lord help us if we had been bent over our devices oblivious to the surrounding world, lost in the siren songs of modern-day Facebook and WhatsApp. I am sure our medical studies would have faltered to a great extent. As it is, it was sporadic bouts of home sickness, or anticipation of calls from parents as well as boyfriends (more credible), that many girls used to hang around the in-house telephones that were available in the nooks under the stairs in every dorm. Sometimes, the phones were answered just for the thrill of it, whether a call was expected or not. Then, the person who picked up the receiver would yell for the call's recipient, and I must say, the voices were at times extremely raucous and loud!

I used to scorn the girls who regularly waited for the calls from their families and paramours. The time they wasted hanging around the phones was unnecessary, but the more I realized my love for Tanya, the more plausible it seemed. Not that she would call me there, because we did meet nearly every evening, but it wasn't beyond me to throw wistful glances to the old rotary devices.

Exams were always stressful and everyone used to be in a world of their own. Including me. One day, while lost in my thoughts, the shrill cacophony of the phone jolted me out of my reverie as I passed it by. I looked around to see if anyone was answering the call and found that there was no one. That in itself was quite unusual. However, it seemed I was destined to pick up the phone that day. The compulsion, or maybe my strong intuition, was too strong to ignore.

Initially, I didn't hear anyone say anything. I just heard someone breathing heavily down the line. "Is anyone there?" I was annoyed. "We are all very busy here, so go and bother your mother!!!" I literally growled.

Just as I was going to bang down the phone (oh, that used to be so satisfying… One can't do that with the phones nowadays. Sad.), I heard a timid, quavering voice on the line.

"Please, talk to me… I'm upset… I need to talk to someone. Otherwise I just… please, I need help…"

At first, I thought it was a hoax. Those were the days when there was no caller ID, so we used to get a lot, and I do mean a LOT, of crank calls. The boys from the neighboring engineering university seemed to have a lot of time to waste and had the audacity to keep trying to connect with one of us. They thought that perseverance was a virtue and they were sometimes successful. I know couples who are still married. Quite happily if I may say so.

There was something in that voice that touched my heart. The person on the other end of the line so forlorn, so sad that I felt compelled to listen.

"Are you a doctor?" I was asked quite timidly.

"No, I'm not. You have called the students' dorm and I am a fourth-year medical student," I answered.

"My name is Riaz… uh Razia, and I desperately need a doctor! I don't know what to do and I have no support from my parents and because no one understands me. I have no help from anyone! Please, please, help me," she said. "I am at the end of my tether; I just want to die!"

I was so alarmed at the despair in Razia's voice that I stayed on the phone with her for at least an hour and made her promise to come and visit me at the outpatient's clinic the next afternoon at 3 pm sharp. Only when I was absolutely sure that she would keep her promise did did I put the phone down and make my way upstairs to my second-floor dorm room. I was quite disturbed by the phone call and hoped that Razia would keep her appointment. I actually sent a prayer heavenwards for her because somehow, I felt that her safety could be compromised. Closing my eyes, I saw the face of a beautiful child that was marred by injuries. I wondered where that unusual thought came from.

The next day, I made sure that I was in the OPD well before the appointed time. I kept looking at my watch anxiously hoping that all was well. I didn't even know how Razia looked. How would I identify her? How would she find me? I hoped that the professor wouldn't send me on an errand or that we wouldn't be in the middle of a lecture when Razia arrived. I wanted her to know that I had kept my promise to meet her there in the clinic. I wanted her to trust me and to know that I was someone she could talk to without recriminations. I knew deep in my heart that she needed help desperately, and that I could help her.

It turned out that I didn't need to worry. At least about her finding me. At the appointed time, one of the ward boys came looking for me with an odd look on his face and informed me that I had a patient in the ER. This patient, Razia, had just asked for me by name and insisted that I was to be contacted immediately.

I found it odd that the ward boy referred to her as a patient instead of a visitor.

"Please, bring Razia to one of the empty seminar rooms. I need to talk to her before I decide what doctor I will refer her to."

"You really need to go to the ER," he said firmly. "Dr. Ejaz is on duty and he said you were to go there immediately."

Wondering what that was all about, I started to walk briskly towards the Emergency Room. I tried quizzing the ward boy on the way, but apart from shaking his head in disgust and clicking his tongue, I got nothing out of him.

The ER was buzzing as usual and I had to ask one of the nurses where the doctor on duty was because I didn't want to violate the privacy of other patients by peeking into every occupied curtained cubicle.

Just as I was wondering what to do, Dr. Ejaz peeked out of one of the cubicles and beckoned me over with a palpable sigh of relief.

"I was waiting for you. I am off duty now, but I didn't want to go before I briefed you about your patient." Why was everyone referring to Razia as my patient?

"Listen to me." Dr. Ejaz sounded exasperated. "Razia has been brutally beaten by her father and two male cousins this morning. It so happened that one of her younger cousins heard her talk to you on the phone and narrated most of the one-sided conversation to her uncle, Razia's father."

He went on to say, "Razia's father was frustrated, sick and tired of her emerging femininity, which was getting more and more obvious as Razia matured. His male relatives were pressuring him to be firm with his child, and he repeatedly threatened to send her to a *Hijra* camp. Her phone call to you was the breaking point and her father just snapped." Dr. Ejaz shook his head in a mixture of sympathy and disgust at the cruelty of a father to his child.

I entered the cubicle and what I saw brought tears to my eyes. I didn't know what to do. This poor soul was only eighteen years old and had seen so much suffering in her short life. I had to pull myself together and control my emotions in front of my patient, for that is what she definitely was then.

I stepped closer to the gurney on which she lay and saw

that her pain was etched deeply in her face. From her expensive but ripped and blood-spattered clothes, I could see that she was from a well-to-do family, and her speech, even though it was slurred due to the painkillers she had just received, indicated that she was well educated. Physically, she had a willowy feminine body, with softly rounded hips and a burgeoning bust, but the most prominent thing I noticed about her was her beautiful, thick eyelashes that framed her sad light brown eyes. Her face was marred by bruises and cuts. One eye was swollen shut, and her lower lip had a deep cut that definitely needed stitches. Her nose was bleeding profusely, and I was certain it was broken. Despite being injured and disheveled, I noticed that her shiny auburn hair was cut stylishly and tangled with a woefully crushed garland of jasmine that was interwoven in her hair. The natural fragrance of the bruised flowers was so strong that it was nearly overpowering in the small cubicle.

How could anyone willfully hurt such a delicate child? Were her problems so terrible that her own family was willfully cruel to her?

Before I sat down to talk to Razia, I scribbled Tanya's name and phone number on a piece of paper and asked a nurse to request her to come to our ER as soon as she could. This had now become a medicolegal case, and if we wanted justice for Razia, we had to handle her situation through the proper channels and with kid gloves.

"Hi, Razia. I am Sarah. You talked to me on the phone yesterday. Remember?" I talked to her in a low and what I hoped was a soothing voice. I started to talk about innocuous things to make her feel comfortable with me. I didn't want to push her to tell me about her problems immediately. She needed to heal physically before we could even address her mental wellbeing.

The doctors and nurses bustled around as usual, trying to make our patient as comfortable and pain free as possible.

"I would like to wait for Inspector Tanya so that you can tell both of us your story." I put my hand reassuringly on her arm.

"Please, no! Not the police! My father knows many influential people and there might be a big scandal!" She was clearly agitated.

"Tanya is my friend. Why don't you talk to us and I promise we won't file an official complaint just yet? Since she knows the law, she could tell you what your options are in this situation."

I reassured her that it would be her decision whether to talk to us or not once she met Tanya.

As soon as Tanya arrived, seeing that Razia was still quite groggy from the painkillers, she decided to speak first with the ER doctor. She went over the file where Razia's injuries were documented in detail and jotted down her own notes. I noticed that she wrote everything down in painstaking detail and even took photographs of the injuries. Going through the list, we were appalled at the amount of physical abuse that had been inflicted.

When we turned Razia over to examine her back, she let out an involuntary whimper of pain. When the hospital gown was gently pulled aside, we saw lacerations caused by a whip. While most of the injuries were fresh, there were a few that were older and hadn't received any medical care. I was overwhelmed.

"Who did this to you?" I couldn't hold myself back anymore.

"Sometimes my father would whip me, and sometimes, with his consent, my cousins would. They enjoyed torturing me." Razia started to cry again.

Once Tanya was finished with her examination and documentation Razia began to talk. It took effort on her part, but it dawned on me that she had so much grief and pain bottled inside herself that it just had to come out and overflow like a breached dam. I was glad that she trusted us.

"When I was born the doctors couldn't determine my physical sex. I was labeled "*Ambiguous Genitalia.*" That means that I have a rare condition where I don't appear to be clearly either male or female."

I knew most parents of a baby with Ambiguous Genitalia, and even some doctors, found this very confusing.

A medical team plays an extremely important role when it comes to providing information and counseling. Being well informed could help guide decisions and the overall consensus about the baby's gender and any necessary treatment if required.

It is also important that the appropriate physiological gender is assigned from the beginning because that is necessary for the healthy development of the child. The psychological implications of assigning genders according to the family's preferences or burying one's head in the sand and not doing anything at the time could be devastating for the child. Especially when they start puberty.

At the time of her birth, Razia's father already had five daughters and obsessively craved a son. His wife's doctor was adamant that this had to be her last pregnancy because she wasn't strong enough to bear any more children. Therefore, despite the advice from the pediatrician, the father refused any gender investigations and said he would take his chances and raise the baby as a boy. He proudly called the baby Riaz and introduced him to his friends and family as the long-awaited son he had wanted.

As time went by, Riaz's mother continued to persuade her husband to have the baby tested. She intuitively knew that they were inflicting wrong gender values and expectations on the poor child. She was aware that Riaz was consistently bullied and physically abused but being a weak woman with health issues of her own, she could not do anything about it except offer solace to the poor child when it was sought. Without any thought of the impending psychological impact on his child, the father continued to stubbornly refuse any investigations or doctors' visits to assess him.

When Riaz started to show overt feminine tendencies, his father would try to "beat the girl out of the boy" and threaten to send him away to a *Hijra** camp, but instead of "straightening" out little Riaz, the beatings caused him to behave even more like a scared little girl. Eventually he became an introvert, nearly a hermit. His natural personality was subdued with the beatings and the abuse he consistently had to suffer. He refused to go out and socialize and was scared of his own shadow.

When Riaz hit puberty, all hell was let loose. He started showing signs of feminization with strong female puberty traits. He developed breasts along with the feminine type of body hair distribution. Even though he had monthly cramps that progressed to being more severe in intensity every month as time went by, there were (as yet) no physical signs of menstruation. That convinced the father that his child was male. Additionally, a trusted friend of his had told him that some boys had temporary breast enlargement at puberty, so he wasn't too concerned about the changes he saw in his son.

Riaz, on the other hand, insisted that he always felt like a girl. He loved playing house with his sisters and his favorite toy was a cute little baby doll. When he could, he would dress up in his sisters' clothes and called himself Razia.

He would hide when he did that because he knew if he were caught he would be beaten black and blue. If not by his father, then by his male psychopathic cousins, who were always on the lookout to bully him. The worst part was when he was shamed in front of the whole family.

Razia had a brilliant idea. Since they had just started the national database that issued ID cards to citizens from eighteen years and over that same year, and as Razia's birth certificate had been damaged in a flood the year before, she was able to register herself as female. When her father found out he became incredibly angry and even more abusive. He tried his best to change the data, but due to the usual red tape, he had to ultimately give up. This was a small but painful victory for Razia.

She desperately wanted to see a doctor and she was

glad of the unusual circumstances that led her to meet me. She said she needed the long delayed genetic and chromosomal tests to be done so that she could once and for all determine her actual sex. Her feelings and the changes in her body were driving her insane and the situation in her home was becoming unbearable. The day of her first visit, when she landed in the ER while coming to see me, she wore her feminine clothes to convince me and any other doctor who could have examined her that she was definitely female inside and out, no matter what. That blatant flaunting of overt femininity had led to dire consequences when she was caught leaving the house and was beaten within an inch of her life by her own relatives.

No one was willing to help her as she lay bleeding and crying in her driveway. Everyone, including her own sisters, turned their back on her. Not because they didn't want to help her, but because they were scared of their father's wrath.

Finally, her old nursemaid took pity on her and got a taxi to bring her to the hospital to get her injuries treated and to meet me.

Razia took a deep breath and stopped talking. I could see that she was exhausted, and her face echoed her body's excruciating pain. She clung to my hand like a child as we tried to reassure her.

"If you feel like a woman, you definitely are one, no matter what the test results show," I told her fiercely. "The main thing is that you have to be comfortable in your chosen persona. That's all that matters."

I wanted to convince her that she was a loveable person and it wasn't her, but the people around her who were flawed, to the point that they had made the life of an innocent child a living hell.

Some people are quick to abandon or ostracize a child on gender or sexuality issues, but they would go out of their way to seek treatment if the baby had something like a cleft lip. I could not even imagine pushing away or not loving a child that shared my DNA.

I peeked out of the cubicle and intercepted a gynecology intern. I asked whether the Professor of Gynecology, Professor Imrana, was available to see a last-minute patient of mine. We were in luck. She had just finished with her outpatients clinic and was kind enough to come over to the ER for a consult.

I introduced Razia to Professor Imrana and meant to leave the cubicle out of deference to Razia's privacy, but she frantically clutched my hand and looked pleadingly at me. "Please stay; I'm scared," she said.

Since the professor had no objection, I stayed while Razia narrated a shortened version of her tale and her medical history once again. Professor Imrana got up and walked towards a microscope that was provided for the use of the ER doctors and picked up a mysterious disposable kit. She said that getting to know Razia's actual sex could be determined within a few minutes.

"This kit will help me do a short, simple, and fairly reliable procedure. I will scrape mucus membrane from the inside of your cheek and examine the cells under a microscope for *Barr bodies.* If they are present, your phenotype is definitely female," she said while she was preparing the sterile kit.

Adding a little factoid here: A Barr body is the inactive

X chromosome in a female cell. The buccal (inside the cheek) smear Barr body test is usually performed to identify the inactive X-chromosome in the female cells and compare them with the male cells.

Razia was so overwhelmed that she squeezed my hand so tightly that I thought the circulation might be cut off..

She was asked to rinse out her mouth a few times with cool water and then Professor Imrana used the kit to scrape the inside of her cheek and swab it with a soft probe. The cells thus harvested were set in alcohol on a glass slide to be examined under the microscope.

Professor Imrana took her time to examine the specimen in detail.

"Keeping in mind the medicolegal implications of the case, I need to be absolutely sure of my findings."

In the meantime, I kept talking to Razia in a low voice and tried to take her mind off the impending life changing results.

After about thirty minutes, the professor twirled around in her stool and beckoned me over to have a look in her microscope. Not having seen such a specimen before, I was not very sure what to look for. I saw an array of cells which were magnified manifold. Most of them had a shadow that clung to the nuclear membrane. They were Barr bodies! I looked towards my teacher with barely concealed excitement and she nodded. Razia was genetically female! The Barr bodies had confirmed it.

"Well," said Professor Imrana, "this is just the springboard from where we start our investigations and assess if any treatment is required."

Now the hard part was just about to begin. We needed

to do a complete physical evaluation to see whether Razia had adequately developed female internal organs, and what her external malformations entailed. Most importantly, whether she needed hormones and major or minor surgeries.

The technology of ultrasound was new at the time, but Professor Imrana had a machine in her clinic. The images were not as sharp as they are today, but a scan confirmed that there were no signs of any male organs or male features.

Razia's external examination showed that she had fused labia and an imperforate hymen, so she needed corrective surgery. Once the more severe of her injuries had healed, her mother was contacted and she was told of her daughter's predicament. She wasn't home that day, but once she got to know, was appalled at the merciless beating that her husband and nephews had inflicted on her poor child. She immediately gave her consent for the surgery, which was scheduled within a week.

Professor Imrana said that the procedure would be easy, but she made sure that Razia was absolutely certain that she wanted to proceed. It was a big decision. Razia was thrilled that she wasn't considered different anymore. Her intuition had been accurate and she now looked forward to a normal life with no stigmas or recriminations. As a matter of fact, having the foresight to register herself as female to get her ID card, she had actually saved herself a lot of unnecessary red tape and paperwork!

Just to be sure that they covered all of the medicolegal and ethical concerns before she underwent her corrective surgery, Razia and her mother, with Tanya's help, consulted a lawyer. The future implications of living with a different gender than what her parents had stipulated at the time of her birth was discussed in detail. Finally, they consented to intensive family group counselling, but in the end, the result was a done deal since Razia wouldn't need any additional hormonal enhancements. Therefore, the surgical corrections were the only therapies required to set her on her new path in life.

As we got to know her better, Razia told us about her story. "I have been very scared of my father's threats most of my life. He would get extremely angry and tell me that he would banish me to the *hijras* where I could openly live as a transexual woman."

She suppressed a sob and went on. "But that would have meant that my family wouldn't acknowledge me in any way. I was always terrified that I would be forced to leave home."

Blowing her nose on the tissue I gave her, she tried to smile bravely. "I just want to finish school and enroll in a university. I want a career. Preferably one where I can help abused women and children." It was so nice to see her think about her future. Though she still looked sad at times and there was still a lot of counselling to be done, we were happy that we had saved her from a dire fate.

The only jobs a person could possibly have by joining a *hijra* camp in those days were to be a street dancer, a beggar, or worse come to worst, a prostitute. Razia believed her father when he said that the hijras would haul her off if they laid their eyes on her. He kept telling her that they always were on the prowl for people "like her" and let her know that he would gladly hand her over to the hijras if they came calling.

It's only been recently, thanks to their lobbying, that the hijras have been legally recognized as a third gender. This can now be documented as such on passports, ID cards, and other official documents. Admissions to schools and colleges have helped them get educated and created a considerable shift from the previous traditional occupations of desperation to professions of respectability.

In the case of our Razia, she would go on to finish college with honors. A budding friendship between her and Tanya determined the direction towards an exciting career path. It also happened that as people became aware of their friendship and her prospective profession, the bullying within her family and in the neighborhood stopped very quickly.

While she was still in college, Razia enrolled in martial arts classes and then when she graduated she joined the police force. Her chosen career suited her and she earned a name for herself as a hard-working person with integrity. She was well respected and her keen mind ensured that she was soon promoted to inspector, like Tanya, at a very early age.

We were thrilled when we heard that she had married a colleague soon after she finished her stint at the Police Academy, and she soon became the proud mother of twin boys.

Her father and cousins were arrested at the time of her assault and visit in our ER. After spending a brief time in prison, the cousins were contrite and started to treat her with respect, but her father continued to bully and verbally abuse her, although he never lifted a heavy hand on her again.

It took him a while to come to terms that his boy Riaz was actually another daughter, Razia. Seeing her flourish and her success in her academics and the police academy, he finally embraced Razia's true persona wholeheartedly. After all, according to Razia's mother, he wasn't a bad man. He was just brain-washed by the perceived norms of society and influenced by the sarcastic barbs from his friends and relatives. However, I do believe that one of the factors that helped change his mind was that one of Razia's boys was named after him. That was surely a catalyst to his mellowing demeanor.

Tanya

I hadn't heard from Sarah for a while and felt like a callow teenager whenever I was away from her. Maybe it was because I was planning our future without even telling her about it, but I needed to have something solid in hand when I finally told her how I felt. It made no sense to tell her that I loved her and then sit back and live just for the present. That would be foolish and dangerous for both of us. She definitely needed to finish her education first, and I was driven by my career, and I was not ready to be outed as yet.

I had a very productive day. I sent letters to Interpol and the local police in Amsterdam. I was sure that I could be accepted there—I had the qualifications. A friend of mine had told me that Amsterdam was the most tolerant city in the world, especially where same sex couples are concerned. There was a strong advocacy group lobbying for marriage there and that would be ideal for us. Now there was nothing to do but wait anxiously for answers to my letters.

A knock on the door startled me out of my daydream. The constable strode in and saluted smartly. It amused me when I remembered how sloppy he used to be when I first arrived. I was proud to say that my training had created a precinct that was becoming well known for its integrity and vigilance.

"The Emergency Room from the hospital called, sir."

"Did they tell you what it was all about?"

"No, sir, but they said that Ms. Sarah said it was an emergency."

Sarah didn't panic easily. She would rather handle things on her own than call for the police so I knew it was serious.

"You are with me, Constable," I called over my shoulder as I hurried toward my jeep while cramming my cap on my head.

The receptionist at the ER pointed towards a curtained off cubicle when I asked for Sarah.

I rapped my nightstick on the frame and announced myself.

"Thank God you are here!" Sarah came out of the cubicle with a relieved expression. "This is Razia, an eighteen-year-old that has been severely beaten by her father and her cousins."

I was shocked to see the condition of the poor girl that was lying helpless on the bed. I stepped immediately out and asked the ER doctor to tell me what had happened.

Since he was also the medicolegal officer of the ER, I could access Razia's files.

"Have you photographed the injuries yet?" I asked him. "We need to do that as soon as possible while they are still fairly new."

"I would have done it, Inspector, but the patient is only letting Sarah near her. I think she distrusts men at the moment."

"All right. Please, clear the cubicle and I will ask Sarah to help me." He looked relieved. It was part of his job to get as much data as he was able to, but the terror Razia felt was a block to his work.

Sarah was trying to keep calm, and anyone would have said that she was coping pretty well, but I recognized that flicker of panic in her eyes. She looked at me and I saw relief and… was that love? I could only hope.

Razia told me what had happened in her own words. She was encouraged and prompted by Sarah. I put her story together, and the more I heard the angrier I got. The ignorance and intolerance of Razia's father was unacceptable.

Razia calmed down enough to let me take photographs of her injuries. No wonder she had turned to a stranger in despair. No doubt Sarah had saved her life with her soft words and encouragement.

"She has been beaten so brutally!" Sarah had tears in her eyes. "Look at these welts and lacerations. The whip used had metal spikes on it." She couldn't keep the horror out of her voice.

I was definitely appalled but this was not the first time that I had seen something like this. Ignorant people who think someone is different are very quick to inflict violence on them. You don't even need to be gay—just anything that is out of the norm is attacked. It's sickening!

"I need to lodge a complaint against your father and cousins," I told Razia firmly.

"Please, no! They will continue to beat me if you do!" She started to sob uncontrollably.

"I promise we will take care of you."

When the gynecologist told us that Razia was genetically female, the case against the men of her family became stronger. Indiscriminate terror of a child is a grave infraction.

Such cases were the reason why I wanted to take Sarah away. I wanted to take care of her physical and mental well-being. I wanted to shelter her from a cruel ignorant world.

"Constable, please call Judge Majeed." I had to work quickly because I suspected that the culprits would abscond if I waited any longer. "Tell the judge I need an arrest warrant for Razia's father and cousins. Once you have the warrant go immediately to their house and lock them up."

Thanks to Sarah's gentle persuasion, Razia told us the names of her attackers, and the constable left immediately to get his team together to settle the legalities.

As the days went by, Razia became a good friend. She saw both of us as mentors, but I think she was so resolute in learning how to take care of herself that she latched on to me more than Sarah. I was happy that I could direct her towards a career that I had pioneered to create a niche for girls in the future.

After about two weeks, I received a prompt answer

from Interpol—they were happy to consider my application to join them. The only proviso was that I had to learn French. My minor subject in college was advanced English Literature, so that was a part of their requirements out of the way. The only negative thing was that there was a long waiting list of candidates worldwide. While they had officially put me on their list, they suggested I started French classes while I waited. Thank God they had a Berlitz Institute in Nawabshah. Things were looking up. I was getting excited and there seemed to be a light at the end of the proverbial tunnel.

CHAPTER 11

THE DEADLY INTERNSHIPS – SURGICALLY YOURS

"Cover her face; mine eyes dazzle. She died young."
— John Webster, The Duchess of Malfi

Sarah

"This is ridiculous!" I shouted to the ceiling while I packed my books away. "I know she loves me as much as I love her! And yet she says nothing? Doesn't she know that I am on the verge of leaving?"

I made up my mind. I was going to talk to Tanya right away. I needed to tell her how I felt. Otherwise, I had that niggling feeling in my gut that I would regret not telling her my whole life.

That the stressful exams were over was a double-edged sword. I wanted to get out of there, and yet I couldn't leave the love of my life behind. A serious conversation was vital. Immediately.

While I mulled over what I was going to say, I packed up or gave away all the stuff that I had accumulated over the years. Giving books back to the book bank and closing accounts with the cafeteria and the canteen were also amongst my last-minute tasks. It was quite surprising to see the amount of junk I had collected. I was actually relieved to know that one milestone in my life had been achieved. I was looking forward to the next one… getting an internship/house job in a well-known teaching hospital, preferably in a large city. The large tertiary hospitals were where the real teaching occurred and the limited slots for the interns/house officers were always awarded based on the marks achieved in the finals.

And yet I felt hollow inside. I knew what I had to do and by God I would.

Tanya picked me up on the evening before I left to go home. We had planned a quiet evening at her home. I looked forward to that with hope as well as dread.

After a delicious dinner which Tanya cooked, we were relaxing in front of the TV when I turned to her.

"Tanya…"

"Sarah…"

"You first," I said chuckling. Tanya looked so stunning that night... and the look of uncertainty added to her appeal. Just as I was wondering what she would say, she cleared her throat and began to speak. I heard her out with a mixture of joy, wonder, and dread.

"Sarah…" Tanya was so adorable in her uncertainty.

"We have been friends for the whole time that you were studying here in college. I think I fell in love with you when I first noticed you getting off the bus. Just looking into your eyes that day hit me like a lightning bolt."

There was a soft expression in her eyes, a sincerity that pulled me to her. Like a magnet, I was helplessly drawn to her.

"I have been planning our life together… that is if you want to be with me…"

There was nothing I could do but lean over and softly kiss her. Our first kiss! It felt so… electric! I moved back to see her reaction, but she had her eyes closed and was leaning towards me as if she wanted more. And more she got. I had never kissed anyone before, but she definitely knew her way around it. It was amazing! She held me in her arms as if I was the most precious person in the world.

"I love you so much Tanya," I finally said when we came up for air. "I had made up my mind to tell you before I left. I could not go without letting you know that you are the light of my life."

I didn't know what to do, and I didn't want to go home in the morning, but Tanya told me about the plans that she had already set into motion, and I needed to be there for her as she executed her plans. She wanted me to continue with my house job while getting ready to work thereafter either in the UK or anywhere else in Europe.

I spent the night with Tanya. She didn't want to go further than kisses and cuddles till we made a firm commitment to each other. I understood where she came from… and yet I wanted a sensuous reminder of our last day in Nawabshah together. But I knew we would be together again. The sooner the better.

The next day I left the college for the last time. The mood was very different to the day I entered the gates—exhilaration at my successes, melancholy at leaving the love of my life behind, and a feeling of gloom that I would be leaving friends. One never knew if we would ever meet up again. We had all been together for over five years and the camaraderie was inevitable.

When I reached Karachi, I realized the competition for top house job slots was fierce. Therefore, instead of enjoying my time off, I opted to go to the popular hospitals for honorary part-time clinical attachments till our final results were announced. This was so that when the actual official house job started, I would be somewhat familiar with the routines and processes of a busy hospital. Didn't I say I was quite competitive?

Soon thereafter, our final results were announced and that was when the real race started. The prospective house officers were to be interviewed personally by a panel made up of the heads of the various departments. There was no preliminary mail-in application procedure. House job hopefuls had to personally present their papers on the specific dates announced in the local newspapers and then come on their allocated day for their interviews.

On the day of the interviews, you could see many young doctors hitching their portfolios under their arms and keeping their fingers crossed, hoping against hope that they would get into their preferred department.

My application to one of the largest hospitals in South

Asia was thankfully accepted and I was duly invited for the requisite interview. We were called in one by one to appear in front of the interviewing panel in the order of our compiled marks. I was aware that I had passed with good marks in all of my subjects, and I knew what the total aggregate of my marks was. To me, they seemed impressive if I may say so. What I didn't know at the time was that I was considered to be in the top slots for the coveted departments; therefore, when my name was called out almost immediately, I was pleasantly surprised.

Much to the amusement of the panel, I chose orthopedics surgery. That was a department that had never had a female doctor working there, so it was considered quite a novelty.

"Little girl, do you think you can manage the heavy schedule?" My octogenarian professor wheezed at me.

"I assure you that this will be a challenge. I tend to enjoy myself while learning a lot from you and my colleagues in this department."

My job as an orthopedic house officer was varied. I had to be on duty for thirty-six hours at a stretch, and had to be present in the ER, operation theater, outpatient department, and the wards, as and when I was required there. It was frantic, exhilarating, and tiring, but I loved it so. The only downside was that any social interaction with friends and family was limited to my coming and going and my extremely busy schedule. I didn't even have time to think about what Tanya was planning for us. Our sporadic telephone conversations helped to some extent, although sometimes I felt there was something missing inside me.

After I left college, she started to lobby with her superiors to transfer her to Karachi. One day, after a lonely six months, I heard a firm rap on the door of my duty room. To my surprise, Tanya walked in!

"Tanya!" I shouted happily, running to hug her. "You have the pips of a chief inspector shining on your shoulders! Congratulations!"

"Well, in their infinite wisdom, the powers that be decided to promote me for the exemplary work I did in Nawabshah." She smiled shyly while I stroked her shiny new silver badges of rank. "However, I have told them I would stay here only till such time I am recruited by Interpol."

Her superiors were only too glad to have her as long as they could. Promoting her and giving her the premium posting to the central headquarters was a perfect opportunity for her. It would look good on her resume when she sent it to Interpol for review.

Once again, I flung myself into her arms and hugged her so long that she grunted as her breath whooshed out with the force of my embrace. Her kisses were wonderful, and I poured all my love, yearning, and loneliness in them. It was so good to hold her once more.

"My love, I missed you so much," I said, happy to see the reflection of my feelings in her eyes.

She looked around the duty room in interest. "Look at you! *Doctor* Sarah," she said proudly. "Are you happy working here, sweetheart?

"Oh, yes," I said. "When I started to work in the massive ER, one of the first things that I learned was how extremely busy it was compared to the college hospital. The cases are phenomenal, and our hospital not only caters to a city of over twelve million people, as you already know, but also to the rural and urban areas surrounding it. There are so many varieties of interesting cases to learn about." Tanya smiled at my enthusiasm. She knew how obsessed I would get about my patients.

It was wonderful having her in the same city once more. I felt as if my heart was whole again. She also kept hugging me as if she couldn't believe that we were together again.

My favorite place in the hospital was the ER. Not only could I practice my shiny new skills there, but I also conducted minor surgeries in the little operation theater attached to it. Most of the time, that meant setting bones and applying plaster casts and splints.

Whenever I swaggered into the ER, a few colleagues would nudge each other and come to see what I was doing. Some bright sparks would call out to each other to announce that "Dr. S is in the house to pull your leg!"

Hmph! They couldn't believe that a skinny young woman like me could be strong enough to set a burly policeman's leg. Setting a leg with simple break is actually quite easy, trust me, but I still was the entertainment of the day.

On the whole, the atmosphere was friendly and conducive to learning. The hospital administration and the senior consultants put a strict emphasis on proper ethical healthcare of the patients visiting the institution. That was commendable because the majority of the patients received free treatment as the hospital was completely funded by the federal government.

The best part was that no one objected when Tanya visited me in the evenings for dinner or just a hurried cup of tea if she or I were busy. Just to see her, even for a short time, was a boost to my energy and a balm to my soul. Of course, making out in the duty room helped tremendously.

I made friends with the ER and the medicolegal supervisors and we would review patients together and discuss difficult cases. They say you make friends for life when you start your house job, and they are right. To this day, one of my best friends is Professor Jahan Ara, an eminent endocrinologist and the ER in charge back then.

The orthopedic department dealt predominantly with accidents and traumas with relation to bone injuries, but we were also one of the best known hospitals in the country that specialized in post-polio deformities (PPD), and we would treat children who were suffering the debilitating and crippling effects of poliomyelitis. Our ward had some long-term regulars who had to be operated on a few times for fine corrective surgeries, which was a long and painful process. One of these patients was an eight-year-old little girl called Nomi. She was a pretty little girl with reddish brown ringlets. Her big brown eyes were what drew me to her—they were always twinkling and so full of life. She had a sunny disposition and was friendly with almost anyone she came in contact with, so she was well known in the whole surgical unit and her pockets were always full of the treats that she got from doctors and patients alike.

Nomi had a Post-Polio Deformity of her right hand that

needed corrective surgery in well drawn-out stages with multiple and varied procedures. I had assisted with three of her surgeries and it was amazing to see how her hand progressed after each procedure. She was in a lot of pain, but her positive attitude could be set as an example for our much older patients. She was determined to have a more or less fully functional hand one day.

I really admired the little tyke's bravery. Whenever she was in the recovery room after her surgeries, I always made it a point to sit with her so that she knew someone was there for her.

"Stay with me, Doccy *Appa* (big sister)," she would say, still groggy from her anesthesia-induced sleep. If I wasn't on duty, or if she didn't see me immediately, she would always ask for me and wouldn't rest till I went to her bedside.

After her hospital stays, Nomi was usually sent off to recuperate at home, but she needed to come for regular follow ups and readjustment of her pins and cast, and I always looked forward to seeing her sunny face. On one of her follow up days, as the busy OPD gradually emptied, Nomi was still nowhere to be seen. I asked the ward boy to keep a look out for her, but after a fruitless search we all gave up. We thought that her mother was probably busy and had missed Nomi's appointment, which was unusual, because she had never missed a surgical follow-up before.

The next day, while I was eating my hurried breakfast before I left for the hospital, I saw a news bulletin on the TV of an attack on a mother and child.

"Nomi Ahmad and her mother were on their way to the

hospital when they were mugged in Kalamoo Colony. The mother has survived with minor injuries. Regrettably, eight-year-old Nomi succumbed to her wounds." My heart broke while the newscaster spoke in a monotone devoid of emotions. "Nomi and her mother were on their way to the hospital when they were mugged for the paltry sum that they carried with them. The muggers hit Nomi on her head and she died almost immediately." The newscaster went on to say that this was the sixth mugging that had occurred around the hospital area, although this was the only one so far that had resulted in dire consequences. Apparently, patients coming to the hospital were being targeted because they were almost certain to have cash for their or their relatives' treatment. Though most of the procedures and treatments were free, there were some departments like radiotherapy that charged the patients for the sessions. It was therefore inevitable that some of them would have money on them.

Leaving the rest of my breakfast untouched, I rushed to the hospital to find out more about what had happened. There were a million thoughts swirling through my mind and I was distraught.

Once I reached the hospital, the first thing I did was call Tanya. She was my rock and I also wanted her to see what the police could do to catch the killers.

The medicolegal team had just brought Nomi's battered body to the ER. They had laid her down on a gurney and she looked very small and delicate. She had such an angelic expression on her face that I could have thought she was just asleep, but her beautiful head was marred with an ugly skull fracture, and her clothes were soaked with blood. I was horrified when I saw the poor mite.

Nomi's parents had vehemently refused an autopsy, though they did allow us a thorough external examination before they took her away.

When we examined her, we saw that there was a scrap of silk cloth in her right hand with an unusual button sewn on it. The button was striated with rainbow colors and had a mother of pearl sheen. It looked expensive.

Tanya, who had just arrived, looked over my shoulder and said, "It seems there was a struggle and Nomi ripped the button off the shirt of her attacker."

Her other hand was encased in her post-operative plaster cast. The tips of two of the pins on the cast were covered with blood and there was some sort of organic tissue stuck on them. It seemed that she had not given up without a fight and had managed to scratch her assailant with the pins.

"We now have some clues to work on—the blood on the stabilizing pins, the scrap of cloth, and the unusual button," said the medicolegal officer. He immediately collected the items and handed the evidence bags to Tanya to take to the police laboratory.

Before they left, I realized that there was one thing missing from Nomi's body. I had given her a pin for her birthday that was unique because it had her name engraved on it. If we could just find that pin, we could find the culprit.

Nomi's death affected me deeply, as if I had lost a baby sister. Tanya took me aside and talked to me in a low voice, and her kind words calmed me down and reassured me that she would do her utmost to bring Nomi's killer to justice.

When the police from the local precinct arrived for the medicolegal report after an unprecedented delay, they were lackluster and I realized that they were not at all interested in solving the murder. For them it was just a run of the mill mugging that had resulted in an unfortunate tragedy. They were not overly optimistic that they would be able to catch the culprits.

"Such muggings happen on a regular basis, and it is difficult to pinpoint any suspects without any tangible clues or reliable witnesses," said the overweight, greasy looking constable.

He looked around in a desultory manner and noticed Tanya. His demeanor changed almost in a comical manner when he realized Tanya was a higher-ranking officer. He saluted her and immediately obeyed her crisp orders without demurring.

"Please, don't forget to look for the silver engraved pin that I gave Nomi for her birthday," I reminded Tanya. "She loved it dearly and was never without it. It was so touching to see that she would make it a point to pin it on whatever outfit she wore. It would even be pinned on her hospital gown or her pajamas when she was admitted for her surgeries."

The medicolegal officer confirmed that there was a small rip in Nomi's dress that could have been made by her pin. Maybe the tear was there because the pin was pulled violently away? But first, the police had to go to the murder scene and look around very carefully. If it was not there, then there was a distinct possibility that her murderers had stolen it.

I was allowed to tag along with the police only if I promised that I wouldn't get in the way or touch anything. I readily agreed because I wanted to see the crime scene for myself.

The police had already cordoned off the area, so Tanya put on her investigative cap and had her nose to the ground. From where I stood, I could see a concrete gutter cover garishly stained with blood. It was probably where Nomi fell when she was struck. We were disappointed that nothing of significance was found even after the police went over the area with a fine-tooth comb.

While I was observing Tanya and her team, there was a sudden shift in the atmosphere and I felt a warm, benevolent wind envelope me. I looked up to see Nomi standing in front of me, her injuries quite prominent and in vivid colors. She was crying bitterly and kept saying, "They took my pin, my beautiful pin. Doccy *Appa*, please, get me my pin back. I want it back!"

Even though I should have been used to these "visitations" by now, I was still disturbed to see the pain Nomi was in even after she had passed away. As Nomi's image faded away with a sigh in the bright sunlight, I vowed that my friends and I would do our best to bring her murderers to justice.

The shopkeepers and people living in the area were unusually tight-lipped and not very forthcoming with information. Even though they must have seen what had happened, no one came forward with any statement or evidence whatsoever. Everyone seemed frightened.

Nomi's funeral was the next day and most of us that knew her in the hospital attended to bid farewell to our little friend. It was a very solemn occasion, especially so because the loss of a young child with such joie de vivre who was at the threshold of experiencing life's wonders was painful. Prayers were recited and repeated by the people coming and going in Nomi's parents' house.

They say that Lady Luck smiles if you persevere, and definitely if you keep your eyes and ears open. I hadn't believed that till one hot stuffy day when I was fielding patients in an overcrowded outpatient's department.

A cherubic but grubby little boy named Taimur came to see me for a twisted ankle. From his appearance and lack of hygiene, I thought that he was from the gypsy colony that camped in the empty plot behind the hospital. The strange thing was that his shirt seemed fairly new and was made out of silk. It had these eye-catching buttons on it, exactly like the button found in Nomi's hand at the time of her assault. What's more, he was wearing Nomi's pin! You could have knocked me over with a feather.

I quietly beckoned my nursing aide and told her to phone Tanya and ask her to come to the hospital as soon as she could. I had some information regarding Nomi's murder.

To buy some time, I dawdled with the little boy's examination and applied and re-applied a compression bandage as if I were looking for the perfect way to do so. If I had mentioned that we were waiting for the police, I am sure Taimur's mother, Sadiqa, would have taken her son and gone. For now, we didn't have any legal reason to put her in custody.

I started to play with Taimur and rummaged in my cabinet for a lollipop to appease him, because he had started to get restless in the big bad doccy's room. I asked Sadiqa where she had got his beautiful shirt. As a pretext, I explained that the buttons were the exact match for my new shirt and I was sure that they would look classy on it.

Sadiqa was happy that I admired her handiwork.

"The original shirt belonged to my brother," she said proudly. "He is a well-to-do political worker in the area. He told me that the shirt tore while he was doing some physical work and he was about to throw it away."

She went on to tell me that she asked her brother to give it to her because she had six children and always needed old clothes that were in good condition. She would remodel and sew them to her children's sizes.

"Taimur just loved the pretty rainbow buttons, and it had this little pin on it, so he keeps showing it to everyone as if it was a badge."

They were getting restless now, but before they could leave, Tanya entered the OPD. The presence of the police didn't cause the usual knee-jerk reaction that come from guilty people—it was good to see that Sadiqa was calm and not bothered by their presence at all.

"Salam, my name is Chief Inspector Tanya." I really loved the way she spoke with such authority. Without wanting, I let out a sigh of pleasure.

Tanya gave me an amused look and went on, "We would like to know about the shirt your brother gave you. It will help us with one of our investigations."

Sadiqa was cooperating with the police and wanted to help as much as she could. She gave Tanya her brother's name and address quite readily, since she was convinced that he was innocent. Tanya left immediately with her team to investigate the address, and to interrogate Sadiqa's brother.

"You, my dear little doctor, will stay where you are. I promise I will let you know if there is anything of significance." Tanya knew I'd want to come along, but I agreed that I would stay behind and not interfere with her work.

I did trust Tanya, of course. After all, she was *my* amazing policewoman and I was certain she would find and arrest the culprits.

As promised, Tanya visited me later on at the hospital and told me in detail about what she found out. I was appalled at the lengths people would go to obtain money and power, but also grateful that Nomi was able to get justice. She was finally at peace, and I know because she did come to me in a very vivid dream and told me that she was now happy.

Tanya

I was so proud of Sarah. She's Doctor Sarah now. The compassion and empathy that she had for her patients was amazing. I hoped she would always have the enthusiasm and love for her patients that she had at the start of her career. Just to see her with the children was so moving, and my love for her grew even deeper. I was a bit insecure when she left Nawabshah. Would she forget about me? Would her love for me diminish over time? When I finally made it to Karachi, the way she greeted me with such love and joy washed away all my doubts. My soul mate was mine.

The six months apart were hard for both of us. I was fortunate that the political tide of the country turned and they needed a female figurehead in the police. Going to the general headquarters was nothing short of a miracle. Where I was concerned, just a transfer would have been enough, but I wore the new silver pips of my promotion with pride.

Sarah and I had to bide our time for a while because they took their time with the processes in Interpol, as was the norm. They had to be absolutely sure who they recruited and a thorough background check was necessary. They sometimes took up to a year, but that suited me fine. Sarah would have finished her house job by then and we had a lot of plans to make and a future to build. I was excited at the prospect of having her with me all the time, but I was also scared of the consequences of our actions.

Sarah had told me about Nomi. As a matter of fact, she used to talk a lot about her in our telephone calls and I knew that she loved the little girl very much. The harrowing news bulletin of her murder was dreadful. I recognized her when they flashed her photo on the TV because I had brought her sweets when I visited Sarah at the hospital. I knew that Nomi was the sweetheart of the ward, and her death affected a lot of people, especially Sarah.

Sarah insisted to be there when we examined Nomi's body and the crime scene. I thought that she was very brave and it was clear she had come a long way since I saw her lose her lunch over her first autopsy.

As predicted by the lackluster constables, we couldn't find any evidence or clues and Nomi's attackers remained a mystery.

We did get a lucky break when Sadiqa walked with her son Taimur into Sarah's OPD. What were the odds? It definitely was karma.

My team and I immediately obtained a warrant and went to the address she had given us. I didn't want to leave anything to chance. Everything had to be done by the book so that nobody could say that we hadn't worked according to proper procedures and protocols.

Sadiqa's brother lived behind the hospital in a not so well-planned colony for lower income people. The narrow streets were laid out like an untidy maze that made it easy for unsavory inhabitants to lose themselves easily if they so desired. There were stinking piles of rubbish and overflowing gutters, which were endorsements that this colony was not legal and the municipality cleaners were not obliged to work there. These types of colonies usually sprouted up nearly overnight to accommodate the ever-growing influx of immigrants from other parts of the country. They housed people who were usually seeking their fortune on the gold-paved streets of the vast metropolis and would sadly end up in the stinking cesspools of the illegal colonies.

When we reached the specified address, we were surprised at the resistance-free entry into the house. The door was immediately opened by a young woman who introduced herself as Jamila. She was pretty but a bit ungainly because she was in the mid stages of her pregnancy. Nevertheless, she invited us in to wait for her husband, who was expected home soon.

Jamila was quite hospitable and she set some refreshments in front of us. The strange thing was that her responses and hospitality were a bit too quick, as if she knew we were coming, but I let it pass... for now. I wanted to see how this played out.

Our hostess indicated with a wave of her hand that we should help ourselves. The offer of refreshments seemed more or less sincere, and a cool drink on that extremely hot day was welcome, so I reached over to pick up one of the glasses filled with iced buttermilk from the tray.

Just as I was about to lift my glass to my lips, I saw some green particles swimming in my drink. I looked sharply up at Jamila, who had a strange expression on her face. It wasn't very noticeable and she became poker faced almost immediately. In all fairness, we could have missed it if we weren't already on high alert. "What are these green flecks swimming in my drink?" I asked Jamila tersely.

"I have just added some finely chopped mint to the drink to add some flavor." There was a slight quaver in her voice.

Not completely trusting her, I sniffed my drink and didn't notice the smell of mint. However, there was a distinct, faintly pungent smell that made me put the glass down and signal to my constables not to drink. I cautiously dipped my little finger into the concoction and tasted it. That was definitely not mint.

The friendly atmosphere in the room shifted—an antagonistic mood suddenly emerged and started to become palpable.

"Start searching the house! Don't leave any corner unturned!" I barked the orders abruptly to my police officers.

"What in the world are you trying to do, Jamila?" I was angry now. "How dare you try to poison police officers! I will have you arrested and you will be very uncomfortable in jail with your condition."

Jamila crumbled. I realized then that she would tell us what we wanted to know.

"Our neighbor told us that the police were on their way to our house," she broke down sobbing. "My husband is hiding somewhere and he told me to stall you in any way possible. It was his idea to spike your drinks with bhang." Now she looked really scared. Bhang was an edible form of marijuana, and though commonly used in the villages, was illegal.

I rapped on the table with my night stick. Jamila jumped in reaction and started to cry even harder.

"I didn't put much bhang in. You have to believe me! There was just enough in each glass to see that all of you would have fallen into a deep sleep. We had men on standby who were to take your bodies far away from here while we escaped."

Lord knows where they would have dumped our bodies, or worse. Just imagine what it would have done to our reputation if the press had been alerted to a story of "drunk" senior police officials bumbling around.

Jamila was handed over to a female constable while we searched the house for her errant husband. I didn't think he had had time to leave.

The narrow house they lived in had two floors. The top

floor was reached by a narrow, almost vertical rickety wooden staircase that led to two crowded bedrooms. One of the rooms was used as a makeshift storeroom or office. It was stuffed with all sorts of political literature in English, Urdu, and Sindhi. There was also a large collection of flags, pins, banners, and other paraphernalia strewn all over and stacked on all the available surfaces. In one corner was a scarred, dusty desk and a rickety chair. There was a discarded half-full cup of tea on the table and a cigarette butt in an old beat-up cashew nut tin that seemed to regularly serve the purpose of an ashtray.

"This tea is still warm," I said when I touched the cup. "The cigarette butt is also still smoldering." Those two clues were red flags for my team.

"We have to look deeper. I am sure there are hiding places. We have to be very meticulous."

On inspection of the immediate surroundings there was no apparent way in or out of the house except by the front door, and we had not seen anyone in the house besides Jamila and a servant girl.

We persevered though. There had to be another exit and we had to find it no matter what. I was sure the culprit was still hiding nearby. He couldn't have gone far.

With a stroke of luck, one of the policemen found a ladder leaning against the wall. He saw a nearly invisible trap door on the ceiling, much like one to enter an attic or access to a roof. At a silent signal from me, the policeman climbed up and noticed that it was unlocked. The trapdoor led onto a flat-topped roof.

There were a few rope cots set out along the waist-high balustrade surrounding the roof. In a corner were terracotta urns still full of fresh water, with steel drinking mugs tied to them with hemp ropes. A rickety table with more political literature and books was placed next to one of the corner beds. From the wear and tear of the cots and the stack of beddings found in a large tin box that was shoved flat against the wall in one corner, we assumed that these cots were used to sleep outside when the heat inside became oppressive.

My police team inspected every nook and cranny, especially the dead space under the large overhead water tank which would have been just big enough to hide a single man. In spite of being thorough, we were disappointed that there didn't seem to be anyone there. Where could he have gone? The next house was too far away to jump over to the next roof. There just had to be another hiding place.

All of a sudden, I heard someone sneeze. The sound was so faint that it could have been easily missed.

"Go over the roof area once again. There is someone hiding here!"

The adrenaline made my heart pound in anticipation. I knew that we were on the verge of arresting the murderer.

On a hunch, I pulled the large tin bedding box away from the wall, not exactly thinking that I would find anything, but to my surprise, I found Jamila's husband, Ansar, cowering in a crudely hacked out alcove that was cleverly hidden behind the large box.

“I… I… I will tell you everything!" Ansar was on the verge of tears as the constable read him his rights and slapped handcuffs on his wrists. "Just leave Jamila alone.

She doesn't know anything! She is pregnant and she doesn't deserve to go to jail. She doesn't know anything!"

Ansar kept babbling on and on but we understood that his wife had only put the bhang in our drinks because she had been threatened by Ansar's boss, and she obviously just wanted to protect her unborn child.

Once he was hauled out of his hidey hole, I could see that one of the major factors incriminating Ansar in Nomi's murder was the three deep wounds running diagonally down his face and neck. The angle of the injuries was consistent with an attack from a much shorter person. They were too deep to just be called scratches, and someone had clumsily tried to stitch the wounds together. It would definitely make an ugly scar when it healed.

Later on we matched the blood type and DNA from the residue on Nomi's pins. They were a match for Ansar, implicating him even further.

Before he started to talk, Ansar asked whether he and his family could be placed in the witness protection program, and he wanted to be incarcerated in a jail out of state if and when he was convicted. He was petrified because, once he became an informer for the police, he, his parents, and his wife would be in mortal danger from immensely powerful and influential people. Additionally, he requested immunity from some of the charges against him and hoped that he would be considered for a shorter sentence in exchange for the information he had for the police.

Once he was reassured and the requisite legal documents of intent were signed, Ansar became a font of information that solved not only Nomi's murder, but he also had incriminating evidence to implicate a number of people for past unsolved murder and robbery cases, including some planned coups for the future.

Ansar told the police that he and Jamila were from a small village in the interior of Sindh. As a high school graduate, he thought that he could use his reading and writing skills to do better than being a hired hand at a farm near his ancestral village. He did not want to become a bonded laborer to the farmers or the waderas like the other men and women in the area. His intellect and leadership skills soon stood out and he caught the attention of the supervisor who mentioned him to his boss, who happened to be the wadera of the area.

Soon, with the help of his boss, he migrated to Karachi to have a better life with his wife and their future children. The wadera was friendly with the local politicians and had put in a good word for him so that he could have a lucrative job. Little did Ansar know that this was a ploy to get him and his independent influence away from the farm. They had to get rid of him quickly before the others started to think for themselves as well, which would have disturbed the balance of power in the area. He was lucky that he wasn't killed for his so called transgressions.

At first it was like a dream. He was given a house to live in and a job as an assistant to a prominent political worker in the region. The salary was more than enough to put food on the table, and he could also set a bit aside for his future. Moreover, he was happy that he was able to and send some money to his ailing parents. Soon thereafter, Jamila became pregnant and that was the zenith of their happiness.

Not long after he comfortably settled into his new life, they announced the local body elections, and that was when his nightmares started.

The local bully and gang leader succinctly announced that he was going to contest the elections and wanted to represent the area in the provincial assembly. Ansar was asked to meet the candidate, whose name was Ali Shah Khaskheli, and to be his assistant so that he could ensure that Mr. Khaskheli won the elections. Ansar was categorically told that the candidate had to win by any means possible. Legal or illegal.

When Ansar protested, he was forcefully reminded that he had been sent to Karachi due to the wadera's benevolence. If he didn't comply with the orders and carry out the tasks he was expected in order to put a bully and a crook in the provincial assembly, he should be very afraid. They knew where his parents lived and that his wife was pregnant, and they said it would have been a shame if anything happened to them. As the threat against the lives of his loved ones was held high above his head, his life of crime started right then.

At the time of the elections, funds were needed by the Khaskheli camp, not only for the campaign itself but also to pay off corrupt officials. In a country where many lived below the poverty line, buying votes was not uncommon. The poor, illiterate voters were not aware of the significance of their votes. If they could get a warm meal and a few coins with a free outing, they didn't care. It was probably exciting for them to be transported to and from the election venue at the back of a shiny truck.

Usually, the legitimate election candidates in Pakistan

are from well to do families who are descendants of political dynasties. In theory, the assembly seats are handed down from father to son (or daughter) as per the votes of their constituents, but if someone unknown tries to dip their toes in the political maelstrom, especially with the intention of earning tainted money and bullying their constituents, money has to be raised by "public donations" by any means whatsoever.

When the elections drew near, carjacking, mugging, home invasions and other forms of illegal activities tended to increase. One of Ansar's main tasks was to coordinate with the thugs who collected the "donations" and consolidate them into a common election account.

The people who weren't openly robbed were visited by the party workers, and were not so gently told that they needed to pay protection money so that they weren't bothered by crooks… namely them.

Ansar also hired children to work as pickpockets. The younger children who weren't as dexterous or as skilled as the older ones were hired to paste posters on every surface available around town, whether it was legal or not. Banners and other election paraphernalia were meted out to political workers with the only objective of creating a strong presence of the candidate. This subliminal sensory overload meant that, when people went to vote, they didn't have much choice since they would not even remember the names of the other candidates.

On election day, Ansar's team would hang around the voting booths and use their menacing presence and a few words growled under their breath to intimidate the voters. Their candidate would obviously win because of duress rather than popularity. The people knew what side their bread was buttered and they wanted to just live in their area in peace. Even if it meant voting for a crook. Their logic was that once they won the election, they would leave and life would go back to normal.

Ansar was one of the three people who attacked Nomi and her mother that fateful day. He said the little girl was very brave and fought like a tigress, but she was overpowered. In her struggle for survival, she scratched him with the pins on her cast. Those pins caused deep lacerations on his cheek and he bled profusely, but he was afraid to go to the hospital, so he had asked his wife to stitch them for him. He confessed that the pain had been excruciating. It was maybe a little schadenfreude, but it pleased me, more than I cared to admit, to know he suffered. In their struggle, Nomi ripped his new silk shirt, but he was not aware that a part of it was found with one of his funky buttons in Nomi's death grip. The biggest clue of them all was Nomi's pin. Ansar said she didn't want to hand it over. He thought it was expensive and would fetch a good price. If nothing else, it could have been melted down just for its silver. Unfortunately, the pin was small and didn't have enough precious metal of any value, so Ansar gave it to his nephew together with the ripped shirt that his sister Sadiqa refashioned for little Taimur.

"I had to hit Nomi to render her unconscious to stop her from struggling and hurting me further with her lethal pins, but I miscalculated and hit her much harder than I should have." He seemed contrite. He didn't look like a killer, just a person who had lost his way in the evil fulminating bowels of the city. Unfortunately, he had become a murderer from the second Nomi was pronounced dead. "I heard that she had succumbed to her injuries that day. That's why I was alert to the police movements and was hiding."

While Ansar confessed his role in Nomi's murder and his involvement in other illegal activities, he gave the police a concise list of criminals and political workers involved in unsolved muggings and carjackings. Mr. Khaskheli was disqualified from contesting the elections and arrested immediately. However, since he had powerful political connections, he was released soon after, but the majority of his gang were behind bars and the evidence against them was so solid that no political strings or bribes could get them out of their predicaments.

Much to Ansar's relief, his parents and his wife were spirited away under the agreed upon protection program. He was, as requested, kept in a separate lockup before his trial and then sent to prison in another province after he was found guilty on many counts, mainly of theft and manslaughter.

Justice had been served. Rest in peace, Nomi.

That evening, a despondent Sarah came to dinner. She was relieved that Nomi's killer had been caught.

"As usual, you were amazing, my love," she said while snuggling up to me on the sofa.

"Can you stay longer?" I asked.

"I can't. My parents will stay up till I get home. But we can watch a movie together… or make out." She grinned expectantly.

"I need talk to you." I had to tell her what I had

planned. She was so busy in those days that I had to take advantage of her sitting down for a short while.

"Sounds ominous." She laughed.

"Be serious and listen to me, please"

"I'm listening, I'm listening."

"As soon as I get the green light from Interpol, I shall be going to Paris for training and orientation. I want you to follow me to Europe. You can get a specialization internship near where I shall be working. From what they say, it would be in all probability in London." I tried to talk as fast as I could because I was nervous.

"I have already started to prepare for the General Medical Council exams in London," smirked Sarah. "I had hoped that you wanted me with you when you went there."

"Oh, thank God!" I said, relieved. "I was worried that you might have wanted to stay back and ultimately be coerced into marrying someone of your father's choice." I heaved a sigh of relief.

"I wish I could marry you," exclaimed Sarah. "I don't want to marry anyone else." She pouted, folded her arms, and sat sulking in the corner of the sofa.

"Sweetheart, why do you think I am going through all this effort of getting into Interpol? They are already lobbying for same sex marriage in Europe. Holland is on the verge of approving legal unions."

"Really! Are you serious?" Sarah was in awe. I wanted her to realize that I was determined to spend my life with her.

I went down on one knee and pulled out a plain gold band. I didn't want to get anything ostentatious because Sarah didn't wear anything while she worked and we didn't want to alert her family to our relationship… well, not just yet.

"Sarah Shahzad Shah, will you marry me?" I was so scared that I was trembling and I had tears shimmering in my eyes. I didn't know what to expect, but I did love this woman to distraction.

"Yes! Yes! Yes!" Sarah threw herself in my arms and we toppled over on the carpet. She tenderly kissed me, but her kisses soon became deeper with promises of much, much more.

CHAPTER 12

DEGLOVE THE GLOVE

"God needs to bless the works of our hands, but you still need to do some work for God to bless it"
— Sunday Adelaja

Sarah

Oh. My. God! I was engaged! Tanya and I were engaged! I knew it wasn't conventional and I was worried… no, I was scared what the reaction of my parents would be. But we were adults and we had been so patient all those years. What could have been thought of as a college fling was something much deeper and precious. We were made for each other. We were soul mates!

Even though my parents were modern and enlightened, I had heard them speak many times of same sex liaisons in derogatory tones. Being a child of WW2, my mother had the same attitude towards gay people as the government had in those days. My father was the result of a strict upbringing. Though he gave my siblings and I a lot of leeway, he still was strict where his principles were concerned. However, I didn't want to think about the implications of what we were about to do. Not yet. Since we had time till Tanya was settled in Europe, I flung myself as usual into my work.

My work was exhilarating at the best of times. Sometimes it used to feel like riding a roller coaster, while at other times it felt like I was just plodding along. However, the run off the mill cases were just what we house officers did every day and were not overly exciting. Not every case had disastrous consequences and having fortunate outcomes for some of our extremely difficult cases was satisfying as well. More so when the lives of the patients and the families we connected with at the time were able to heal and go on with their lives.

We met Aslam on a sultry day. The weather was typical for July—hot and humid. A few of us house officers had been asked by the chief inspector of police (that's, of course, my Tanya) and our medical director to go and visit a community center in the inner city to talk about health awareness and disease prevention. That was considered a mandatory exercise for the junior doctors because it was supposed to give us credits for our final assessment. It was also part of a collaborative initiative by the hospital director and the government to educate the general public.

That sweltering day was typical of the pre-monsoon season. The temperatures were not that high, but the sky was thick with dark, low lying pregnant clouds and the humidity was nearly 90%. It felt as if we were literally swimming through the moisture in the air, so we were exhausted, damp, and very dehydrated. Tanya accompanied us since it was a joint venture with her department and I did feel sorry for her—she must have been boiling in her uniform.

We spent about three hours in the shabby community hall, which wasn't air conditioned. The cranky ceiling fans were only adding to our discomfort. The hall was packed with women and children who were as hot as we were, and the body odors were ranging on the scale from rank to putrid. Once we finished our presentation and answered the enthusiastic questions from the audience, we sat in our car and immediately cranked up the air conditioner. On our way back to the hospital, we noticed a vendor's cart under a tree on which there was a curious contraption that looked like an instrument of torture. I immediately thought of those horrendous ones used by the Spanish Inquisition. There were also many bushels of sugar cane on the cart itself, as well as a large amount stacked in crates and sacks behind it. To the side was a small table where clean drinking glasses were stacked three apiece. The hand painted board affixed to the cart read "Aslam's Sugar Cane Juice. The Nectar from Heaven".

There was something about this vendor that called to me. I had never stopped in the street for juice, because I was always thinking about the way the things are prepared and the chances that I might get a bad tummy if things weren't very clean. But Aslam sort of drew me to him. As if it was written that we had to meet. Well, by then I had learned that I had to trust my instincts and feelings.

Aslam was doing brisk business by crushing the cane with the contraption which turned out to be a press with vicious looking wheels, levers, and sprockets of heavy stainless steel. The resulting fresh sugar cane juice that was being poured over crushed ice was like a vision from heaven to our dehydrated souls. Tanya and I decided to park our car nearby and order some drinks. We sat under the large ancient banyan tree where Aslam had set down a few rickety benches for his customers. The tree itself was a historical landmark and we were told that it had been there for nearly one hundred years. The dense canopy of green branches had spread over an area of approximately fifty meters with roots reaching from the upper most branches to make their way towards the bottom to become additional satellite trunks growing around the main trunk. With the gentle sea-breeze making the branches and the leaves sway, it was certainly a cool haven on a hot day. Someone had sprinkled water on the ground to ensure that it wasn't dusty, and the damp area increased the cooling effect of the area under the branches of the majestic tree.

Another enterprising young vendor had set up a stall nearby. He was selling seasonal garlands of roses and jasmine. Their perfume was pleasantly heady and added to the relaxed ambience under the tree.

Aslam was thrilled that we had stopped at his juice cart because, as he said, very few "educated" people stopped for juice over there.

"Many people think that they will get sick, because they think that my juice isn't prepared hygienically or the glasses aren't cleaned properly."

However, I think that his apparent cleanliness was

what actually drew us to him, and we were sure to let him know that we appreciated his efforts. Not only were his clothes clean, but we noticed that he also wore disposable gloves while washing and handling the sugar cane, especially when passing it through the intimidating manually operated juicer. We were also pleasantly surprised to see that one of his teenage daughters was sitting by a large tub a few meters away, constantly cleaning the used glasses with proper detergent and water that was endlessly heated in a kettle set on a massive kerosene stove. The truth is that street vendors were not very well known for their cleanliness, and you had to have a constitution of a rhino if you frequently indulged in their wares and concoctions.

Aslam saw us looking towards his daughter and smiled proudly.

"I watched an educational program on my neighbor's television that showed how cleanliness could prevent diseases. I want to be known for the quality of my juice, so spreading disease is not on the cards for me."

Since teaching health and hygiene to the community was one of the prime reasons for our outing that day, we decided that we certainly needed to encourage him, so we continued to chat with him in a desultory manner.

When the juice arrived in the cold misted glasses, it was fresh and crisp, just like the interesting conversation we had with Aslam.

"I couldn't finish school, but I want my children to have a good education." He smiled at his daughter as he spoke. "Maria wants to become a doctor, and Asghar, my son, an engineer." He had a dreamy look in his eyes and he believed that if he worked hard, he would be able to fulfill his children's dreams.

It was relaxing sitting under the ancient tree and watching the world go by. We indulged ourselves for a while until a colleague reminded us that we had to go back to the ward. The short rest did us good—four sleep deprived doctors on sugar highs were now ready to tackle whatever the ER sent our way once more. Tanya had to go for an important meeting, so she had left before we did. We wished Aslam well and went off after leaving a large tip for our health-conscious new friend.

It was just two weeks later that I met Aslam again. This time in our ER. His pristine white clothes were spattered with blood and his right hand was tightly wrapped in a grubby towel. I recognized him and went over to his cubicle to help him with his injuries. Once the towel was carefully unwrapped, I realized that he didn't just have a simple wound. His whole hand was bloody and looked quite mangled.

"What happened, Aslam *Bhai*?" I asked.

"It's all my fault!" he wailed. "I was trying to keep up with the demand of my… what did you call it before? Signature sugar cane juice, and I started to work as fast as I could." Tears were streaming down his cheeks. "My hand slipped as I was pushing the cane into the machine. I could not stop the lever in time and my hand was pulled in by the momentum of the machine."

His hand had been cruelly squashed between the rollers and the sprockets viciously tore at his skin. His accident with the juicer from hell had caused what we call a *Degloving Injury.* This is a type of avulsion in which an extensive section of skin is completely torn off from the underlying tissue, severing its blood supply. It is so named by the analogy to the process of removing a glove. He also had multiple crush fractures in three of his fingers.

"My hands are essential to my livelihood," Aslam went on. "My family depends on my income. If I lose my right hand, it would be devastating for them all. My children's dream of an education would be shattered!"

While trying to stabilize the wound, I couldn't help feeling sorry for him. At that point, no one was sure what the outcome would be.

This type of injury was something that I had never seen before, so I referred him to a senior resident. I was a bit wary to call the specific senior resident on duty that day because he was one of those gung-ho surgeons who had a God complex. He used to work predominantly for the experience and the thrill of surgery with minimal empathy for the patients themselves. For him, the patients were just case numbers to be treated.

As I feared, after taking a cursory look at Aslam's injuries, the senior resident said that he would have to amputate the hand because the bones were shattered, and he doubted that the skin would regain its blood supply. I was upset at how laissez-faire he was about it.

"You can't just decide to cut off a man's hand and livelihood without trying to save it!"

I argued with him for over an hour, but he insisted that nothing but amputation could be considered. He would not be swayed at all. Ultimately, I asked him to let me try and repair the damage as much as I could.

"Since the injury isn't life-threatening, we could

observe Aslam in the ward and see if gangrene sets in, or whether his hand starts to heal." I tried to persuade my senior colleague because I didn't want Aslam's amputation on my conscience if there was a way that we could save his hand.

I was so upset that I called Tanya. I wanted to hear a kind voice, a few words of encouragement. She came immediately and the first thing she did was hug me.

"I know you are the most compassionate person and care deeply for your patients," Tanya said gently. "If you really want to try to save the man's hand, then go to the top. Ask your professor."

I could always rely on Tanya to help me focus, calm me down and give me sound advice. Bless her.

Much to the chagrin of the senior resident, I went to the head of the orthopedics department and explained Aslam's case to him.

"I admire your enthusiasm and willingness to help people while learning, so I won't discourage you," he said. "But first I need to examine the patient myself before I can allow you to proceed further."

After examining Aslam, he was a bit reluctant and tended to agree with the senior resident, but then, seeing how determined I was, he gave me permission to perform the surgery under supervision. I hoped we could save as much as possible of Aslam's hand. I wasn't that naive or uninformed to think that we could save the whole hand, but even if he lost just a finger or two, he could still function.

The surgery wasn't easy. It took six hours of microfine stitching and repair, but eventually the hand looked good.

We kept checking the circulation, and thankfully, the tissues remained pink and continued to look viable.

Now we had to wait and see. We admitted Aslam to the orthopedic ward and set up a complicated contraption with pulleys that kept his arm elevated. It looked as if it was going to be a tedious and long process.

Aslam's dressings were changed when needed and I was pleased that there were no signs of infection in the wounds. However, after a couple of days, there were signs of gangrene starting at the tip of the ring finger. We discussed this with the professor and he advised us to wait for a few more days to observe whether the gangrene would spread any further. Thankfully, by the end of the week it was just the ring finger and the tip of the pinky that had to be amputated. The rest of Aslam's hand remained healthy and healed well. I was thrilled. Not every degloved injury turns out well, but I took a chance, fought for it, and Aslam's hand was more or less saved.

Aslam was immensely grateful. He kept thanking me to the point that it became embarrassing, and his wife tried to slip a "tip" into my hand many times, sometimes even on the pretext of shaking hands. I had to explain that that wasn't the way we did things in the hospital. In any case, the relief and happiness on Aslam's and his family's faces were truly satisfying.

Aslam's initial emergency surgery was followed by a long bout of physiotherapy and another two surgeries, but after a few months, he was finally able to move his hand with just a very slight restriction of movement on the lateral side.

To this day, he is still plying his trade under the ancient

banyan tree. I am sure he is much more careful when he uses his horrific juicing contraption. It was the big crowd of demanding customers that had caused him to work faster and be careless, but he told me that he had learned his lesson.

Whenever I drove by on my way to work, I waved at him, but I didn't stop for juice anymore because he refused to let me pay and I knew he couldn't afford it. Every penny matters when there are children to educate. If I had stopped at his juice cart and hadn't accepted his generosity, his feelings would have been hurt, but I think he understood why I was keeping my distance, because he sometimes came by to the hospital to give me some iced juice in a thermos flask. I couldn't refuse that now, could I?

Tanya

She said yes! Without hesitation, without trepidation. She said YES! I was so happy that I couldn't think straight. Now I had to double my efforts to get our life in order. Just like Sarah said she was working towards and internship in London… I never thought that I would have the opportunity to get married, and yet here I was, making plans.

We spent the evening together when I proposed to her. It was surreal and amazing all rolled together, creating a kaleidoscope of senses and emotions. It was the first time for her, but being in love, making love, was the first time for me as well, so we both savored the sensational roller coaster ride together. Why did we wait so long? Maybe it was because we were afraid of society and the taboos that we were continuously made aware of. But it was worth it… so worth it.

Sarah is amazing. The more I got to know her, the deeper I fell in love with her. One day we had to collaborate with a health care institution to create health awareness in the community. I had nominated Sarah's hospital since it was the largest teaching hospital in the region. I knew she would volunteer in such a venture since she loved teaching her patients on an individual level. Here she would have the opportunity to reach many more people.

Her presentation was precise and I could make out that many understood what she was saying because she made it a point to use simple language, but the oppressive heat was enough to try the patience of a saint. And saints we were not. Therefore, our little side foray under the banyan tree was such a relief.

My Sarah makes friends wherever she goes. She had the sugar cane vendor and his daughter chatting away with her as if they were longtime buddies. I do admire that trait in her.

A few weeks later, Sarah called me while I was at work. She was very upset. At first, I couldn't understand what she was saying and I became apprehensive. Had she told her parent about us and there were already dire consequences?

"Sweetheart, take a deep breath. Now, slowly tell me what's happened."

I heard her inhale sharply. "Aslam has injured his hand very badly and they want to amputate it!"

Aslam? I thought *Oh yes, the sugar-cane juice vendor!* That was bad.

I was on my way to the railway colony nearby, so I made a quick stop at the hospital to console Sarah. I had an ulterior motive as well—hugging her always made me feel good.

Finally, after an intense bout of advocacy for him, Sarah was so proud that she could save a part of Aslam's hand. He would not be as incapacitated as if he had had his hand amputated and he would be able to continue to work.

It became the norm that whenever Sarah had the evening off, she would come for a short while to me, or I'd go and meet her in the hospital. Now that we had expressed our love for each other in every possible way, we couldn't keep our hands to ourselves. She said that she was addicted to being with me, but then, I was addicted to her as well.

My correspondence with Interpol got more precise and their paperwork increased. I had passed two levels of French from Berlitz and would be starting the third level very soon. I got positive commendations and feedback from Interpol whenever I sent my completion certificates to them. I never thought that I would learn a new language. Yet, it was fun and I looked forward to pretending I didn't understand when I was around people who were trying to hide things from me by speaking in a language they supposed I didn't know. I thought I might try my hand at Italian or Spanish next. I was on a roll and wanted Sarah to be as proud of me as I was of her.

CHAPTER 13

REFUGEE DESOLATION

"*War is a soul-shattering experience for the innocent.*" — Suzy Kassem, Rise Up & Salute the Sun: The Writings of Suzy Kassem

Sarah

Tanya's paperwork was nearly complete. If all went well, she would be travelling to her new job and new life in France within six months. That gave me enough time to finish my house job and join her, but maybe not in France. I couldn't master the French verbs in school. I admired Tanya for picking up languages so quickly. She is a genius. My genius.

My application for the PLAB (Professional and Linguistic Assessments Board) for the British General Medical Council exam had been accepted. I was happy to know that I could take the exam locally in the British Council office. My exam was soon, so I spent most of my free time studying. It cut into my "Tanya time," but we both realized that this was a necessary hiccup for us to be together in the future.

The major hurdle we had to face next was to tell my parents. I was scared. Just the thought made my insides quiver. I hoped and prayed that they might surprise us, but realistically I felt that I could lose my family. At least for a short while... till the shock wore off… maybe. I knew Tanya loved me as much as I did her, and we had to be strong for each other. There was no other way.

I drew inspiration from my work and the brave souls around me. Just like Gul Khan, who was one of the many hopefuls that arrived in the big city to make his fortune. He had travelled from up north, near the Afghan border. His dream was to earn enough money to drive his own truck back to his parents' hovel in the refugee village on the outskirts of Peshawar and whisk them away from their dreary existence. It pained him that after all the years of being considered a refugee from war-torn Afghanistan, his father and brothers still lived on the mercy of the refugee agencies that were already strapped for funds. Gul had never seen Afghanistan; his home was now here. He knew no other.

When he eighteen years old, Gul had saved enough money from his odd jobs to finally hitch a ride on a transport truck and travel to Karachi, where he thought he would have better prospects. When he arrived in the big city, he spent a few weeks looking for jobs and he finally managed to get one as an unskilled laborer on a big construction site. The work was hard and he was paid on a daily basis. That meant if he took a day off or was sick he wasn't paid at all. Health insurance was an unknown factor for the workers.

One day, in his haste to climb up the side of the building using the network of poles as a support, Gul's foot slipped and he lost his grip on the pole he was hanging from. He fell feet first down six floors and was impaled on a vertical ribbed steel rod, like a macabre puppet. The rod had entered his body from the groin and exited somewhere near his right collar bone.

Thankfully, his co-workers had the presence of mind to cut the rod above and below him with a blow torch as fast as they could, and got him down to the waiting ambulance.

When Gul was brought to the ER, the doctors were shocked at his predicament. How was it possible that he was still alive after such a freak accident? Curiously, there was not that much blood, but then, the rod was in all probability applying pressure to the injuries internally.

"How do we remove the rod without damaging his already compromised internal structures and organs?" said the perplexed ER doctor. "We have to sedate him immediately; he is in a lot of pain!"

Gul was painfully conscious of his injuries. "I am ok," he kept saying. Even though he tried to act brave in front of his friends, his eyes reflected the excruciating pain he was in and it was no surprise that his tears flowed freely.

"I have never seen such bizarre trauma before," the surgical resident said and started to bark orders to anyone who was available to help.

Our objective was to stabilize him until he was taken

into surgery. Everyone realized that a detailed strategy to handle his injuries in the best possible way was tantamount to our surgical team's success in saving Gul's life.

We knew that pulling out the rod without proper surgical supervision would cause massive internal bleeding and further organ damage. Therefore, a multi-specialist team was assembled to try to pull the rod out centimeter by centimeter and repair the damage.

The surgery lasted for nearly nine hours. I focused on the cardiac monitor in the background beeping regular heartbeats indicating that Gul's heart was still going strong.

All of a sudden, the cardiac monitor emitted an ominous continuous flat sound which meant Gul's heart had stopped. The anesthetist and the surgeons started resuscitation procedures and while all that frenzied activity was happening, as I turned to change the empty blood bag, I felt a breeze blowing near the nape of my neck. That familiar sensation that I usually had when something inexplicable and out of the ordinary happened was there once again. I looked towards the operating table and saw Gul standing there looking down at himself while the doctors were working on him. There was a beautiful glow surrounding him and he looked peaceful. When he looked up, he was startled when he realized that I could see him.

"Doctor! Can you see me?" he asked, surprised. My hair stood on end and I felt goose bumps all over my body.

I didn't want to attract attention to myself, so I just nodded.

"If I don't make it, please, tell my mother I tried. Just tell her that. My address is on my ID card… tell her… I… tried…" His voice faded away as I heard the cardiac monitor start its regular beeping once more. The resuscitation had been successful.

Another two hours went by and Gul was still holding on. His will to live was strong and that was recognized by the team working on him. He was a medical miracle. No one had thought he would even last that long.

Now the biggest test after the surgery was whether he'd survive the massive abuse his body had suffered and manage to live a normal life.

I thought back to my predicament. Would I be strong enough to survive the wrath of my family? Would I live a normal life? My feeling of disquiet just kept growing, but I still knew it was the right thing to do. I needed Tanya in my life, just like Gul needed the blood transfusion we were forcing into his body.

The care that Gul received in the in the Surgical Intensive Care Unit (SICU) was remarkable. He stayed there for ten days and continued to have blood transfusions and a medley of IV fluids. We were thankful that all of his wounds, internal as well as external, had started to heal well with no signs of superadded infection.

One day, while I was changing his dressings after his second surgery, he idly traced his massive scar with his fingertips and had a speculative look on his face. He started to say something, then he shook his head and kept quiet.

After a while he tried again. I looked at him with what I hoped was an encouraging expression, but he still had that anxious round-eyed look of a person who is about to do or say something that's out of his comfort zone.

"You saw me in the operation theater, didn't you?"

I knew what he meant, but I wanted to know why he

was questioning me. "Of course. I was there as part of the team."

"No!" he nearly shouted. "You saw me there! I had died for a while. I was looking down at my body and I know that you saw me as well." He was now getting quite agitated. To calm him down, I put my hand on his arm trying to find the words to talk to him. It was a bizarre situation.

"Yes, I did see you. You gave me a message for your mother."

"Oh, thank God! I thought I was crazy, or I had dreamt that." His relief was palpable, and we shyly smiled at each other but didn't mention the incident anymore.

Gul was in no physical condition to work at hard manual labor anymore. Therefore, I garnered some information about an adult literacy program that was run by a local philanthropist who not only looked after runaways, but ensured that they were either repatriated with their families or went to school.

That was the perfect solution for Gul. He was incredibly happy and left the hospital as soon as he could. True to his promise, he would frequently call and let me know how he was doing. He finished high school and wanted to study further. Therefore, to encourage and help him, a group of doctors and I collected enough money to pay his fees to go to Law College. We were all proud of him because he did well and graduated with honors. He is now an eminent lawyer working for human and refugee rights. He even liaises with the United Nations High Commissioner for Refugees (UNHCR) and is well respected in his field of expertise.

He finally fetched his mother from the refugee camp,

and not in a truck as he thought he would, but in a nice comfortable sedan. She now lives with him and his wife in a beautiful house in the outskirts of Peshawar, but she still dreams of peace for her country. She desperately wants to go one day to see the mountains and the green orchards of Kabul from the stories her parents had told her.

It is such a blessing when our patients survive. The belief in the divine does incorporate itself even more in us. Or so I think. Maybe there is hope yet for us?

Gul's case gave me hope, a direction towards believing in positivity. I needed to have faith. In myself, in Tanya, and in all that is holy. It was meant to be, so we would be all right.

We went to see my parents one night. They thought that I was bringing home a friend for dinner. They were not wrong. Tanya was my best friend. And my lover.

I met Tanya after work and she realized that I was tense and nervous. I think she was as well, but her stoic nature helped her bring her anxiety under control.

"Sarah, sweetheart, don't be afraid. I am always here for you. I love you." Tanya made it a point to reassure me of the strength of my love before we talked to my parents.

"I love you too. So much," I answered.

She hugged me close and her kisses became passionate. Making love to me at that time was the most beautiful gift that she could give me. Her love and support ensured that all was going to be all right, and my anxiety faded away, for the time being.

Tanya

My papers arrived. They wanted me to join within two months and I was excited. It was another step towards a new life with Sarah. I hoped we'd manage to go without much conflict. Sarah's family is close, and I understood. I envied and wished I was as close to my parents as she was. How different my life would have turned out to be.

I was grateful for my superiors' encouragement at work. It was a feather in their cap that a person from their department had been chosen to work in Interpol. My boss kept telling me to make them proud and always remember that I was representing my country. It wasn't as if I didn't know that already.

Tying up loose ends meant trying to settle all the cases that were on my desk. My team was good, but they needed a nudge now and then.

Sarah called and told me about her bizarre case in the hospital. I had to go over and see it anyway. All suspicious cases came under my jurisdiction. I had to make sure that the victim wasn't pushed. After that, I had to meet with my counterpart in the labor department to discuss the workplace safety of the construction site. If there was no foul play, we had to at least fine the contractor and ensure that the victim received proper medical treatment.

As I stepped in the ER, I became aware of the controlled chaos there. I watched from afar how efficiently and fast Sarah worked with her colleagues. I was so pleased to see her. I was proud that she was mine and I was hers. I couldn't help but smile.

Sarah waved at me when she saw me but didn't miss a beat with what she was doing. I understood that she was busy, so I waved back, talked to the medicolegal officer, and left. I had glimpsed the patient from afar. It gave me the chills. The doctors are so brave for the way they handle the battered humanity on a day-to-day basis.

We were seeing Sarah's parents that night. She was a bundle of nerves and I wanted to alleviate her anxiety and reiterate that I was always there for her. After all, she was my love. My soulmate. I had to be her pillar of strength as she was mine.

Calming Sarah down was easy. My love for her was absolute. We made gentle and sweet love. The glow on her face showed that she was sure of my feelings for her. She just needed to know that I would love her for as long as I humanly could.

Sarah's parents were quite cosmopolitan and entertained a lot. When we arrived at their house, we were quite surprised to see that there were a few cars in the driveway.

"What is going on, Sarah? I thought it was just us for the evening today." I was puzzled. It seemed there was a party going on.

"I don't know." Sarah was just as puzzled as I was. "I specifically told Ammi that I wanted to talk to her tonight and that I wanted Baba to be there as well." She frowned.

"Well," she said climbing out of the car, "Let's go and see what the fuss is all about." Holding her head up high, she walked into the house and called out a general greeting to everyone.

Sarah's mother met us at the door. She had an air of excitement, as if she had a wonderful secret and just couldn't wait to tell us. I had met her a few times and she had always been nice to me.

"Finally you are here!" she exclaimed. "Come into the drawing room. I want you to meet someone."

She held me by my arm and guided me towards the other guests.

"Come on, Sarah, don't dawdle," she said playfully over her shoulder. "Hurry up."

"I'm coming, I'm coming." I could see that Sarah did not like what was happening and she was sulking.

"I wanted to talk to you and Baba alone, Ammi," Sarah whispered to her mother. "It's important. Why did you invite these people over?"

"Patience, child, and you will know in a minute." She was clearly excited.

When we walked into the drawing room, we saw that there were a few people already partaking the buffet dinner laid out on the dining table, but the most prominent person in the room was Dr. Farooq, a colleague of Sarah's. She disliked him because he always made derogatory and lecherous remarks whenever he saw her in the hospital. She would always try to avoid him at all costs at work.

"What is that creep doing here?" Sarah asked her mother through clenched teeth.

"Behave yourself; he is our guest!" Her mother's voice was laced with steely reserve. She turned around and looked at both of us. Sarah had reached out and grabbed my hand. Her mother sighed and took us to another room and closed the door.

"I know what's going on with you two. I wasn't born yesterday!" Her friendly demeanor changed as if she had flipped a coin. "Tanya, you go to France. Forget about Sarah. She is not like you. We are not like you." She tried to keep her voice down, but it still rose a few octaves. "Sarah has had this silly crush on you since she was in college. This has to end now!" She sat down and rubbed her temples as if there was a headache developing. "Dr. Farooq and his parents are here because they have asked for Sarah's hand." She sounded jubilant. "We have agreed to the proposal and the marriage will be in three months."

"How can you do that, Ammi?" Sarah was appalled. She couldn't go on as she didn't know what to say. "I-I-I want to go to London to study. I want to be with Tanya!"

"You can go to London. Farooq will also be taking the PLAB exam. He has promised to take you as well. That was one of our conditions."

"You can't make decisions for me!"

I just stood there with my arms around Sarah. I was speechless. This was an unprecedented hiccup, but a hiccup that could be remedied. I swore to myself that I would find a way out.

"I don't think it's appropriate for you to stay, Tanya," said Sarah's mother. "You are welcome to have something to eat, but after that I would like you to go."

Sarah gasped at the insult. "If Tanya goes then I go with her!" she shouted.

"Calm down and behave yourself! I can't handle this. I am calling your father." She stomped away and left us alone in the room staring at each other in dismay.

After a short while, Sarah's father walked into the room.

From his cheerful expression we deduced that her mother hadn't said anything yet.

"Congratulations, Sarah! You are going to get married!" He said jubilantly at the top of his voice.

"Baba!" said Sarah in dismay. "You could have at least asked me."

"What do you mean?" he said with a frown. "Farooq is a doctor from a well to do family. He has promised to take you to London with him. What more do you want?"

"He is a lech and a bad-mannered person." Sarah started to cry. "He is always making derogatory and sexist remarks to me and the other doctors at the hospital. We all hate him."

"Oh, it's just high spirits of youth. Once he is married, he will settle down. I am sure of it." He scoffed at Sarah as if she was being foolish. "You will be a good wife for him and steer him in the right direction."

"But you and Ammi are so modern in your outlook... Why are you being so archaic with me?" Sarah was seriously crying now.

"Your mother and I thought it was for the best. We don't want you to associate with Chief Inspector Tanya anymore!" He turned towards me. "Go to France, Tanya. Leave my daughter alone. If you don't, then I am well connected. I can not only destroy your career, but I can also make your life miserable!"

I heard Sarah gasp. "How can you do that, Baba? How can you even say that you will ruin someone's life?"

Sarah looked at me with such love in her eyes, and then she said with a broken voice, "Go, Tanya. Remember that I will always love you, but I don't want your hard work to be unraveled by some vindictive person." She looked at her father angrily.

"Yes, go. And if I even hear that you are near her, I will not hesitate to carry out my threat."

What in heaven's name was happening?

"Don't even try to see Sarah. Henceforth her brothers will be taking her to the hospital and will pick her up. She is to come straight home. After three months, she will be her husband's problem. Now go!"

I saw that Sarah's heart was breaking, but she was being held back by her father even though she reached out to me. I knew that if he hadn't threatened me, she would have come with me.

I looked at Sarah with as much hope and love as I could and tried to convey to her that all would be well. We would find a way. Love would definitely find a way.

CHAPTER 14

THE DEADLY INTERNSHIPS – PAEDIATRIC TALES

"There is no greater inhumanity in the world than hurting or belittling a child." — childinsider.com

Sarah

How could my parents hurt me so? Was I not a child of theirs? Was what society and people thought of more value than I was? Their flesh and blood? They were pushing me into a marriage with a person that I couldn't stand at all. Even if I hadn't been in love with Tanya, there was no way I would marry a man like Farooq. He was two-faced, cruel, and thought he was God's gift to women. Even when we are supposedly engaged, he would openly flirt in front of me while sending me challenging looks. Most of the time I felt like wiping that smirk off his face with my fist.

"Hey, Sarah! Give me a kiss!" he shouted in front of our colleagues, trying to stake his claim on me.

"Behave yourself, Farooq. We are at work. There should be some decorum." I was irritated, and though it seemed initially funny, it became tedious for the others as well.

"I shall go home and say some special prayers," said my colleague Fiza.

"Why?" asked Farooq, absolutely clueless.

"That my parents refused your proposal to marry me!" she shouted.

Apparently, he had tried to marry nearly every female in the hospital. It was only my spiteful parents who had finally said yes to him, and now I was a laughing stock as well.

My brother Adam used to bring me to the hospital and pick me up when it was time to go home. He noticed my stress and that I had lost a lot of weight. My eyes were permanently red-rimmed because I couldn't stop crying. If anyone asked, I just lied and said it was an allergic reaction to the smog in the city. Little did they know that I would cry at the drop of a hat.

Adam and I were close. He didn't like Farooq either because he had heard stories of his womanizing and gambling from his friends. They were surprised that I had "consented" to marry him.

"Let's go to the beach and talk. We can have a cup of tea from the kiosk there," Adam said one day.

Since going home wasn't pleasant anymore, I agreed. I was curious. What did my brother want to talk to me about?

It was high tide and the sea was a bit turbulent. It was

monsoon time and the waves crashed angrily on the rocks off the shore. Just like I was feeling. We found some high boulders to sit on and quietly sipped our cups of tea.

Finally, he spoke. "When is Tanya leaving?"

"Next week." I looked despondently to the horizon, where I just could make out the twinkling lights of the ships in outer anchorage. I wished that I could have the strength to swim over to one of them and stow away. One of them was sure to sail to France.

"Look, Sarah," Adam said. "I love you a lot. You have always been there for us, no matter what." I turned to look at him in surprise and motioned him to go on.

"Do you really love Tanya? Enough to leave us and make a new life with her?" I was suspicious. Maybe my parents had asked him to talk to me. So I kept quiet.

He must have realized what I was thinking. "No, it's not the parents. I am the one asking. I love you and I can't see you fade away like this. Moreover, I keep hearing about Farooq's indiscretions and uncouth behavior. I know you won't be happy with him. Ever. So please, answer my question so that I can help you if you want me to."

My eyebrows rose in surprise. My brother, my dear, dear brother wanted to help me!

"I love Tanya more than life itself. I cannot think of living without her. Just the thought of marrying that lech Farooq is revolting to me!" I was talking so fast that my sentences ran into one another.

Adam laughed and rubbed my back, which I found calming.

"Don't worry," he said gently. "My friends and I will help you."

We sat there for a while. Since he was with me, my parents wouldn't question us if we were late. It wasn't unusual that he had to wait for me while I finished off with a patient.

"Running after Tanya at the airport when she flies off is too obvious and very movie-like," Adam said. "We need to plan something that will not be predictable so that Baba's spies are duped."

We brainstormed a bit more and decided on a plan. It was quite elaborate, but we needed to talk to Tanya before we could start anything.

For now, I rented a safety deposit box at the bank. I hid my salaries, pocket money, gifts, and jewelry there. It was in one of the smaller banks, which meant it would be almost untraceable. Of course, with Tanya's help, anyone trying to investigate would get a run around and it would be quite some time before anything could lead towards me. I slowly smuggled my clothes and shoes in to my ward locker. It got more and more difficult to close and lock each day, but I didn't show it to anyone. Just a slip of the tongue could have been treacherous for what we had planned.

In the meantime, I passed my PLAB exam and I already had a few interviews lined up in the London area, but I had to finish my pediatric house job first.

I longed to see Tanya. I would see her fleetingly when she came to the hospital and we would gaze at each other from afar. I knew that she tried to project her love through those looks. As did I.

I hoped we would get a case in the ER where she just had to interact with me. How else could she talk to me with Farooq and other spies of my parents around? I did not want Tanya to leave her job under a cloud of disgrace. Knowing my father, he would carry out his threats. The insult to Tanya hurt me more than it did her. I was devastated.

I often attended wards that were in a separate building from the main hospital. They had their own autonomy and were collectively called the Children's Hospital. It was a bit disconcerting to see everything shrunk to kiddie size as compared to the adult wards. The rocking horses, swings, and mechanical cars that worked if a few coins were inserted gave the massive lobby an ambience that would chase away the anxiety any child could have when entering a hospital. It would probably work with adults too, or maybe even with a nervous house officer.

The first day at work, after our orientation, I was asked to help the senior residents in the Out-Patients Department. That was quite a revelation. I walked down a quiet glassed-in corridor admiring the manicured gardens on both sides and then opened the door to the OPD. Oh, my! It was as if I was hit with a supersonic boom that was made up of a cacophony of different sounds.

The OPD was massive, as big as two basketball courts. I looked around trying to make sense of all the chaos, and I could see that there was a central area with rows of benches for the patients, and the periphery was lined with rooms where the doctors worked. Right in the middle of the massive room, a triage station was set up where nurses and nursing aides were taking the patients' height and weight as they came in, while another station was documenting the symptoms and handing out slips to the allocated clinics.

At one glance I could see that there were over three

hundred patients along with their parents sitting on the long benches waiting for their turn with the doctors on duty. The children were either playing "Battle of the Yells" with each other or they were just too sick to do anything except cuddle or sleep in their mothers' laps. It was easy to see which patients were there for their follow ups and which children were really ill. I had to clap my hands over my ears and then gradually pull them down to get used to the noise. Once I started to tolerate the sound, I walked in confidently and marveled at the almost party-like atmosphere there. Mothers were huddled together, catching up on gossip while simultaneously doling out treats from bags or picnic baskets.

The other epicenter of chaos in the hospital was the pediatric ER. Thank God it was separate from the adults so it was much easier to triage the sick children and deal with them accordingly. It was an area where prompt actions and decisions were required to save lives.

My chance to meet Tanya came sooner than I thought. One night, I was elbow deep in dealing consecutively with five patients from a single family with acute gastroenteritis. I noticed the senior nursing supervisor walk into the room. She looked disturbed, but she came over to me and asked me to hand over my patients to another doctor. I had to come as soon as I could into the ER receiving area. It took me a few minutes, but once I was satisfied that my colleague had things under control, I hurried after her.

The pediatric surgical intern was examining a two-year-old toddler who had been brought in by the ambulance. His name was Sikander and he was unconscious and unresponsive. His breathing was ragged and his heartbeat rapid. I had been called to examine him because he had a fever and he needed to be medically cleared before he could be taken to the operation theater. He needed to have surgery on a depressed fracture of his skull, as well as to stitch the multiple cuts and lacerations he had all over his body. The surgeons also needed to evaluate him in case he had internal injuries. His left leg had to be splinted because his femur was broken in two places. Having had orthopedic experience, I was asked to help out there as well, because time was of the essence, and we couldn't wait for an orthopedic consult.

After he was stabilized, we handed Sikander over to the surgical team. Then my prime focus was to calm the mother down and to find out what had happened. The receiving staff told us about the cause of injuries documented, but we all agreed that they were far too severe for a simple tumble down the stairs.

Once they took Sikander to the operation theater, I told the nurse to call Tanya immediately and then tried taking a detailed history from Amina, Sikander's mother, but she was so distraught that she could hardly speak. She couldn't stop crying and just kept rocking back and forth repeating that her little Sikoo had fallen down the stairs. It was as if she was trying to convince herself that was what had actually happened.

Amina spoke in a difficult colloquial Indian dialect, but with a bit of effort we began to understand each other. The only problem was that she was not very forthcoming with the information required. You could see that she was either too terrified to say too much or she was protecting someone, but after reassuring her safety she started to tell us her horrifying story.

"I come from an extremely poor family in the Indian Punjab. My father had eight children, six of them daughters. He was a poor tenant farmer and his income depended on the share that he would get from the harvest of the lands that he cultivated for his landlord." I wondered why she was telling us about her origins, but I let her go on. Maybe there was some method to her going off the tangent?

She went on with her story. "My father was a chronic worrier and was always wondering where the next meal would come from or how to clothe his family, and hoping for an abundant harvest or a way to marry off his daughters without being financially broke." She made a rueful face. Thinking about her family made her sad and homesick.

"My father thought he was quite successful since he had arranged passably suitable marriages for his two elder daughters, my sisters, but he still had four more daughters to worry about."

Amina started to breathe rapidly as if she was having a panic attack. I gave her glass of water and let her compose herself before she went on.

"Our neighbor introduced my father to a strapping handsome young man who was visiting from Pakistan. The way the young man, Abid, presented himself, the quality of his clothes and shoes indicated that he was well-to-do. His demeanor also implied that he had a good job and would take care of one of us if he were allowed to marry."

Amina, with her delicate features and clear skin, caught

the young man's eye immediately, and after only two weeks, the village joyously celebrated a wedding.

Once she reached Karachi, Amina's eyes were rudely opened and she realized that the stories of abundance and respectability were just that... stories. On her arrival she was ferried from the railway station on a rickety *tonga* (horse drawn buggy) to a slum area where most of the houses were constructed with scrap corrugated iron and bricks. There was no drainage system and the area was immersed in a stench so foul that one was surprised that human beings actually lived in that makeshift slum.

Amina realized that Abid had lied about his circumstances. It seemed he was just sporadically employed, only working when it so pleased him. Basically, he was a *rickshaw* driver by profession. He had recently damaged his vehicle in a senseless accident, and it was beyond repair. Therefore, he would just accept odd jobs if and when they came his way, but going out and specifically looking for a job was something he just did not want to do. On top of that, she found out that he was a drug addict and slept most of the day away, while he spent the nights getting high and gambling with his cronies.

Abid thought that if he had a wife, she would work and take care of the household while he would have a life that was relatively unchanged. He still wanted to live the life of a bachelor while having the comforts of married life. However, Amina was pregnant and didn't know her way around the city, which meant it wouldn't be easy for her to find work. Things went from bad to worse and whenever she would timidly ask for money to get food or other household necessities, Abid would lose his temper and start brutally beating her. It was only because of the kindly neighbors who regularly came to her rescue that she was able to carry both of her pregnancies to term.

When her children were born, first little Sikander and then soon after Baby Lyla, they also became the target of their father's ire. Amina was terrified because she knew in her heart that their lives were in danger, but it was difficult for her to travel back to India. Logistically and economically.

The day Sikander was brought to the ER, the customary shouts, slaps, and slurred insults had already started early in the morning. The toddler was grousing and irritable because he had a fever and there was nothing in the house to help bring it down. The incessant crying and fussing irritated Abid to the point that he brutally beat the child and flung him roughly down the stairs. A neighbor witnessed this gruesome act and volunteered to help Amina to take Sikander to the hospital.

Thankfully, Tanya came immediately when the nurse called her. She looked to me like a beautiful avenging angel. She hated it when children were hurt or molested.

"Good Evening, Dr. Sarah," she said formally. "What is the problem? How can we help you?"

I was trembling and nearly tripping over my tongue with the emotion of seeing her at such close quarters once again, I tried to be concise as I gave her the facts of the case. I could see how affected she was by Sikander's plight, and I was sure that he would get justice now that Tanya was on the case.

My professor suddenly appeared. "Dr. Sarah, Chief Inspector Tanya, may I talk to you both in the office?" I had not seen him walk into the room. I was told that he was listening to us for a while and it made sense that he wanted us to discuss the case in private without people butting in.

As we sat down in the sofa across the massive desk he said, "I am the father of a friend of Adam's and he asked me to find an opportunity for you to speak with each other. I will leave from the other door. No one will notice that I have gone. In the meantime, Tanya, please, for God's sake, bring the twinkle back in Sarah's eyes. She has been moping around long enough now." He chuckled and quietly left the room.

We just sat there and stared at each other not believing that we were together once more, albeit for a very short time. Then we gravitated to each other and hugged as if we were never going to let go. It felt so good to hold her once again. My Tanya. My love.

"Does this mean that your brother will help us?" Tanya was pleasantly surprised.

I nodded happily. "We will have to talk about Sikander, but let me tell you quickly what Adam and I have planned."

I urged her to go to France the following week as planned. I assured her that I would meet her after about a month in London. I apprised her of how we were going to do that.

"What? No movie-like finish with you dashing after me to the airport?" She laughed.

"In your dreams." I nudged her shoulder.

Just then the nurse knocked on the door and told us that Sikander had succumbed to his injuries. I guess it was inevitable with the extensive injuries the poor child had received. We both felt sad about the unnecessary loss of an innocent life. But we felt for his mother even more.

Once Abid realized that his wife and son were in the hospital, he had absconded and was nowhere to be seen. He had been told by the neighbors that the police were investigating Sikander's death. He was in trouble and had to get away fast.

There were no dry eyes in the hospital when we released Sikander's body and signed off the death certificate. Everyone had the same question in their mind. How can such innocence be violated by the evil of one man who valued getting high more than his own family?

Tanya would bring the monster to justice and I was in a happier frame of mind since I was seeing a light at the end of the tunnel once more.

Tanya

I had never been so insulted in my life. The derogatory way Sarah's mother treated me was despicable, but what bothered me more was the hurt look in Sarah's eyes when I was humiliated. I tried to tell her that I didn't blame her parents' bad behavior on her. I hoped she got the message when I looked at her. I was smartly escorted out of the house by her brother Azan and her father so I couldn't say a word to her. That hurt. A lot.

I was leaving for Paris in a week. As the days of my departure drew near, I tried to keep my mind occupied by tying the loose ends of my cases. I needed to keep busy so that I would fall exhausted into bed and sleep dreamlessly. Otherwise, I was sure I would become crazy.

I tried to see Sarah in the hospital, thinking it was neutral ground, but it seemed her father's influence was widespread. If I saw her in passing, she was surrounded by her colleagues, her brother, or that irritating Dr. Farooq, who had announced to all and sundry that he was going to marry her in a couple of months. Many knew of his reputation as a womanizer and sexual predator. Genuine friends of Sarah's were appalled that her parents had consented… nay, forced her into this engagement. I asked a mutual friend to talk to Adam and tell him of Farooq's true nature. If she couldn't be with me, if she had to get married for the sake of her parents, then she at least deserved to marry someone decent.

Finally there was a breakthrough in the stalemate when I was called for a case of child battering in the pediatric ER. I hoped, nay prayed to get a chance to see Sarah. I needed to talk to her at least once more before I left. We both needed closure if at all.

To my surprise, Sarah's professor called us together into his office and made us sit and talk to each away from any distractions. Holding her once more in my arms was like heaven and hell all rolled together—heaven because she felt so good to hold, and hell because I knew that this wouldn't last long.

We talked about her amazing and nearly impossible plan to join me soon, but since I had been summoned to the hospital for a specific case, I had to officially see to it. We made plans to try to "fine tune" her impeding adventure towards our life together.

The case for which I was called had tragically become a homicide case, so I had to go to the colony where Sikander and his family had lived. The neighbors and tradespeople of the area were questioned, and information was sifted through with the proverbial fine-toothed comb.

From our methodical investigation and intense questioning, a horror story emerged. How could a person be so cruel to their own flesh and blood? How can there be pleasure in cruelty? Sick and twisted people are all over the world but being so close to the case was horrifying. And yet there were people like Sarah's parents, who were cruel to their own children and justified their acts as kindness.

Amina had two children. The baby, who was just six months old, had also died a violent death just two months before Sikander was brutally beaten. On further investigation, we found out from the neighbors that little Lyla was a colicky baby and cried a lot. Her pitiful cries would echo in the neighborhood in the evenings, specifically when Abid came home. He was rarely sober and was either drunk or stoned. The incessant crying bothered and enraged him so much that he ended up silencing Lyla by smothering her with a pillow and dumping her like garbage outside the door. He threatened to kill anyone who tried to pick up the body, so she stayed outside in the heat, decomposing till someone told the municipality cleaners about her. Finally, they found her remains under the rubbish heap. She was unceremoniously hauled away because Amina was terrified of the whole situation. She did not dare say anything to anyone because Abid had threatened to kill her and Sikander with the large kitchen knife that he kept with him at all times.

Since Amina didn't know anyone to tell her story or solicit help, and since she wasn't allowed to be friendly with the neighbors, she quietly went on with her life for the sake of her surviving toddler. For her, it was a living nightmare.

When Sikander was physically abused and succumbed to his injuries, it was the final straw for her. She realized that if she did not leave immediately, her life would be in danger a well. She had lost her children due to her fear. Now she had to at least take care of herself, but she didn't know where to go or who to turn to.

By a sheer stroke of luck, we were able to contact a women's crisis center for Amina. Not only did they have a place for her, but they also had adult literacy classes as well as artisan and technical courses. I am glad to say that after she got over her grief and shock, she thrived there and was in her element. She was only twenty-two years old and was looking forward to a new and better life. She took computer and ticketing courses and started to work in a travel agency. You could see that there was a positive change in her and she enjoyed her new career.

Abid did not fare so well. After leading us on a merry and convoluted dance, he was finally arrested in an opium den in Kathmandu. A long-drawn-out trial followed where there were many who gladly testified against the brutal child abuser, and he was convicted with a life sentence. The verdict? Willful homicide. The keys to his prison cell were metaphorically thrown away.

But that is not the end of this saga. Abid continued feeding his drug addiction even while he was incarcerated. On one fateful day, a guard went to inspect the wing where

Abid now lived and found him dead in his prison cell. Someone had slipped him some heroin that was contaminated with a high quantity of *strychnine*. He had overdosed and died after having a massive convulsion.

The Child Abuse Committee liaised with a local TV station, and a well-known script writer wrote a play based on Sikander's life. The TV drama was well received and, as a consequence, child abuse groups, pediatric organizations, and legal advisors stated working with the government to lay down guidelines and adopt stricter child abuse laws with tangible consequences to the offenders.

That was the last of my cases before I left for my new life. Sarah had once again given me hope that we would be together once again. Her journey was going to be treacherous, but I also asked some friends to help along the way, and I was so glad that one of her brothers would help her as well.

CHAPTER 15

THE GREAT ESCAPE

"It is always fair sailing when you escape evil."
— Sophocles

Sarah

Tanya was leaving in just two days. I was counting down the hours, minutes, and seconds when she would be taking my heart with her. I was so grateful that we had a chance to talk and I could tell her of my plans. Adam heard the whispers in the hospital and his social circle about the Farooq's debaucheries and he gradually became indignant about the situation. He repeatedly tried to talk our parents out of committing to the marriage. Baba would insist that Farooq would settle down once he was married. But his reputation in the hospital was exceptionally bad, and my brother became increasingly aware of that and worried for my well being.

By now I had just a month left to complete my house job, but my professor was kind enough to issue me my completion certificate before that time because I had unofficially joined the ward for practice work in the beginning. My convocation in Nawabshah was also in a week's time. The designated chief guest was the President, and they hadn't invited parents because of so-called security risks. I was excited because that was definitely in our favor.

The easiest way would have been to barrel over to the airport and hop on a plane just as it was about to close the boarding process, but we all agreed that knowing my father's influence, I could have been stopped and put under house arrest till I was to be married. Thinking back, I was sure he would do that.

I collected the clothes that I had smuggled to the hospital and put them in a suitcase that I had asked Adam to buy for me, and then I went to the bank and emptied out my locker. I had enough money for my "adventure" and a bit left over to set myself up when I reached London. The jewelry was also a solid backup in case I needed to sell it in case of an emergency.

Convincing my parents that I had to attend my convocation was a bit tricky. I had to argue that after studying in the college for so many years, it was my reward to be awarded my degree personally rather than receiving it by courier. My father had to verify from the principal's office that parents weren't invited. It was sad that he had stopped trusting me. It was also sad that I had stopped trusting them as well. It pained me that they thought I was a burden and needed to be thrown out onto the garbage heap, aka in the direction of a despicable person like Farooq.

My parents finally agreed to let me go on the proviso that Adam accompanied me. That suited me fine. After all we were co-conspirators, weren't we?

The train ride to Nawabshah was uneventful. As a matter of fact, it was fun connecting with other ex-students on the train, and as it edged nearer to our destination, I felt my heart become lighter. I smiled at my brother, who was so glad to see me in a better mood once again.Wanting to show me his love and support, he reached over and squeezed my hand affectionately.

I loved the pomp and the show of the convocation. Getting my degree, the photographs, and catching up with friends were all a balm to my bruised soul, but after all the festivities were over, the serious part of my journey was to begin.

We had planned that I shouldn't spend the night in the college like most of the ex-students did. Instead, my brother was waiting for me at the gates after the gala dinner. I had changed into a peasant woman's clothes, but covered myself with an immense *chaddar (sheet-like shawl)*. I was known to travel with a chaddar in the past to prevent the grime and the dust from settling on me while travelling in the open third class compartment in the trains, so no one raised an eyebrow at my attire.

Adam and I hurried to the station and were just in time to hop onto a train travelling up north. We had deliberately left it to the last moment so that we bought our tickets on board and couldn't be traced in case the ticket seller at the station was questioned.

We ambled along the aisles of the overbooked compartments and found two empty seats in the second class coach. We hadn't initially wanted that. We were hoping to get a sleeper compartment to ourselves. But since we were hopefully for the time being untraceable, we claimed those seats and and settled down for the night. We were undisturbed the whole night and were able to get a well deserved rest while being lulled to sleep with the rhythm of the train.

In the morning, we were woken up by the slowing of the train and the gradually increasing cacophony of a busy railway station. Peeking out of the carriage window, we saw that we had arrived in Rawalpindi. Since that was the twin city of Islamabad, where we knew our father must have alerted someone to look out for us, we hunkered down in our seats waiting for the train to move on to the next station.

At one instance Adam looked out of the window and sharply pulled me back.

"Cover your face immediately!" he whispered. "There are a few soldiers showing your photograph to some passengers."

"How did they find out so quickly that we have gone?" I was afraid and very upset, but I knew that no one would rip the cloth away from a woman who was trying to cover herself. There were too many people around who would react to the perceived insult to a local woman.

When we saw two soldiers making their way to our

compartment, Adam went to the WC and locked himself in. He was too recognizable to stay with me for now.

"Who are you and where are you travelling to?" A soldier stood near me and shouted. "Is there someone with you?"

"My husband has gone to get some food," I answered in a thick northern accent. Travelling in the train had made me quite grimy, so I was sure they didn't have a clue who I was.

"Please, don't bother me. I am not feeling well," I said pathetically. "I am pregnant and I need to throw up every little while." I made a retching sound and jerked my body. Alarmed, the soldier went hastily ahead. Soon they had given up, but I was glad that Adam joined me when the train started to move once more.

We decided not to get out at the main station of Peshawar. Without doubt, the same search would happen there. We chose a smaller, lesser used station that was used to water the trains as they passed by. Adam had already called ahead to Hamza, a friend from his university who met us there in his battered jeep. Thankfully, he was already there when the train pulled into the station and we didn't have to wait for him.

"Will this jalopy take us to the mountains?" asked Adam looking at it suspiciously.

"The engine is brand new; I have just fitted it in the beaten-up shell so that no one is suspicious. There are brigands in the mountains who wouldn't think twice to steal a roadworthy car. So the shabbier it looks the better. It will definitely be reliable. Don't worry." Hamza laughed.

Since it was now dark, we waited in the shadows for the

train to move away from the station and then started our journey after we were sure that no one else had stepped off the train after us. Hamza took us right into the middle of the tribal area where the government didn't have any legal jurisdiction. We were safe as long as we were considered guests of Hamza and his family. He had arranged that we were to spend the night in his ancestral home at Parachinar, which was just near the Afghanistan border.

The next day, after we had a substantial breakfast prepared by the matriarch of the family, we readied ourselves to go, but Hamza walked in right when we were in the middle of breakfast and told us it wasn't feasible for us to leave that day.

"I am sorry, but I think you might have to wait a couple of days before you leave. The airports and railway stations have your father's cronies looking out for you. Adam, please, don't shave for a few days—a beard would be an excellent disguise for you." Hamza feared that our father's reach could even get within the tribal area. "A young man travelling with his wife would not look suspicious, and since you are as fair as the people of this area, no one will find anything odd… unless you look like your own selves." Hamza looked a bit worried. "I am glad you decided on the disguises, but I think you need to keep them on till you are on the final stretch of your journey."

Having nothing else to do, we sat down to plan our route. It seemed that my great escape was now a convoluted and maybe even dangerous journey into the unknown. I kept Tanya's image in my mind and drew strength from the thought of the love we had for each other.

"How about taking the Karakoram Highway into

China? We can get visas on arrival at the border," Adam said.

"That is a very good idea," I said. "We could probably get a flight to Dubai from Urumqi, the capital of the Xinjiang province. It's the nearest to the border."

"I am impressed with your knowledge of geography," laughed Hamza. "Or did you just read up on that for this trip?"

"I have to confess it popped up when I was researching routes to get out of the country." I smirked.

"Well, China it is then, but we travel at night." We all nodded in agreement. I had a permanent pit of fear in my gut. I wanted this to be over. As long as we were still in the country, there was a chance that I would be dragged back and sentenced to a life of cruel drudgery with Farooq.

Adam hadn't told Hamza about Tanya, but he did tell him what he called my "Farooq predicament." I was grateful that he didn't ask more questions.

After a few days, when Adam finally sported a thick unruly beard, I donned my peasant garb once more and shrouded myself in the chaddar. It was comfortable because it also warded off the chilly mountain air. We left before sunrise so that we could be in the Karakoram mountains as early as possible. It was better to drive along that high treacherous pass in daylight.

Though we couldn't see much in the pre-dawn dark, occasionally the moon peeped out from the clouds and shone on the beauty of the Karakoram Highway, which was built by Pakistani and Chinese engineers. I hoped to come back one day and see it in happier times.

We crossed over to the Chinese border with ease just

after dawn. The road to Urumqi was well paved and we reached there tired but happy in the evening. While Hamza went to look for accommodations for the night, Adam and I went to look for a travel agent to arrange for my airline tickets.

"Please, come with me, Adam!" I pleaded to my brother. "I don't want you to take the brunt of our parents' anger."

Adam looked at me with brotherly love and cupped my cheek tenderly. "Go and be happy, little sister. Write to me when you can. I will be all right. I love you."

I was overcome with emotion and clung to him while I sobbed with the strength of the pent-up frustration and sorrow that I had felt all those weeks. I wouldn't have been able to come so far without this stellar brother of mine.

The travel agent turned out to be a nice man named Shin Li who understood English well. He was happy to talk to us and practice his English speaking skills. We asked him to arrange for a ticket to Dubai for me, from where I planned to get a ticket for my onward journey.

"It would be cheaper to buy a ticket right up to London," he advised us. "I have a limited quota to give discounts to my passengers, so I can give you a good deal," he continued in his British/Chinese accent.

"I don't want anyone to know where I am flying. I am running away from home with the help of my brother because my parents are arranging a marriage for me that will end in disaster if it ever happens." I thought that if we were honest and recruited his help, he might be more cooperative. "I don't want anyone to know that I am on these flights, at least for now."

Shin Li understood my predicament and chuckled softly. He arranged for me to fly to Dubai with China Airlines, and from there on to London with Emirates. I had a two-hour transit stay at Dubai. The only catch was that I had to leave for the airport immediately. Which I gladly did.

I was so happy I nearly hugged Shin Li. He was so helpful. His cheerfulness had lifted my sprits immensely. Instead, I hugged my brother and once more tried to control the tears in my eyes. He hugged me back. He turned quickly away but not before I saw the suspicious glint of moisture in his eyes.

Adam stood at the departure gate waving at me till I went through the security checking area and I couldn't see him anymore. I only heaved a sigh of relief once the plane was in the air.

When I reached Dubai, I was able to have a shower at the airport lounge and change into comfortable jeans and a sweater. Due to my journey over the mountains and the limited facilities to bathe, my hair smelled quite ripe and it had to be washed. The shampoo I had bought from the duty free shop made it shine and bounce once more.

My flight to London was uneventful and I managed to eat a substantial on board meal and catch some much-needed sleep. As soon as we touched down, I let the other passengers go before me. After all, there was no one waiting for me, was there?

After retrieving my baggage, I walked out of the airport via the Green channel. I noticed a tall slim person standing near the entrance with a sign in front of their face. It simply said, "Dr. Sarah S. Khan". Was that me? Were there any others with my name? I tentatively went up to the person and cleared my throat. They still had their face hidden behind the sign. As the sign was slowly lowered, Tanya's twinkling eyes emerged, and then her beautiful face. My Tanya! My dear Tanya had come to receive me at the airport!

I flung my bags aside and jumped into her arms. I was crying and laughing at the same time.

"How did you know?" I finally asked her.

"Adam got a message to Razia, who let me know." She smiled tenderly at me. I hugged her once more and then kissed her. With everyone to see. I wanted to shout my love out loud to everyone. My world was now whole once again.

Tanya

With a heavy heart I boarded the Air France plane to Paris. I noticed that there were some people who were observing and surveilling the surroundings. I was checked a few times till I was allowed access to the passenger lounge. It was as if they were trying to find something illegal on me. But I didn't give them the satisfaction of getting irritated. At one security check they tried to make me lose my temper, but I realized what they were up to. I didn't even tell anyone that I was from the police. I let it go. Sarah's father may have forgotten my profession, but I know these tactics. If I had lost my temper, they would have had an excuse to arrest me for unruly behavior in a public place. Clever.

"Have you packed your bags yourself?" I was asked for the tenth time. I just nodded and went along with the almost robotic procedures. Let them have their fun. I wondered what they were trying to achieve by examining my hand-luggage for the fourth time. Anyway, I would be away, out of their jurisdiction soon. Hopefully, Sarah could also carry out her plan as soon as possible. I looked forward to holding her in my arms again. Who would have thought falling in love was such sweet sorrow? Oh, yes, Shakespeare knew.

Our flight refueled at Beirut, and we had a four-hour stay there. I made myself comfortable in the airport café and took out my book to read. Suddenly, the airport's comm system crackled to life.

"Chief Inspector Tanya Karim, please come to the customer service desk!" The message was repeated two more times before the comm system crackled once more and went quiet.

Intrigued, I made my way to the nearest customer service desk and told the woman behind the counter who I was.

"I have a telegram for you, Inspector Karim," she said handing it over to me.

I thanked the woman and sat down on a nearby bench to read the mysterious telegram, which I saw was from my friend Inspector Razia.

"Sarah on flight to London-stop-Emirates flight from Dubai-stop-If you can do receive her at Heathrow-stop"

I was overjoyed. She had gotten away! I had to go to London. I still had a few days before I needed to report to the office in Paris. I had left early because I wanted to use the free time to orient myself in the new city. But this was more important.

I went back to the customer service desk.

"May I send a telegram from here, please?" I asked.

"Not from here, but there is a post office on the second floor. They send telegrams for the passengers."

I thanked her and followed the signs for the post office. I sent a telegram to Razia, and then one to Paris telling them that I would be delayed for a couple of days. After that, I went to the British Airways office and booked a ticket to London. I was lucky to get a seat within the hour and they promised to get my luggage from my Air France flight. I was so excited that I was trembling. I would even stutter while talking and that wasn't like me at all. I think they thought I had a speech impediment.

Once I reached Heathrow I checked the incoming flights. Sarah's flight was to arrive at another terminal in a couple of hours. That gave me enough time to call Paris and arrange for our accommodations in London for the night. I also bought card paper and a marker from the newspaper stand and wrote Sarah's name on it. She would be so surprised! We were going to create a new life here in this world where our love and our preferences would not be looked at with as much venom and revulsion as at home. We would live as two loving individuals. With no restrictions and no prejudices. There was hope for us. For our love.

CHAPTER 16

ONE YEAR LATER

Sarah

After all our worries and adventures, I still sometimes feel it's a dream that Tanya and I are together, but I just need to look out of my office window and see the impressive ancient Tower Bridge and I know my reality is that I am living in London, working at the prestigious St. Thomas's Hospital, and on my way to qualifying in advanced pediatrics.

Tanya has completed her training at Interpol, obviously with flying colors, and has finally been stationed at the Interpol headquarters here in London. The icing on the cake is that we have bought a beautiful duplex house with a large garden in Surrey. The commute to town is twenty minutes by train, but the peace and quiet once we get home makes it all worth it. We are happy together. We live and love like a married couple without fear and without looking over our shoulder all the time. While we are aware that the laws are still being challenged and will hopefully change soon, our commitment ceremony in front of a Justice of Peace and our new friends was just as serious and just as legally binding for both of us. Our hearts are at peace. We have each other.

When I first arrived here, I was able to initially ask for asylum with the help of Tanya's Interpol connections, based on the threats my parents had been heard to continuously make on my and Tanya's life. That helped alleviate my fear and anxiety. A lot.

Tomorrow is a special day for me. Tomorrow I will be awarded British citizenship. They have fast tracked my application because of our situation. I am ecstatic. Now I know that the Queen's government will protect me. Or at least I think so… Though I am sure my intrepid Tanya wouldn't leave any stone unturned if anything happened to me. She says I should think happy thoughts. And I do. But there is always this undercurrent of fear that tinges my happiness. My intuition is sometimes very irritating, but it has always helped me out of precarious situations and it's always better to heed the warnings. Even though they might not lead to anything at all.

Every day we read in the newspaper of British Pakistani girls who were kidnapped by their own family members and forced into marriages in remote areas of Pakistan. Never to be heard of again. I believe that is a threat that can always hang over our heads like a dark cloud. Hopefully, if that ever became an issue, being a British citizen would ensure that I am not lost in the dark hidden areas of the country forever, and someone would have the authority to look for me and pull me out. Till then, I revel at my freedom to be with my soulmate and work at my dream job. Fate has been good to me, and I thank God every day for His kindness to me and Tanya.

Tanya

At last, we are together. Living in harmony. Sarah is on her way to becoming a brilliant pediatrician. I am so proud of her. Her colleagues always have nice things to say about her when I meet them, and the children love playing with her in the ward. Apparently, they know in which pocket she hides the lollipops.

She keeps telling me about these "feelings" of hers. I am worried because they are often correct. While she reassures me that her ESP is not an accurate science, I have learned not to ignore her when she says something out of the blue.

I haven't told her yet that I have seen some unsavory characters following her. I could intercept them twice, but the problem is that I am not there all the time, so yes, I worry. I have to go on assignments, often outside the country, but I am grateful for the liaisons and friends we have made in our brief time here. I believe that is mostly due to Sarah. She does make friends wherever she goes.

I am aware that Sarah spends a lot of her time at work, and that is a relief for me because the security at her hospital is very good. Since she is allowed to stay in in the country because she requested asylum, it is not difficult to get someone to tail her when I am not available. It seems that her parents haven't given up—they want their girl back. If it was for love I would understand, but it seems to me that it is their ego what's at stake rather than the well-being of their only daughter and youngest child.

It is wonderful that we have created a new life here. Our commitment ceremony was magical. Sarah was a beautiful bride, and I nearly burst with pride and love when I saw her in her finery. One of my friends, who is a photographer, captured a moment when the wind blew her dress about her, and she looked up towards me. That photograph is priceless. Our love is there for all to see, our feelings frozen in time in that photograph forever. As a present, my friend had it enlarged and framed, and it now holds a place of honor over the fireplace in our living room. The little village where we live on the outskirts of London is amazing and our neighbors are friendly and kind. Our home is comfortable, and our many friends visit at all times. That is, when we are home—our professions keep us very busy'. However, living without having fingers pointed at us and being evaluated and judged on the way we conduct ourselves as human beings and professionals instead of who and how we love is refreshing. The fates have been good to us. We are together and that is all that matters, isn't it?

THE END (for now)

GLOSSARY

AJRAK

Ajrak is a unique form of block printing on shawls found mostly in Sindh Pakistan. These shawls display special designs and patterns made using block printing by stamps. Over the years, ajraks have become a symbol of the Sindhi culture and traditions.

These unique shawls and their processes can be traced back to the ancient Indus Valley civilization to nearly 400 BC. Till today, the same techniques and dyes are being used as they were over 3500 years ago.

AMBIGUOUS GENITALIA

Ambiguous genitalia is a rare condition in which an infant's external genitals don't appear to be clearly either male or female. The genitals may not be well-formed or the baby may have characteristics of both sexes.

BEEDI

A beedi is a thin cigarette or mini cigar filled with tobacco flakes, commonly wrapped in a tobacco leaf & tied with a string or an adhesive band at one end. It can also contain a mixture of betel nuts, herbs (or marijuana), and spices. It is a traditional method of tobacco use throughout South Asia and parts of the Middle East.

BHAI

Brother

BHANG

An edible form of marijuana, and commonly used in the villages. It is mixed in buttermilk or milk with almonds and drunk on festivals.

CADUCEUS

The medical definition of caduceus is that it's an insignia bearing a representation of a staff with two entwined snakes and two wings at the top sometimes used to symbolize a physician.

CHADDER / CHADOR

Chadder or Chador is an outer garment or open cloak worn by many Muslim women It is a full-body-length semicircle of fabric that is open down the front. The garment is pulled over the head and is held closed at the front by the wearer; it has no hand openings, buttons or clasps. It may also be held closed by being tucked under the wearer's arms.

CHARPOY

Abed with a light frame (wood or steel) strung with tapes or light rope.

EID

Muslim festival marking the end of Ramadan and fasting.

FARSI

Persian/Iranian language.

HIJRA

A South Asian term for a person whose birth sex is allegedly male but who identifies as female or as neither male nor female (hermaphrodite).

HUMERUS

The humerus is a long bone in the arm that runs from the shoulder to the elbow.

MALLEUS, INCUS & STAPES

Three little bones in the middle ear that help with conduction of sound.

NAAN

Naan is a leavened, oven-baked or tawa-fried flatbread which is found in the cuisines mainly of Western Asia, Central Asia, Indian subcontinent, Indonesia, Myanmar, and the Caribbean.

NEEM TREES

Neem Trees are evergreens erupt with large clusters of fragrant white blooms and bear a vibrant yellow (inedible) fruit. Neem has been used traditionally for many centuries. In the subcontinent it is known as "the village pharmacy".

But neem is still relatively unknown in the Western world. However, the word about neem's remarkable healing properties is slowly spreading.

PARATHAS

a flat bread of thin batter fried with butter on both sides. Usually on a flat iron griddle.

PETIT MAL EPILEPSY

Another name for absence seizures which are one of several kinds of generalized seizures. These are sometimes referred to as petit mal seizures (from the French for "little illness", a term dating from the late 18th century). They are characterized by a brief loss and return of consciousness, generally not followed by a period of lethargy (i.e. without a notable postictal state). Absence seizure is very common in children. It affects both parts of the brain.

PLAB

The **P**rofessional and **L**inguistic **A**ssessments **B**oard test provides the main route for International Medical Graduates to demonstrate that they have the necessary skills and knowledge to practice medicine in the United Kingdom.

PPD

Paraphenylenediamine is a chemical substance that is widely used as a permanent hair dye. PPD is used in hair dye because it is a permanent dye that gives a natural look, and the dyed hair can also be shampooed or permed without losing its color. It can be used in other substances like henna (which can also used as a hair dye).

RAMADAN

The month of fasting for Muslims. A fast is usually held from sunrise to sunset.

RICKSHAW

An auto rickshaw is a motorized version of the pulled rickshaw or cycle rickshaw. Most have three wheels and do not tilt. They are known by many terms in various countries including auto, auto rickshaw, baby taxi, and tuk-tuk.

SALAM

A shortened version of the Islamic greeting "Asalam Alaikum" which means peace.

SINDH

Sindh is one of the four provinces of Pakistan. Located in the southeastern region of the country, Sindh is the third-largest province of Pakistan by total area and the second-largest province by population after Punjab. It shares land borders with the Pakistani provinces of Balochistan and Punjab to the north, respectively, and the Indian states of Gujarat and Rajasthan to the east; it is also bounded by the Arabian Sea to the south. Sindh's landscape consists mostly of alluvial plains flanking the Indus River, the Thar Desert in the eastern portion of the province along the international border with India, and the Kirthar Mountains in the western portion of the province.

The Greeks who conquered Sindh in 325 BC under the command of Alexander the Great referred to the Indus River as Indos, hence the modern *Indus*. The ancient Persians referred to everything east of the river Indus as hind. The word *Sindh* is a Persian derivative of the Sanskrit term *Sindhu,* meaning "river" - a reference to the Indus River.

TONGA OR TANGA

A tonga is a light carriage or curricle drawn by one horse used for transportation in the subcontinent. They have a canopy over the carriage with a single pair of large wheels. The passengers reach the seats from the rear while the driver sits in front of the carriage. Some space is available for baggage below the carriage, between the wheels. This space is often used to carry hay for the horses.

WADERA

A feudal lord or baron from the rural areas in Sindh.

ABOUT SHIREEN

Dr. Shireen Magedin is a practicing pediatrician who has studied in Pakistan, England, and Ireland. Lifelines is her first novel.

She has always had psychic abilities, and in the beginning they scared her, until she received guidance from trainers and connected with people who had similar abilities, thus knowing she wasn't alone. Connecting psychically and intuitively with her patients has helped her hone her medical skills.

She lives with her cat Pompi (aka Madam Pompadour) and enjoys visits from her daughter Sharmeen, son Nadir, and daughter in law Mariam.

Website:
https://shireenmegedin.com/

Facebook Group
https://www.facebook.com/groups/shireenmagedin

AUSXIP Publishing Author Page
https://ausxippublishing.com/authors/shireen_magedin/

ABOUT AUSXIP PUBLISHING

AUSXIP Publishing showcases authors who inspire, strengthen and enrich our souls with their storytelling. We bring you quality stories with strong characters that will build you up, to create a sense of achievement and most importantly, entertain. We love reading about people who strive to change their world, and we know you do as well. Come with us on our journey and lose yourself in our books and grow with us.

Discover our Authors
https://ausxippublishing.com/authors/

Subscribe to our Newsletter
https://newsletter.ausxippublishing.com/

Discover your next read!
https://store.ausxippublishing.com/

Printed in Great Britain
by Amazon

77531289R00183